CW01370570

George Bellairs was the pseudonym of Harold Blundell (1902–1982). He was, by day, a Manchester bank manager with close connections to the University of Manchester. He is often referred to as the English Simenon, as his detective stories combine wicked crimes and classic police procedurals, set in quaint villages.

He was born in Lancashire and married Gladys Mabel Roberts in 1930. He was a devoted Francophile and travelled there frequently, writing for English newspapers and magazines and weaving French towns into his fiction.

Bellairs' first mystery, *Littlejohn on Leave* (1941), introduced his series detective, Detective Inspector Thomas Littlejohn. Full of scandal and intrigue, the series peeks inside small towns in the mid twentieth century and Littlejohn is injected with humour, intelligence and compassion.

He died on the Isle of Man in April 1982 just before his eightieth birthday.

ALSO BY GEORGE BELLAIRS

The Case of the Famished Parson
The Case of the Demented Spiv
Death in Dark Glasses
Half-Mast for the Deemster
Corpses in Enderby
The Cursing Stones Murder
Death Treads Softly
Death in High Provence
Death Sends for the Doctor
Corpse at the Carnival
Murder Makes Mistakes
Bones in the Wilderness
Toll the Bell for Murder
Death in the Fearful Night
Death of a Tin God
The Tormentors
Death in the Wasteland
Death of a Shadow
Intruder in the Dark
Death in Desolation
The Night They Killed Joss Varran

The Tormentors

An Inspector Littlejohn Mystery

George Bellairs

ib
ipso books

This edition published in 2017 by Ipso Books

First Published in 1962 in Great Britain by John Gifford Ltd.

Ipso Books is a division of Peters Fraser + Dunlop Ltd

Drury House, 34-43 Russell Street, London WC2B 5HA

Copyright © George Bellairs, 1962

All rights reserved

You may not copy, distribute, transmit, reproduce or otherwise make available this publication (or any part of it) in any form, or by any means (including without limitation electronic, digital, optical, mechanical, photocopying, printing, recording or otherwise), without the prior written permission of the publisher. Any person who does any unauthorised act in relation to this publication may be liable to criminal prosecution and civil claims for damages.

Contents

Chance Acquaintance	1
Deep Waters	16
Alibi	28
Ballacroake	40
The Bishop's Arms	53
Teddy-Boy's Lament	67
The Ghost at Ballacroake	80
The Man in the Upper Room	93
Croake's Saturday Afternoon	109
The Treasure of Ballacroake	124
The Little People	137
The Inventory	150
The Confidences of Joseph Croake	158
Feminine Gossip	168
The Tormentors	177
The Elder Brother	193
Hard Luck on Littlejohn	203
The Cliffs at Keristal	214

CHAPTER ONE
CHANCE ACQUAINTANCE

A Sunny Morning in mid-August. A clock somewhere in the maze of streets along the waterfront struck half-past ten. The sailors manning the gangway on the Manx boat from Liverpool hauled it nimbly in, the engine-room telegraph clanged, and the trim cross-channel packet slowly moved into the river. The crowd on the pier gradually melted away and those aboard waiting for the bars to open, pushed their way to find a drink. The rest slowly settled down about the decks, talking excitedly, making new friends, eager to be starting their holidays right away.

'The Isle of Man's too risky these days. The police meet you at the boat, and, if they don't like the looks of you, they turn you round, give you a free ticket back to the mainland, and you've had it. And if you do get in and they cop you at any racket, they give you the birch. They can still do it there, you know.'

When his pals had told him that, Alf Cryer had accepted it as a challenge. He was more than a match for any meddling bobby. He'd packed his bag and taken the next boat.

The main thing was to establish a respectable front in case the police over the water questioned him too closely. His pocket was stuffed with pound notes, but that wasn't enough. He had a bad record and didn't want it to come to light if any questions were asked or they decided to check him up. He had three and a half hours in which to find a way out. By the time the *King Orry* passed the Mersey Bar, he'd found a solution and got it all sewed-up.

Alf was attractive in his scruffy way to those who fancied that kind. Some of the girls, prowling about the decks in jeans and tight jumpers and with their hair dishevelled, seemed to think so and turned to take a second look as he strutted past them looking as if he owned the boat. He gave them scornful looks, which was, he knew, the way they liked it.

He was dressed in black stovepipe trousers terminating in long pointed shoes which had cost him quite a lot, and he wore a plastic jacket and a pink holiday shirt open at the neck. His friends had also advised him against putting on his ted's clothes if he wanted to be let-in at the Isle of Man. He had a complexion the colour of putty, pimples on the back of his neck, a snub nose, and dark curly hair shining with oil. His eyes were black and cunning, with the almost sightless look of someone concentrating hard on his own devices. He was nearly six feet tall, thin, and well set-up, with long arms and legs and huge ill-kept hands. He carried himself like the cock o' the north and walked like a cat.

Perhaps it was the evil in Alf Cryer which attracted Sid Wanklyn. Or it may have been his impudence and self-possession. Nobody, not even Sid, will ever know. But, as the boat slowly nosed her way into the river, Sid introduced himself. He was on his own, too. He indicated the shabby fibre suitcase Alf was clutching.

'Want to get rid of that till we land? I'll see to it. I know my way about these boats.'

'O.K. See I get it back.'

Alf said it roughly, almost ignoring the other. In the mob he moved about with, he was almost a nonentity. He did as he was told. Now he was on his own with a chance to give orders himself.

'Sure.'

Sid almost ran to put the tumbledown luggage beside his own bag in a corner near the funnel.

'That's safe enough.'

He was a good four inches smaller than Alf. Stocky, square-headed, pale blue eyes, and crew-cut fair hair. He, too, wore narrow trousers, an imitation leather jacket, and brown shoes with thick rubber soles.

At first, Alf was disposed to dismiss him roughly. Tell him to drop dead. Then he changed his mind.

'You on holidays?'

'Yes. You?'

Alf didn't answer the question. Except as a part of the scheme he had in mind, Wanklyn was less than the dust to Alf.

'Booked your digs?'

'No. I'm staying with my aunt.'

Alf actually smiled. It was a poor effort, a mere predatory baring of the teeth, but Sid thought it betrayed good will.

'She lives in Castletown.'

'Where's that?'

'In the south. About ten miles from Douglas. It's a nice quiet town...'

Alf wasn't interested in geography. He was thinking. He stuck a fag in the corner of his mouth without offering one to his companion, lit it, flipped the spent match over the side of the boat and spat out a mouthful of smoke.

'Douglas is the top town, isn't it?'

'Yes.'

'Busy at this time of year they tell me. Plenty of lolly about.'

'That's right. The place to have a good time. Been before?'

No answer. Alf was doing the asking. Sid didn't seem to mind. He was used to being ignored. An orphan, without any relatives except his aunt, who was religious and invited him over now and then for the purpose of inspecting his moral welfare and respectability. It was something to do when he got a week's holiday. Otherwise he just had to loaf about. On the Island he could pick up a girl when he'd money in his pocket, and swank a bit and throw his weight about. In the quarter where he lodged, off Scotland Road in Liverpool, his pals were older and larger than he was: chiselled-in if he found himself a girl, sheered off and left him when they were up to anything worth while. He earned eight pounds a week in a railway warehouse and now and then increased his labourer's income by swiping and flogging worthwhile stuff which passed through his hands, when the rest weren't looking.

'Cigarette?'

Alf decided he'd better be affable. If there were any plainclothes men planted aboard and he wanted to make use of Sid, he'd better behave like a familiar.

'Thanks. My name's Sid Wanklyn.'

'You can call me Alf.'

'What about a drink, Alf? The bar's open.'

'Lead me to it.'

The decks were crowded with holidaymakers and the day was fine and sunny. The passengers were growing noisy and good-humoured in a sort of thanksgiving for a calm crossing. There was music everywhere. Someone was playing an accordion; sad music. *Paris, ma Tristesse.* Some beatniks leaning over the rails looked ready to throw themselves in the water. On the other side of the deck, portable radios were picking up a jazz band. *Riverboat Rock.* Some of them were twisting and rock-and-rolling. The decks were so crowded that it almost became a riot.

Riverboat Rock, sailin' to the sunset.
Riverboat Rock, rock ma baby in my arms.
Yoo Hoo! Rock ma baby an' me.

They were still in sight of land. Liverpool Bay was full of shipping. In the distance, a liner on its way to Canada and another heading for Liverpool. The air was like wine and the sun was warm and kind. Just the sort of day for starting a holiday. Already some of the passengers were half seas over, celebrating the joys to come.

Alf and Sid elbowed their way through the crowd to the bar at the end of the deck. Sid's eyes were everywhere, taking it all in. Alf, on the contrary, seemed to see nothing with his half-dead gaze which, nevertheless, missed nothing at all. Now and then, a couple of girls, hunting for someone to finance them through the holiday, gave the pair the glad eye. Alf ignored them, but Sid was slightly exhilarated by it. He'd had his amorous adventures now and then, but some of the girls on the boat, dressed in their best and got-up to kill, put to shame the partners of his fumbling amours in sordid corners round Scotland Road.

Alf wasn't interested, however. The girls who took his eye had men with them. Men he'd have pushed aside in his normal surroundings. But now he was going to behave himself. Just in case…

'Come on. Time for that when we get there.'

They fought their way to the bar. Alf paid for two.

'You can buy the next. Then, that'll be the lot. Got to arrive sober. Respectable place, the Isle of Man. Or don't you know?'

Sid giggled. He felt that way. It looked as if they were going to have a good holiday after all. He and Alf. Already he could see them. Women, wine and song, with Alf to show him the way, to set the pace.

Everybody was merry and bright. Offering to pay for drinks for men they'd never met before; all pals together, out for a jolly good time. Now and then, somebody jostled them. Alf looked like thunder and seemed ready to start something. His dead eyes would light up and flash and the jostler would cringe away or smile a sickly smile. Then Alf would smile back. He'd remembered to be on his best behaviour. Just in case…

As the two of them got back on deck, the nine o'clock boat from Douglas was passing the *King Orry* on her way to Liverpool. She was a pretty sight, clean and graceful, her decks crowded with people returning home, cutting through the water like a racing dog. Passengers crowded to the rails to give her a wave and a cheer as she sped past. Some sang her a verse of the latest top hit.

Yoo Hoo! Rock ma baby an' me.

'Another 'oliday over.'

A tottering little fat man in an off-white suit and a fancy tweed hat, lifted his glass of beer to her with one hand and raised the hat with the other.

'It'll be the same with us in a fortnight,' he added sadly and drank his beer in one to help him forget it.

Alf and Sid leaned over the rails. They were now almost out of sight of land. All that remained behind them was a dim patch of it, like a cloud on the eastern horizon.

'Know any good digs in Douglas?'

'No, Alf. I daresay, if you wanted, my aunt could find you a place in Castletown. We'd be together there. I know the Island well. I could show you about.'

He didn't like the idea of their parting now. With Alf the holiday would be made.

Alf made an impatient gesture.

'I want the lights and crowds. I'll find me a place if you don't know one. We'll meet. You can come down to Douglas and we'll ....'

He halted there. The very idea of having Sid hanging around didn't suit him. He wanted to be on his own. He'd things to do.

'There's one thing you can do for me. I hear they're a bit choosey on the Island. They don't fancy the likes of you and me ...'

He passed his hand up and down, indicating the way they were dressed.

'... They think everybody wearing clothes like you and me are up to mischief.'

'I've never found it that way, Alf. Who's told you that?'

'I've heard of the police turning back fellows they didn't like the look of. Sending 'em back home by the next boat.'

He looked hurt.

'They won't try it on with us. I'm going to see my aunt, I tell you. She's Manx. Her name's Mrs. Creer. If I tell them that, they'll give us the welcome handshake. That is, if they do ask questions, which I doubt.'

'If they do, then, just tell them I'm your pal, see? We're *both* going to see your aunt ... That'll put it right.'

Sid brightened up.

'Decided to come with me, after all?'

Alf was disgusted. The man was just too dumb.

'No. I said Douglas, didn't I? If there's any questions, that's what you say. Get me?'

'Yes. I'll see to it.'

'There's the Island. See it? Good ole Isle of Man.'

The little fat man in the fancy hat was going the rounds again. He'd another glass of beer in his hand and started toasting the island loudly.

Ahead, land was slowly forming, building itself up on the horizon. A long, low outline, which gradually grew larger. A panorama of gentle hills, then a sudden clearing of the air, revealing their green slopes sweeping down to the sea and ending in massive cliffs. People began to crowd on deck to see it. Some of them were even making bets about how far the Island was still away and how long they'd take to reach it.

'Another hour yet,' the man in the hat was shouting. 'Time for a few more drinks.' He went off to have another.

They could see Douglas. The harbour and then a long crescent of promenade with white boarding-houses and hotels shining in the sun. Passengers began to gather their baggage, jostling one another for pride of place in the queues forming at the gangways. The boat blew a blast on her siren. Those who couldn't bear sailing in any weather began to emerge from below. They looked incongruously sick and green, but grew miraculously well again as the boat entered the harbour and docked.

'This is it...'

For the first time, Alf looked tense.

'Nothing's going to happen. I know some of the police here. One of them used to live near my aunt...'

Alf felt like telling Sid to take a walk. He sounded so cocky and pleased with himself. The kind that normally Alf picked quarrels with, just to cut them down to size. The gangways were out and they all began to shuffle off the boat. It was amazing how many the boat held. They seemed as if they'd never stop. Like a river trickling down the planks and then forming a huge lake of excited humanity on the quayside.

Alf's dead eyes picked out the helmets and even recognized the plain-clothes men, apparently idly standing by, casually watching the newcomers. Now and then, one would help a woman with heavy luggage and no porter to get her bags safely on the quay. One of them even carried a child shoulder-high, because she couldn't keep up with the mob. Then he calmly turned to Alf. He was a large, powerful officer with a fresh, gentle face.

'Here on holiday, sir?'

He looked mildly into Alf's dead eyes. He knew the type.

'Yes. Anything wrong with that?'

'No. You seemed like a stranger to the Island. Ever been here before?'

Alf had to struggle to keep his temper. Nobody pushed him around and that was what the detective was trying to do.

'This is the first time. So what?'

'Have you booked your room?'

And then Sid appeared, lugging his own and Alf's bags, like a strange gentleman's gentleman trailing behind his betters.

'He's with me.'

'I see.'

The policeman smiled affably. Actually, he wanted to laugh. He compared the two of them. One was full of it; the other, his admirer, a lad who'd fallen for his phoney bravado and cocksureness.

'Have *you* been here before, then?'

'Yes. I come every year. My aunt lives here. We're staying with her.'

'Where, if you don't mind telling me?'

'Castletown. Her name's Mrs. Creer. Lives on the estate near the airport.'

'That's different, isn't it? Almost Manx yourself, aren't you?'

Sid produced a grubby letter.

'If you don't believe me, here's her invitation.'

The policeman smiled.

'That's all right. We just have to make sure. Sometimes people arrive who make it a bit noisy and unpleasant for those who want a quiet life... Get along, then, and have a good time.'

Alf was almost exhausted with keeping his temper and by his efforts to behave civilly.

'Who the hell do they think they are, anyway? Keeping us standin' there like a couple of crooks and everybody staring at us. I'll get even with him for this. Nobody treats me like that without me getting even. Well... That's all for the time being, young Sid. Thanks for the good turn. I'll not forget it, in spite of the way we've been pushed around. Did you hear him? Bit noisy and unpleasant, are we? We'll see. So long, then. Perhaps I'll be seein' you before I go back. On the other hand, perhaps I might not.'

The sudden turn about, even the tone of Alf's voice, took Sid's breath away.

'You don't mean...?'

Alf's mouth widened in his cruel grin again.

'Look. What would I want with a kid like you? You'd be more a hinderer than use. Get off to your auntie and have a good time...'

Suddenly he stopped. He wondered if the police might put a tail on him. He stood there at the pier gates looking around with his cold eyes without moving his head.

The approaches to the piers were almost empty. A clock struck three. The promenade was filling-up with crowds dressed in holiday wear. Horse trams were moving to and fro, stopping to pick up a few passengers and the horses off on their ways without so much as a ring of the conductor's bell or a twitch of the reins as soon as they saw all were aboard. The next boat was due out to Liverpool at four o'clock and a ragged queue had formed already. The plain-clothes man was talking to the harbour master and looking in the direction of Alf and his companion. They'd better be careful.

'Sorry, Sid. I didn't intend to be rough with you. But that damned copper... What about eating? Then we'll find me some digs and you can get off to your aunt's.'

Sid perked up.

'It's all right. Let's eat, then. After that, we can arrange something and fix to meet again. I'll come to Douglas any time you say.'

The restaurants in Victoria Street were empty by now. The owner of one was taking inside the blackboard on which he chalked the dishes and prices. He eyed them dubiously as they entered.

They had little to say to one another over the meal. Sid respectfully left the talking to Alf and Alf remained lost in thought, eating slowly, holding his knife and fork clutched in his fists, tackling his meat violently, as though it might be an enemy. He chewed with a rotary motion, opening his mouth and showing all inside it as he did so. He didn't seem aware of what he was eating. As the meal went on, Sid's spirits fell again. This was going to be a disappointing holiday after all.

Alf paid and they left the place and entered the crowded street, Sid still carrying the bags like a servant. Alf took the middle of the pavement, forcing passers-by to walk round him. Now and again, one of them would resist, and then give way for the sake of peace when he saw the sneer and the cold eyes.

They wandered in the direction of Peel Road and then Alf suddenly seemed to become aware that Sid was still with him.

'We've passed the bus station, haven't we, just down there? You'd better get the next one to Castletown and leave me here...'

'But...'

'I said, leave me here. I'm tired. I'll find some digs and then have a rest and tidy up. Then I'll see what the place is like. Your aunt'll be waiting for you.'

He picked up his bag.

'But...'

'Don't keep butting...Just scram, Sid. That's a good boy.'

He moved away and turned down a side street without looking back.

Sid picked up his own bag. He didn't quite know where he was. Alf's treatment and sudden disappearance had given him a shock. He didn't feel like facing his aunt yet. He wanted to sit down and sort himself out. He shambled his way to the old quay, which was full of visitors, strolling about, shop-window gazing, standing in little knots eyeing the coasters tied up to the bollards. Crowds were making their way up to Douglas Head. The concert party at the top was in full blast and the choruses, sung by the audience, wafted across the calm air. Sid turned-in at a small quayside pub and ordered a drink.

There was a girl there, all alone, too. Sid paid for a drink for her. They were both melancholy. Her boy friend had found himself a fresh girl and was leaving with her on the afternoon boat. Marlene herself was returning by the midnight and now she was at a loose end.

By the time they'd had more drinks, both Sid and Marlene (her name was Ida, she confided, but she'd changed it for the holidays) were as merry as the rest. They laughed at each other, pretending to make light of their misfortunes. He told her about Alf and his dirty trick. Marlene said he was better without Alf, who was obviously a no-good. And Sid said Marlene was better without Max (real name Maximilian) who sounded a square. They confessed they wished they'd known each other before and without more ado, went to Douglas Head, heard the concert and sang the choruses. They had some tea there, too, and then as daylight was fading, found themselves a place on the grass slopes, already teeming with amorous couples, and indulged in a little lovemaking themselves.

Sid arrived at his aunt's after eleven o'clock. He said he'd missed the morning boat and caught one in the late afternoon. His aunt's face was sour, for she knew it wasn't the truth. She told him he'd better mend his ways or else he'd end-up like Uncle Arthur, who was the *bête noir*, the bogeyman of the family. He'd left home in his teens and gone to sea and returned a penniless drunkard in his late forties, to sponge on his sister. He had disgraced them by his eccentricities. Drunk at the harbour, singing bawdy sailors' songs; whitewashing somebody's house; in charge of a lot of donkeys on Douglas beach; hawking mushrooms or blackberries he'd gathered in his battered hat... In the end, he'd forgotten to turn right at the quay, walked straight ahead, and drowned himself.

After all this, Sid's aunt told him he'd better get to bed and they'd talk matters over in the morning. His breath smelled strongly of beer and he ended with a violent fit of hiccups. She was sorry she'd asked him over. Still, she'd her duty to do. She'd made a promise to his mother. She gave him some supper.

At one in the morning, the police knocked on the door.

'Is Sid Wanklyn staying here?'

A constable from Douglas, in charge of a car, shouted it as quietly as he could at Mrs. Creer, who was hanging out of her front bedroom window, with an article like a small fish-net keeping her hair in order.

'Yes. What are you after at this time o' night?'

'He's wanted in Douglas. Can I see him?'

There was a terrific hullaballoo. Mrs. Creer started abusing Sid and talking about Uncle Arthur again before she'd even shaken him awake. The bobby was patiently waiting in the hall, whistling under his breath, and she took care that he heard it all, a sort of monologue extolling her own respectability.

Sid eventually appeared, tousled, fastening his braces. Short of sleep, and with his stomach turned-up by the drink he'd consumed the previous evening and the cold pork pie his aunt had provided for supper, he didn't quite know where he was or what was happening. He looked a sight.

The constable soon put him wise.

'Do you know a man called Alfred Cryer?'

'Yes. But...'

'There's been a bit of trouble in Douglas and Cryer's been taken-in for questioning. It happened around half-past ten. One of our men says he saw Cryer come off the boat with you this afternoon and you both said you were coming here to stay with Mrs. Creer. Cryer states you were with him all night and the Douglas police want to verify it...'

'I never...'

'You'd better save your breath till we get to Douglas. There's a car at the door.'

Mrs. Creer was speechless at the lies Sid had told her and the thought of the disgrace he'd brought upon her. She could only ask, 'What's he done?'

'Well, it's a matter of an elderly man murdered on the Old Quay.'

Sid was sick in the front garden.

Chapter Two
Deep Waters

On the way to Douglas, the constable driving the car said nothing. At first, Wanklyn tried bluff; then pretended to be indignant. He asked a lot of questions and made a lot of complaints.

'They'll tell you all about it when we get there. I was just ordered to find you and bring you along.'

The officer was pleasant enough, but didn't seem interested in anything but reaching his destination. Finally Wanklyn settled down in sulky silence, and silence made him more and more afraid.

There was no traffic on the roads and they travelled at high speed.

The lights in the control tower at Ronaldsway Airport flashed past. Then, the illuminated call-box at Ballasalla. A solitary light shone in one of the bedrooms of the housing estate. A lot of farms and cottages, all asleep, silhouetted against the darkness. The glow of Douglas in the sky, and then in the distance the street lights of the town, dotted here and there in the residential quarter on the high ground behind the promenade. The elaborate coloured illuminations had long been extinguished and, visible under plain electric lamps, it seemed dismal now.

They skirted the Old Quay, ghostly and fluorescent, with coasters tied-up and silent in the basin, and, in the distance beyond the swing-bridge, a cargo boat ready for off on the next tide. Somewhere a drunk was singing at the top of his voice.

The car drew up at the police station nearby. Wanklyn grew slit-eyed at the bright lights of the charge-room. There was a sergeant drinking tea at a desk and a constable standing with his back to the fire. They seemed good humoured and showed no excitement at the arrival of the newcomers.

'Where did you find him, Kilbride?'

'At his aunt's in Castletown. He was in bed, asleep.'

'A cool 'un, eh? Did she say when he arrived?'

'Between eleven and half-past.'

'Would she be Sammy Creer's widow, the one who was harbour master at Derbyhaven?'

'That's right.'

The sergeant rose and crossed to a filing-cabinet for some papers. Wanklyn stood there speechless. He was quite bewildered; in a sorry state. His eyes were set in a fixed frightened stare.

The sergeant returned and straightened out a form before him on the desk.

'Name...? Address...? Age...?'

Wanklyn gave them hesitantly, as though he hadn't used them for a long time. They all went down on the form in large, plain writing.

'Parents?'

'I haven't any.'

'Nearest relatives, then.'

He gave his aunt's name and address.

'When did you arrive on the Island?'

'Yesterday afternoon.'

'Morning boat from Liverpool?'

'Yes.'

'What did you do with yourself after you arrived here?'

'I had dinner with a pal who'd travelled with me...'

Then, the whole sorry story. How he'd met Alf; every detail of what they'd done on the boat and in Douglas. Then, of Alf's sudden change of mind and desertion.

'Did you see him again?'

'No.'

'What time did he leave you?'

'About four o'clock, as near as I can guess.'

'You didn't arrive at your aunt's till after eleven. Where were you between four and eleven?'

The sergeant was a large, round-faced, ruddy man, good tempered and quiet voiced. No bullying; no threats. It gave Wanklyn a bit of confidence.

'What's all this about? I've just come over for a week's holiday with my aunt, and this happens. I don't know what you're getting at. I've done nothing wrong.'

Plaintive now. He sounded ready to burst into tears. He was thoroughly sorry for himself. He had dressed hurriedly, and been got out of bed and hustled off without a wash or a tidy-up.

The constable who'd driven the car and his colleague were both drinking tea by the fire. They didn't seem interested in what was going on. They were discussing a school for croupiers somebody was setting-up in Douglas in case a casino was opened.

'What'll be the good of it if the casino doesn't come off...'

The sergeant eyed Wanklyn closely.

'You not feeling well?'

'You ought to know how I feel at this time of night. Being pulled out of bed and...'

'Better give him a cup of your tea, Kilbride.'
Wanklyn gulped it eagerly. It was hot, strong and sweet, but he didn't seem to notice it. Down it went.

'About the girl you said you were with... Her name was...?'

He didn't know it. All he knew was that it was Ida and she called herself Marlene.

It hadn't seemed odd at all after the drinks and with her close to him in the afternoon. Now it was incriminating. In fact, he knew nothing whatever about the girl. He'd held her in his arms on Douglas Head and made love with her and yet, he didn't know her name, where she came from, or where she was going.

The sergeant didn't seem put-out. He was used to that kind of thing in the holiday season. But he didn't tell Wanklyn that, of course. He just opened his eyes wide.

'I know you won't believe me. I left her on the promenade. She was going home on the midnight boat, she said. Going back to her boarding-house for supper and her bag. It seems she'd come over with her boy friend, but he'd fallen for somebody else in the same digs and left her in the lurch. That's all I know.'

The sergeant had to struggle to keep a straight face. The usual penny novelette stuff of holidays. As soon as the spell wore off, Marlene, or Ida, or whatever her name was, would find herself going steady again with her fickle boy-friend. It was like drink. It wore off and left you flat and sorry.

'You got the half-past ten bus to Castletown?'

'Yes. I said so.'

'Your buddy, Alf, didn't by any chance turn-up again later in the evening?'

'I told you, I never saw him again after I left him at four o'clock.'

'He says you did.'

'What's all this about…?'

The sergeant gave him a compassionate look. 'You see what a mess you can get in by keeping bad company. The best thing you can do now is to tell the truth about the whole business.'

'But I've told you the truth. I swear…'

'No need to shout, young fellow-me-lad. I was only giving you a bit of friendly advice. Sit down.'

Wanklyn did as he was told, sank on one of the wooden chairs, his elbows on the table, his head in his hands. He licked his dry lips.

'Well, if that's all you have to tell us, young Wanklyn, you'd better wait in the next room.'

The sergeant nodded to the constable, who took Sid by the arm and led him off to a small room on the right, which looked like a store. There was a wooden chair there and a table. Hanging from hooks on the walls, all neatly labelled, were the firearms collected under the amnesty from owners without permits. Everything from an old blunderbuss and several muzzle-loading carbines to the latest service revolvers. A gunman's idea of heaven! The constable motioned Wanklyn to the chair and himself sat on the table, swinging his legs. He offered Wanklyn a cigarette, which he eagerly accepted, inhaling the first smoke like a parched man in a desert.

'They won't be long. Just calm down.'

Ten minutes later, they sent for Wanklyn again. The same policemen were in the charge-room. The constable was making a fair copy of Wanklyn's statement on a typewriter. His hands were large and he worked daintily, like an elephant gingerly crossing some stepping-stones. There was a newcomer in plain clothes. A tall, well-built, cheerful Inspector with large teeth and a polite way with him.

Wanklyn didn't see Cryer, at first, but when he did, he lost his temper completely.

'What lies have you been telling about me? Isn't it enough...?'

Cryer, in spite of the pickle he seemed to be in, bared his teeth in a malicious smile.

'You're not going to let down a pal, are you...?'

The sergeant didn't let them get any farther.

'Sit down, Wanklyn. And keep your temper. Shouting won't do you any good.'

There was another strange object there, too. A slovenly unshaved man, like a tramp, with large new boots and no socks. They were charging him with breaking-in an allotment and stealing a lot of hens and a shovel. Then, he was led off to the cells to spend the night. He didn't seem to mind. The hens were in a sack in an adjacent room and were squawking and cackling. Their owner was on the way to take them home.

The Inspector stood before the fire, his hands in his pockets, toasting the seat of his trousers. He seemed lost in thought until the smell of hot cloth made him move away.

'The sergeant tells me you deny having seen Cryer after he left you at four o'clock.'

Cryer chipped in again.

'He's a liar, then! He's trying to get out of it and leave me carrying the can. Why should I...?'

'Shut up, Cryer! Speak when you're spoken to. And don't interrupt Inspector Knell...'

The sergeant didn't seem to like Cryer!

Knell smiled. He was used to it.

'You'd better tell young Wanklyn exactly why he's here, I think.'

The sergeant took up another typed statement; the one Cryer had just signed.

'I'll not read all this. I'll just give you a short idea of what it's all about.'

He cleared his throat, put his elbows on the table, and stared at Wanklyn with sad eyes.

'At ten-thirty tonight, an elderly man was found stabbed in a side-street off the North Quay. He's since died without saying a word.'

Wanklyn sprang to his feet, but instead of shouting, looked piteously around him, like a trapped animal which finally resigns itself to its fate.

'I didn't...'

'Will you listen? Your friend, Cryer...'

'He isn't my friend. I hardly know him.'

'Will you keep quiet! Cryer was caught, as he ran out of the side-street into Victoria Street, by a civilian who'd heard the shouts of the victim before he was knifed...'

It was Cryer's turn now.

'I didn't knife him. I'd no knife. How many times have I told you, I picked up the wallet in the street as I left Sid Wanklyn....'

'As I was saying, Cryer was turned over to a constable by the civilian. During the scuffle with the said civilian who, by the way, happened to have been a wrestler when he was younger and stood no nonsense with Cryer's butting and kicking.... During the scuffle, Cryer tried to throw away a wallet which was later identified as belonging to the victim, John Charles Croake. Cryer, as he has just loudly informed us again, says he found it in the street. He also says he'd just left you at the time of his arrest, which was ten-thirty.'

Wanklyn looked round at the surrounding faces. He was like a trapped rabbit. At ten-thirty, he *had* been on the quay, running to the bus station for the last Castletown bus after leaving Marlene. Cryer must have seen him. It was dead on ten-thirty, too, because he'd seen the clock on the quay and started to run for it.

'Cryer says you'll testify to that and say that he couldn't possibly have robbed or killed anybody in the time between leaving you and reaching Victoria Street. I must tell you, the alibi's so thin, we think the pair of you were in it together.'

Wanklyn and Cryer both started to shout at once; Cryer that he'd done nothing, but parted peacefully with his friend, Wanklyn that he'd seen nothing of Cryer since four o'clock.

The interview went on until dawn and then they weren't any nearer. So Wanklyn and Cryer were locked in the cells until breakfast time. Both stuck to their stories. Wanklyn to his escapade with Marlene, Cryer to his tale of finding the wallet after leaving Sid.

Before they locked-up Wanklyn, the sergeant took a description of Marlene. For one who'd been so intimate with a girl, Sid made a poor show. She was smaller than he was, fair hair erected on her head in the shape of a beehive, nails painted red, black shoes with stiletto heels, light blue jeans, a thin yellow jumper with bare arms, and her real name was Ida, although she called herself Marlene.

'Oh... and she'd green eyes. She told me. She was proud of them. I hadn't noticed.'

The sergeant flung down his pencil and cast his eyes to heaven. He had a nice wife, four daughters and two young grandsons, and he was a somewhat sentimental man.

'A real young lover you are, aren't you? I could go on Douglas promenade any time tomorrow and pick-out hundreds answering to your description. Including the green eyes. You'll have to do better than that if you want us to find her.'

And he started with her style of hairdressing and ended up at the way she walked. He went through the whole erotic catalogue, like a judge at a beauty contest. Sid did his best and tried to please to the extent sometimes of gilding the lily. Finally, he said Marlene looked a bit like a well-known French film star, whereat the sergeant said he'd had enough and locked him up for the night. Sometimes, when prisoners were amiable and well-behaved, they were allowed to occupy the same cell, but in this case it was thought prudent to keep Sid and Alf as far apart as possible. Even then, Alf spent half the time until breakfast shouting abuse at his one-time pal. The man who had stolen the hens slept peacefully through it all.

Meanwhile, the sergeant decided he'd better concentrate on the fact that the girl's real name was Ida and she called herself Marlene, she was fair, and probably a hot and tasty dish. A number of constables were, therefore, much to their disgust, detailed to interview landladies in an effort of finding-out more about her.

Inspector Knell went home at four in the morning. He looked as fresh as a daisy, even at that outrageous hour, but he didn't feel it. He was completely confused.

Nobody had seen the crime committed. The knife hadn't been found, although the police surgeon had said the wound could have been inflicted with a flick-knife.

The murdered man, John Charles Croake, was an Island notable. Director of a number of prosperous Manx companies, a J.P., a former Member of the House of Keys, a prominent Methodist. Someone would be out for quick results in this case and quick justice, too. Croake had been alive when they found him, lying there, staring up at the little crowd which had gathered, a puzzled expression on his face, blood flowing from the corner of his mouth. Then he'd simply said 'Ah', and died.

In any case, what was an obvious thug like Cryer doing around at all? They kept his kind away from the Island nowadays. Wanklyn was under a cloud for the lies he'd told to get Cryer admitted. They'd probably prove to have been accomplices.

As for what Croake was doing there at that hour... He'd come in from near Ramsey with his sister and was on his way back to the car-park nearby, where they arranged to meet after parting earlier to visit their own friends. She'd been taken home by the police after making a statement. She was a spinster, he a bachelor, and they lived together at a large house on their estate of Ballacroake, near Lezayre, which had been in the family for centuries. Pots of money. Pots of trouble on the way now, too.

Knell didn't sleep the rest of the night. To prevent his wife from being anxious, he pretended to snore now and then, but all the time he was turning over the case in his mind.

Wanklyn obviously wasn't a killer. A question if he'd much wrong in him. Certainly not the criminal kind. Cryer, was another cup of tea altogether. A bad lot. And yet, cunning enough to know that if he killed anyone on the Island, he'd be sure never to get away with it, for he'd never get past the watch they kept in such cases at the boats and airport. He might bully or butt someone for a pocketbook or a bit of ready cash, but murder...

At ten o'clock next morning, Knell, after calling at the police station drove right on and into the country. As he passed the boarding-houses on the way, he could see lodgers through the windows eating their hearty Sunday breakfasts.

Just through Ballasalla, he turned left at a signpost, the sign of which had been blown off and not restored. The road led into the heart of the lovely Manx countryside, past farms where the milking was over and the men returning home to put on their Sunday clothes. One or two waved to him as he passed and he waved back. Then, suddenly, the byeway dipped through an arch of old trees like a tunnel and he found himself in the hidden village of Grenaby. Over the bridge and up the hill to the vicarage.

The vicar's housekeeper, Maggie Keggin, opened the door to his ring. She was nearer seventy than sixty, a little sturdy woman with bright eyes and a forbidding face for some, but from which the clouds would easily lift for others. She gave Knell a look of thunder.

'You again! You can't even stop away on Sundays now.'

'Yes. The Superintendent hasn't gone home yet, I hope. Is he up?'

'You know very well he hasn't gone yet. Trust *you*. And he's up, and they've gone to church. He's with the Archdeacon. It's Sunday, you know, and they didn't call-off the morning service in case you might call. They won't be back for over an hour.'

'I'll wait, then.'

'Where? I'm turning-out the parlour and the study's private.'

Knell bared his teeth in a grin.

'What's wrong with the kitchen?'

'I can't do with you there. I'm cookin' …'

She paused. After all, his mother had married her second cousin and Knell was in the family.

'Come in, then. You're a nuisance. I suppose it's another murder. You seem to save them all till Inspector Littlejohn comes over for his holiday. I wonder he ever bothers to come at all...'

An hour later, the Rev. Caesar Kinrade and Littlejohn returned from church to find Knell starting to eat his second apple pie and passing his cup for his fifth lot of tea.

'Murder always seems to make that Knell hungry,' Maggie Keggin later confided to the Archdeacon.

Chapter Three
Alibi

Maggie Keggin herself announced that Knell would like a few words with 'the Inspector.' She disapproved of his title of Superintendent, as belonging more to a Sunday School or an insurance company than the police. *Inspector* sounded bigger and better. 'A few words' was an understatement, after the Manx fashion. The story took over an hour to unfold and after half of it, Knell stayed to lunch.

Superintendent Littlejohn and his wife could hardly be described as globe-trotters. Every August, they spent a fortnight at Grenaby with the Venerable Archdeacon of Man; and he returned their visit by staying with them at Hampstead during protracted annual church conferences in the autumn. The rest of the Littlejohn's holidays were spent in France, with policemen. Dorange of the Nice Sûreté had a villa in his father's rose gardens at Vence; and Luc, now retired from the Paris Sûreté, lived in the lovely valley of the Orne in Normandy, near Le Bô. There was always a welcome at either place.

Today, Mrs. Littlejohn and their bobtail sheep-dog, Meg, had gone visiting to Ramsey. Mrs. Littlejohn's friend wrote children's books, and Meg had taken a fancy to her basset-hound, which reciprocated with a frenzy of eccentricities whenever she appeared, eating the carpets, pulling up geraniums in the garden and tossing them to Meg, and, finally, plunging in the forbidden swimming-pool and refusing to come out.

After Knell's long account of the murder, Littlejohn found himself wondering why he had been consulted at all about what was apparently just an ordinary nasty crime. Knell, as though reading his thoughts, was eager to explain.

'Murder is rare on the Island, sir. We don't want to make a mistake when one does occur. Both of these young men say they'd nothing to do with the murder of Croake. I believe that Wanklyn knows nothing about it. Cryer's a different sort altogether. He's a wrong 'un and no mistake. I think he stole the old man's money, but I doubt if he stabbed him. You've had more experience of this kind of crime than me. I'd be glad of your advice.'

Maggie Keggin, who was laying the table, sniffed loudly and muttered to herself. 'As usual...'

'The first move seems to be, Knell, to find this girl who calls herself Marlene. If she can confirm Wanklyn's account of his movements last night, that should put him out of the case. That will leave Cryer to be dealt with.'

'In what way?'

The Archdeacon, sitting still and relaxed, listening to it all without comment, spoke for the first time.

A rugged old man with a fine head of silky white hair, a full white bristling beard, and extremely bright-blue penetrating eyes.

'In what way? If Cryer persists in his denials, are you going to beat it out of him, or question him in relays for hours on end, as the French or American police do, judging from the enjoyable thrillers I read about them, until he confesses to the murder out of sheer exhaustion?'

'No. If Cryer won't tell us, we must find out in other ways. Has he told you, Knell, exactly what he was doing between the time Wanklyn is supposed to have left him and his capture by a passer-by?'

'Not yet. He's for further questioning this morning. We were up till three o'clock with him last night, but the bringing-in of Wanklyn led to some confusion. He denied everything and we let him go to bed finally, to avoid the foreign methods the Archdeacon's complaining about.'

'Let's assume that Wanklyn's telling the truth. That Cryer was left to himself...'

The telephone rang. It was Sergeant Costain, of the Douglas police, asking for Knell.

They'd found the lodgings where Marlene had stayed last week. Or, at least, Mrs. Quilliam, the landlady, had had among her guests a girl who'd left by last night's midnight boat, roughly tallied with the thin description given, and who, after calling herself Marlene Watson for several days, had received a letter addressed to *Ida* Watson. The landlady had only handed it over reluctantly to her after a proper explanation. Ida Watson came from Everton, and the police there had been alerted about her and would, at once, seek her out and take a statement.

'It sounds as though Wanklyn's telling the truth.'

For some reason, Knell, in spite of the heavy weight of responsibility on his shoulders, ate his lunch with splendid appetite.

Manx Plaice, Baron of Manx Lamb, Applie pie and Cream, and a tasty cream cheese made locally. The wine a rosé Château de Selle, a gift from Inspector Dorange, who was a friend of the vintner, made Knell cheerful and talkative.

'I guess what we have to do now is to break down Cryer's resistance and get him to confess...'

'If he's done it.'

The Archdeacon was becoming a devil's advocate on behalf of Cryer. Knell looked hurt.

'There doesn't seem much doubt about it, does there? He tried to throw away Croake's wallet. He'd obviously taken it from him by force. And when Croake resisted, he stabbed him.'

'But he denies it.'

'He's a proven liar. Look at the way he's tried to involve Wanklyn in the affair.'

'The weapon hasn't been found. If Cryer is charged with murder, and doesn't admit the crime, you'll have a case built on circumstantial evidence...'

Telephone again.

Maggie Keggin was annoyed.

'Can't they stop makin' this house into a police station every time Inspector Littlejohn comes here for a bit of peace and quiet. It's not fair...'

The latest bulletin from Douglas police station. Ida Watson had been interviewed by the Liverpool police. They'd found her at her home, sleeping off the effects of last night's crossing. She worked a sewing-machine in a shirt factory. She had definitely been with Sid, she said, until nearly half-past ten the night before. She didn't know his surname, but the description tallied and he'd told her to call him Sid. He had left her on Douglas promenade, saying he'd only just time to catch his last bus to Castletown, and he'd set off at the run, as he'd only a couple of minutes to do it. She said Sid was a nice boy; they'd arranged to meet in Liverpool when he got back.

That seemed to let out Sid. The Douglas police had nothing else against him and proposed to release him on condition that he didn't try to leave the Island without permission.

The police surgeon's report was to hand, too. Croake had received a nasty blow on the head, as well as a knife wound. Judging from the position of the blow, he might easily have been unconscious when the knife was used.

'A pretty kettle of fish, sir. Cryer has no alibi now. He must just have coshed the man and then stabbed him in cold blood...'

'Has a cosh or knife been found?'

'No. He might have thrown them anywhere between where he left the body and where he was caught.'

'He committed the crime, was alarmed perhaps by some one approaching, bolted, and was caught. Did he go down any side-streets on the way?'

'No, sir. He seems to have run straight down the alley from the body to Victoria Street in what you might call a straight line. I suppose he hoped to mix with the crowds there. It's usually full of people having a last walk or going to their digs from the pictures at that hour.'

'Where, then, could he have thrown the cosh and knife on his way? It isn't a big area to search.'

'Our men have been over the place with a fine-tooth comb, but found nothing.'

'Anything would do for a cosh; but a knife would be more difficult to hide. Like me to come back to Douglas with you? Even if I'm not much help, it will be an outing. The Archdeacon might enjoy the trip, too...'

The three of them started out.

It was a lovely day and Littlejohn was loath to spare it. The sun was hot and the sky clear and Grenaby looked at its best. The stream rambling under the fine ivy-covered stone bridge, the old trees, the Archdeacon's next-door neighbour, Joe Henn, loafing in his garden in his carpet slippers, still in his pyjamas with his coat and trousers over the top of them. He waved to Littlejohn.

'Good day... You'll see...'

The latter was a cryptic repetition of a forecast made by Joe Henn that, one day, Littlejohn himself would decide not to go back to London, and would become infected by the Manx atmosphere and stay to loaf the hours away, like Joe.

'You'll see...'

The roads were full of holidaymakers; on charabanc trips, in hired cars, on scooters, a few hardy ones walking. Knell reminded the other two, as they passed over the Fairy Bridge, to greet the little people, as it would bring them luck. He'd need it! They all doffed their hats and uttered the ritual words.

It all gave Littlejohn the holiday mood again. That torpor, that jolly feeling of irresponsibility which seems infectious among a crowd of holidaymakers. He sat with his hat over his eyes, the windows open, watching the passers-by, half-clad and happy in their temporary freedom. When they reached the police station, he felt reluctant to pass the doors, for inside the mood would vanish and the busman's holiday was probably waiting for him.

They never resented his arrival there. The Manx police always seemed to regard him as a friend from across the water, calling to see how they were doing, willing to tell them what was going on at Scotland Yard. They found him and the Archdeacon some cups of good strong tea and again told them the story of the murder of Croake.

Wanklyn had been released and was on his way back to his aunt's. His reception there was assured. He would now take his place in the family records of malefactors, along with the late Uncle Arthur. A no-good, a family disgrace, a skeleton in the closet.

Cryer, his confidence completely undermined by the loss of his alibi, had changed his tune. He continued to swear he hadn't killed Croake; he hadn't even had a knife. The police told him that if he wished to be believed after the lies he'd already told, he'd better make a clean breast of what he'd done the night before. They also reminded him that it was better to be convicted for robbery with violence than hanged for murder. That had shaken him still more. He'd confessed to the robbery, at length. But murder... He even broke down and wept at their thinking he'd stoop so low.

His tale was more coherent this time. He'd had a few drinks at a pub on the quayside. The landlord would confirm that.

The police had expected a beginning of that kind to the account. Most robbers with violence put it down to too much drink. You could almost have the 'few drinks' introduction printed on the charge-form to save time.

After the few drinks, he'd seen an elderly man emerge from the side door of an hotel in a street off the Quay. The man seemed a bit squiffy and, as he got in the street, by the light shining through the glass of the door, he'd seen him holding a wallet as though he was too drunk to put it in his pocket. Cryer said he didn't know what came over him...

They never did! They always seemed to become possessed of the devil before committing an act of violence. As though they expected the police to decide that someone of a different identity altogether had done it, and release the suspect right away.

Cryer didn't know what came over him, but he decided he'd like to take the wallet from the elderly man. So, he told him to hand it over. When he didn't... Well...

'You hit him. With a cosh?'

'I told you, I didn't have no cosh. I'd no weapon at all. Or at least...'

'At least, what?'

'Well, things seemed a bit disorderly in parts of the town. One or two gangs of lads shouted after me. I thought they might get rough. So, I put a stone from the shore in my sock...'

'On the spur of the moment.'

'Yes. I didn't set out from my digs looking for trouble. Premeditated, as you might say. Nothing of that.'

'When you were brought-in last night, you'd both socks on. You don't mean to tell me that after you'd manhandled the man and taken his wallet, you took off your shoe, replaced the sock, and started to run like hell. You left the digs with the sock in your pocket, didn't you? I'll grant it wasn't an offensive weapon then. Just a plain, ordinary sock. But you made it into one by putting a suitable stone in it. Am I right?'

The questioning sergeant had thrust his face close to that of Cryer, who had wilted, hesitated, and then agreed.

'But it wasn't premeditated. I just put it in my pocket in case any of the gangs got rough, see?'

'To return to the old man. When he refused, you hit him with the stone in the sock. What then?'

'I snatched the wallet and went off.'

'You ran hell-for-leather. Why not calmly, so as to cause no alarm?'

'I heard footsteps coming up the street from the quay.'

'So, you took to your heels and ran right into the arms of someone who'd heard the elderly man shout before you hit him.'

'I seemed to, yes.'

'What happened to the weapon?'

'It wasn't a weapon...'

'Just an old sock. I prefer the word weapon. What happened to it?'

'I dropped the stone out as I ran and the sock seemed to get lost in the struggle along with the wallet. I was carrying both of them. I hadn't time to put them in my pocket. But I didn't knife the old bloke. I'd no knife. You've gotta believe me. I'd no knife.'

And with that, Cryer had tried to get to the wall, to emphasise his statement by beating his head against it, but they'd brought him back and sat him down again.

That was the account they gave Littlejohn and they produced Cryer's signed statement to confirm it.

'Where is he now?'

'In the cells. Like to see him, sir?'

'I think I'd better not. It might start him wanting to beat his head against the wall again. So that explains the cosh not being found. I suppose he didn't dare bring one with him, in case the police at this end decided to go through his bag and his pockets and sent him packing by the next boat if they found a cosh or a bicycle chain or such... It doesn't account for the knife, though.'

'No, sir. That's going to be a tougher problem. By the same argument, he wouldn't bring a knife with him. But he might have bought one here. It's Sunday and we'll have to leave that till tomorrow. We'll do the round of the shops. Anybody could get a knife... table or potato-knife... which would do the job, from any ironmonger's.'

'Cryer said the elderly man was emerging from the side door of a pub. Was that right?'

'Yes. The *Bishop's Arms*. The landlord said he was there until about ten-thirty. That, too, confirms Cryer's account.'

'But a big Methodist, an ex-M.H.K., a prominent man... It sounds a bit out of character. What was he doing there? Boozing?'

'No. I suppose he signed the pledge once, and he kept it. He used to call for a lemonade or some other soft drink. It wasn't the drink he was after, though. It was the barmaid.'

'Indeed!'

'Well...The landlord's daughter, to be precise. Jenny Walmer. The old chap was sweet on her.'

'Half his age, I suppose.'

'Thirty. He was sixty-two. It was becoming the talk of the town. All straight and above board, though. It's said he hoped she'd marry him. He seems to have gone up the wall about her. They sometimes do at that age, don't they? Her dad told us and he was furious about it, but I gather Jenny wasn't averse. Croake had plenty of money, you know, and he wasn't a bad sort. Jenny's one of those bouncing, motherly women, good-looking in a lush kind of way. Walmer, her father, told me the old man met her at a charity fete he opened and since then, there's been no doing any good with him. They've been seen here, there and everywhere in his car and whenever he comes to Douglas, he calls at the *Bishop* and drinks a glass of bitter lemon with her in the private room. Very embarrassing for her father, though she doesn't seem to mind. Proud of it, in fact.'

'So, there begins to be more in this than a mere hit and run robbery. Croake, lying unconscious in a dark lane, might have tempted other people to finish the job. What do you say?'

'I hadn't thought of that, Superintendent. It might be so.'

'You haven't had time to think of it yet. Cryer was the obvious suspect, wasn't he? He might turn out to be the killer after all. However, until he confesses, we might take a look into Croake's general background.'

Knell, sitting with Littlejohn and the Archdeacon, listening to it all, gave the Superintendent a questioning look. Littlejohn pretended not to see it, but he knew what was coming.

'You know the Croakes very well don't you, Reverend?'

'Yes.'

The Archdeacon said nothing more, but his eyes twinkled.

'Would it be possible...?'

'Don't beat about the bush, Reginald...'

Knell flushed. It would be 'Reginald' all over the force now for weeks to come. When he was a constable, it had been 'Nellie'. Now...

'I thought perhaps you might call to offer condolences and take the Superintendent with you. If the local police call, the family might not like it. It might look as though...well...'

'We weren't satisfied with their share in the matter? Have they been interviewed?'

'No. Miss Bridget made a confused statement about what they were both doing when she and her brother came to Douglas yesterday, but after that, we took her home. She was prostrated, of course. We thought we'd let it simmer down a bit.'

'Quite right. So, you want me to take Superintendent Littlejohn to Ballacroake and investigate. That will be easy. First thing this morning, Ewan Croake, who is an old friend of mine, telephoned to say he wished to see me urgently. Just that. He didn't say what about. It must have been about his brother's murder. Since it has become known that Superintendent Littlejohn is a close friend of mine, the idea has got abroad that I, too, am a detective. I told Ewan that I would call tomorrow. I've evening service at six-thirty tonight and I must get back to Grenaby. First thing tomorrow morning, we'll go... I beg your pardon, Littlejohn. I hope you agree.'

'Of course. Anything to help. Unofficially.'

'Thank you very much, sir.'

Nobody reproached the Archdeacon for hiding this trump-card up his sleeve. He was often absent-minded or full of surprises. None of them grudged him his bit of fun.

As they said good-bye, they heard Cryer shouting for attention. He knew there was something he wanted; something they always wanted, the big shots in a jam on television. A lawyer. That was it.

'I want my lawyer,' he was shouting.

'They're not open on Sundays,' they told him, and gave him a cup of tea instead.

Chapter Four

Ballacroake

It took Littlejohn and the Archdeacon an hour to reach Lezayre; less than twenty miles of a journey, but the morning was so fine and the country so attractive that they couldn't persuade themselves to go any faster.

Moorland covered in gorse and bracken, graceful sweeping hills constantly changing shades under the shadows of high-riding clouds, valleys thick with foliage through which the road twisted like an intruder. Finally, a long run with the sea in view, and then the mountains suddenly ended and the flat land spread to the north like a fertile green carpet. A huge triangle terminating in the Point of Ayre, with a lighthouse behind which the channel seemed incredibly narrow in the deceptive light of the sun and made the Mull of Galloway appear but a stone's throw away.

Kirk Christ Lez Ayre... Lezayre for short. They halted to smoke and enjoy the scene, sorry the pleasures of the cross-country run were over.

It was eleven o'clock in the morning.

They resumed their journey, turned left, splashed through a ford in the Sulby River, and drove along a narrow country road for over a mile. Tall banks, topped with gorse, on each side. Through the gates which intermittently broke the hedges, were vast fields, vivid in the green of reclaimed marshland, intersected by dykes, and relieved by patches of gorse, bog willow and myrtle and dotted here and there with dark, still pools, fringed with tall, twisted trees.

In a break in the hedge, a white iron gate, slung between two solid whitewashed posts with conical caps. Thence a long, straight road, a 'farm street', climbed slowly uphill to a house in a ring of grim trees. An old painted wooden sign on the gatepost, with a single word just recognisable. *Ballacroake.*

Littlejohn opened the gate, drove through, and closed it again. The road led through well-kept parkland, with sheep feeding here and there. The whole set-up was trim and carefully managed. A workman in rough tweeds and a cap, with two sheepdogs at his heels, was walking in the same direction and Littlejohn stopped the car as they passed him.

The man turned and when he recognised the Archdeacon, touched his cap. He was past middle age, tall and heavily built, with a shock of red hair and a clean-shaven, ruddy face. From his air of self-assurance and the straight look he gave them with his green eyes, he might have been the owner of the place instead of the hired hand.

'Good day to you, pazon.'

'Good day, Juan. Are the family at home?'

'They're all up at the house. You've heard the news. A bad thing.'

'If you're going in, we'll give you a lift.'

'I'd rather be walkin' ...'

They left him. He was locally known as Red Juan. Through the mirror, Littlejohn could see him watching the car until they left him out of sight.

Littlejohn drove slowly. He was in no hurry to spoil the fine day by becoming involved in the shabby business of murder again. A flock of geese led by an old gander crossed the drive and he slowed down to let them pass. The gander stood and hissed at him.

The view from the rising ground was magnificent. In the distance, the Ayre lighthouse with a backing of still green sea. To the left, the tower of Andreas Church, lost in the fields.

Another iron gate cut in a low whitewashed wall which surrounded the house and garden. Again, the ritual of getting out of the car, opening it, driving through, setting it to. They were in a courtyard in front of the house.

'This is Ballacroake. It was once called the Deemster's House. Deemster Croake was a judge on the Island a hundred and fifty years ago. He was shot dead by a madman on his way to Ramsey courthouse. It was built on the site of a previous farmhouse in Georgian times by a notorious rake and it became the haunt of a group of local bucks, a sort of miniature hell-fire club, who gambled here and met their women. It had a bad reputation. Two suicides, a murder, and one or two owners have gone out of their minds. Now there's another murder to add to the list.'

A good start. Now, all the blinds were drawn and there wasn't a sound. You imagined that somewhere behind the blind windows someone was cutting his own or someone else's throat and that at any time the dead quiet would be broken by the wild cries of yet another occupant going crazy.

A good architect or some intelligent local builder must have been responsible for erecting the house. It was Georgian; tall, almost gaunt, with a stucco finish. The exterior had been recently painted and shone in the hot morning sun. A large front door stood at the top of a small flight of stone steps. Two tall sash windows on each side of the door, and above it, a long and splendid window, presumably lighting the staircase, with the two-a-side repetition of the windows on the floor below.

There was a well-polished brass knocker on the front door and Littlejohn left the car, climbed the steps, and beat a tattoo with it. The Archdeacon joined him. They stood side by side listening to the silence.

Behind them, the garden was as tidy as the exterior of the house. Flower beds had been constructed under the protection of the low surrounding wall and were alight with the orange, reds and pinks of marigolds, geraniums, sweet-williams and snapdragons. There was an old well-head in the middle of the yard, with ferns springing from the top, and two palm trees standing at each corner of the wall, absolutely still. Beyond the wall, a kitchen garden, also scrupulously tidy, and then the park, with its old fine trees dotted here and there in the grass. Under the nearest tree, just beyond the vegetable garden, was an iron table and three chairs. And farther still, the magnificent bastion of the Manx hills, suddenly ending and falling away to the plain.

The gate to the yard creaked and Red Juan was there with his dogs. The animals disappeared behind the house, presumably seeking food. Juan didn't seem surprised to see the visitors standing there, waiting for something to happen.

'Have ye knocked?'

'Yes. There doesn't seem to be anybody about.'

'They're about, all right. Nessie must be somewhere in the back. The family are inside, but they won't answer the door. They alwiz leave it to her. I'll go and see.'

He went round the house, his nailed boots clinking on the stones of the courtyard. A door banged somewhere at the back. Then they could hear someone moving indoors, light feet hurrying and boards creaking under her weight. The door opened.

It must have been Nessie. A dark, rather tall woman with plump arms and hips, middle-aged, with white in her hair. Her face was still handsome and full of character; quiet dark eyes and healthy red cheeks. She was soberly dressed in a black cotton frock with a white collar. She greeted the Archdeacon pleasantly and then stood there patiently waiting for them to state their business.

'How's your father, Nessie?'

She was a local girl.

'Middlin', Reverend, middlin'. Ninety-four last birthday. He's beginnin' to feel the weight of his age. He's livin' with my sister down at Bride. He'll be glad to hear I've put a sight on you, sir.'

'Are any of the family at home?'

'They're all at home, sir. Terruble trouble they're in. You've heard?'

'Yes. Mr. Ewan asked me to call. I expect he needs the comfort of his friends. This is a friend of mine. Mr. Littlejohn.'

She gave the Superintendent a dignified greeting, half a nod and half a curtsy.

'They're not seein' anybody, Reverend. They're all that cut-up. All the same... The Reverend Archdeacon isn't *anybody*. I'll tell Mr. Ewan you're callin'. Please come inside.'

'Just a minute, Nessie...'

Littlejohn laid a hand on her arm to prevent her hurrying inside. She turned her placid eyes on his.

'Yes?'

'How many of the family are at home now?'

'Mr. Reuben, Mr. Ewan, young Mr. Joseph and Miss Bridget...'

'Where were they all on Saturday, particularly at night, whilst Miss Bridget and Mr. John were in Douglas?'

'Would you be from the High Bailiff's office?'

She raised her eyebrows and turned her ear slightly for the answer. At the end of the question her voice rose in the Manx lilt.

'The High Bailiff over here is the equivalent of your Coroner in the matter of inquests...No, Nessie. Mr. Littlejohn's from the police.'

'God preserve us!'

It sounded like a prayer and not a frivolous interjection.

'There was only Mr. Ewan at home. He's on the Methodist plan and was takin' service at the Curragh Chapel yesterday. He was indoors preparing his sermon. Mr. Reuben was out with Mr. Joseph most of the day. They left early in the afternoon to go fishin' in Ramsey Bay. Mr. Joseph has a boat in Ramsey. They got home around half-past eleven at night. I'm sorry to say they were the worse for drink. Mr. Joseph ought to know better. He knows the drink isn't good for Mr. Reuben. A good job Mr. Ewan was busy with his writin' when they sneaked in and upstairs...'

'Mr. Joseph is...?'

'The son of the late Dr. Edward Croake, who died in England. Mr. Joseph lives there but spends most of his time here in the summer.'

The house itself remained still during all this talk in the hall.

'Where is everybody, Nessie?'

'They're all inside, Reverend. Mr. Ewan's up in his room, praying most of the time, judgin' from the sounds when you pass the door. Mr. Joseph and Mr. Reuben are in the morning-room and I'm tellin' no secrets when I say there's a bottle of whisky there with them. Miss Bridget is in her room, also, and from what I can guess, she's turning out the drawers in her clothes-chest. She always finds comfort in that when in trouble.'

A door banged in the rear and Red Juan appeared in the hall. His face was livid and he strode up to Nessie and roughly turned her round to face him.

'What's the meanin' of all this? The Archdeacon and his friend called here to see the family, not to stand listenin' to your gossip all the mornin'. Go and tell Mr. Ewan they're callin'.'

He turned her with her back to the visitors and gave her a push. Then, without a word, he left them standing there alone.

Nessie was back quickly.

'Mr. Ewan will be down in a minute. I'm to ask you to wait in the drawing-room.'

For a moment, they could see nothing in the room except the large sash windows at the front. A yellow light filtered through and gradually, as their eyes grew accustomed to the half-dark, they could make out the furnishings and pictures. Exquisite Sheraton and Hepplewhite cabinets, mirrors, a large dining-table on twin pedestals, with Hepplewhite chairs set round it. The cabinets were full of fine china. There were a number of gilt-framed portraits on the walls and the picture opposite the Adam fireplace was a Corot or a good copy. Littlejohn stood there looking round in amazement until footsteps approached and a man entered the room.

Ewan Croake was a large man; taller than Littlejohn by a couple of inches, which made him about six feet four. His enormous body filled the doorway. He had a massive brow and a face which might have been modelled in bronze; firm, strong, fanatical. Even in the badly-lighted room his eyes shone, but when he moved, swiftly and quietly for a man of his bulk, to the window and drew up the blind, it seemed to Littlejohn that he had been weeping. Nothing but the eyes showed it, but it was there; the bright, confused sight which sees through tears. He was not too heavy for his height and his body gave evidence of immense strength. He broke the spell by offering both his hands to the Archdeacon.

'Caesar! It is good of you to come.'

The Rev. Caesar Kinrade offered his condolences and introduced Littlejohn.

'Nessie told me the police were here. May I ask why, Superintendent?'

'I am quite without official authority, Mr. Croake. The Archdeacon said you wished to see him and suggested I might accompany him. I'm his guest at Grenaby. I'm naturally interested in this case; very sorry about it, too. Please accept my condolences. I have a professional interest in the matter, though. A young fellow, as you know, is being held in custody in Douglas. He was found with your brother's wallet in his possession and he is suspected of murdering him. The police case, however, will have to be constructed on more than surmise. I'm sure you will agree. We must be quite certain of all the details before a charge of murder is made.'

'I agree with you. That is why I asked the Archdeacon over. I am anxious that the fullest investigation shall be made. I don't want it assumed that because a young thug stole my brother's wallet, he also murdered him. I am anxious that something more than a circumstantial case shall be made of it. I need advice.'

There was a silence. Ewan Croake was in full possession of himself, quite calm. The only sign of any nervousness was in his stroking his thick grey moustache, which stretched the length of his upper lip.

'You will probably want to know as much as possible about my brother's movements before his death. My sister had arranged to meet him at the car-park in Douglas. When he didn't arrive, she went to look for him. She had an idea where he might be. I suppose the police know of all that.'

'Yes, sir.'

'Probably you have already found out about my late brother's haunts. He had grown friendly with a young woman half his age, the daughter of a publican in Douglas. You know that, Caesar?"

'Yes, we do.'

'And that he was in the habit of visiting her when he was in town? Briefly, my sister knew this, too, and made her way to the side door of the public house. When she got there, she found a small knot of people, including the police, standing round my brother's body. He died as she arrived. The police were kind enough to see her safely home. She was very upset, in fact, prostrate, and they asked her a few questions and sent her here. There seems little more to say.'

'We would like to talk with her quietly sometime, sir, and see if she could throw any more light on what happened.'

'I don't see what good that will do, Littlejohn. She is still too upset to be even reminded of Saturday night. I hope you will not insist.'

'The inquest is tomorrow, Mr. Croake, and after that, I assume, the funeral. When these are over, I hope she will agree to meet us then.'

'We must see how quickly she recovers. I'll let you know.'

'Meanwhile, may I ask *you* one or two questions. If they seem personal, or inquisitive, I hope you'll forgive me. I shall only ask what I think is absolutely necessary.'

'Do. I was prepared to take the Archdeacon fully into my confidence. He is an old friend. But I reserve the right to decline to answer.'

He said it quietly; no suggestion of anger or even irritation.

'Your brother was a wealthy man?'

'Yes. He inherited quite a large amount from my father. He was the youngest, but the inheritance was shared equally. My brother considerably increased his fortune by careful investment.'

'He was a bachelor, I believe.'

'Yes. Are you going to ask me who was his heir? I don't mind telling you, for I am his executor along with his lawyer. There are only two of the next generation, as my sister never married. Joseph is my late brother Edward's son. Edward was a doctor in England and died seven years ago. The other is my own son. He is a farmer in Kenya. He is unmarried, as yet, although I gather he shortly proposes to change that.'

'And the two nephews will inherit your late brother's estate.'

'No. This house and estate and certain farms in the north of the Island are subject to a family trust. My brother's share of the estate goes into the trust for the benefit of coming generations. It has always been a point of honour in our family to keep this home intact and also the income from the farms which keep it going. It has been so for generations. As for my brother's personal fortune...'

He shrugged.

'I am telling you all this in detail, because I know that, if I don't, you can ferret it out if it suits you to do so, and I would not care to have our family affairs surreptitiously investigated by outsiders. You understand?'

'I do, sir, and thank you for your help.'

'It is, from my point of view, not help at all. Merely a safeguard. To continue. My nephew Joseph didn't please my brother John at all. Joseph's ways are not ours. In the first place, he drinks too much. My brother John never touched it and neither do I. It has degraded too many of our family already...'

A bitter twist of the lip betrayed some wound or other which stung at the thought of it. Later, the Archdeacon told Littlejohn that Ewan Croake's wife had died an alcoholic. A member of an old family with not a few rakes in it, she had finally given way to the old weakness.

'...Joseph is a young man of very extravagant tastes and habits. No amount of remonstrance on our part seems any use. My late brother, therefore, left Joseph an income under the trust. To have left him capital would only have encouraged him in increased dissipation and the squandering of his heritage. My own son, Henry, was John's favourite nephew. He left him fifty thousand pounds. I tell you that because you will only go to the Rolls Office and get full details if I don't.'

'One other painful matter which is public property, I believe, sir. It is that your brother had talked of altering his Will?'

There was not a sign in the hard face of Ewan Croake that he felt any anger or bitterness about it.

'You're thinking of the girl Jenny Walmer of the *Bishop's Arms*? He had, I gather, spoken of marrying her and thanks to her father's public outbursts of rage at the idea, it has spread all over the Island. John never mentioned it to me. If he had seriously contemplated marrying the woman, he would have spoken about it. He'd have been compelled to do so. I am one of the trustees of the family estate.

However, what has happened has put an end to that matter. He didn't reach the point of altering his Will, even if he'd thought of it.'

Nessie came hurrying in, her pleasant composure disturbed. She tried to whisper to Croake, but her excited voice almost rang round the room.

'Miss Bridget's had another of her *does*. She wants you, sir. You'd better come, I think...'

Croake shook hands with the two visitors as a gesture of dismissal.

'I'm sorry, if there were anything else to tell you, I'd still have to leave it unsaid. My sister needs me. I must go... The funeral will be at Andreas church tomorrow at two. I would like you to be there, Caesar. You, too, Superintendent, if you care to do so.'

He turned back on his way to the door.

'Please excuse my not offering you the usual hospitable drinks. I am a little confused and am forgetting my duties...'

He smiled blandly. His first smile.

'Nessie will give you refreshment if you care for it. Please do come to the funeral if you can, both of you. Good-bye.'

And he was gone.

Nessie showed them out. As he left the car to close the gate, Littlejohn caught sight of Red Juan, who appeared round the corner of the house, red with anger and determination. He entered by the front door.

Littlejohn walked quietly back again. The front door and that of the vestibule were both open. He could hear angry whispering inside and stopped to listen. It was Red Juan and Nessie. Anxious not to disturb the family, she was keeping her voice down, but sounded in great distress. Juan's voice rumbled angrily.

'Tell me what was said. What did you tell 'em, and what did you hear Mr. Ewan say?'

'I won't. It's none of your business. Leave me alone...Leave me...If you don't, I'll call for help. Let me go...'

Littlejohn turned into the hall. Juan was there holding Nessie in his arms. But it wasn't in any amorous manner. He was squeezing the breath out of her to make her talk. Littlejohn took him by the shoulders and spun him round. Juan faced him with blazing eyes and the Superintendent thought he might turn violent. He was glad he didn't. A powerful man with muscles like iron and the temper of the redheads.

'What are you up to, Curghey? Let her go. And don't let me find you intimidating her again. If I hear you've pestered or bullied her in the slightest next time I call, I shall haul you in for assault.'

Curghey struggled to control himself and then took to his heels.

As he reached the door he turned and faced them with an outstretched forefinger.

'You be careful, my girl...And you be careful, too, policeman. Or else it'll be worse for you both. You leave the Croake family alone, or there'll be another murder.'

And he hurried off to one of the outhouses and slammed the door to sulk in solitude.

Chapter Five
The Bishop's Arms

Littlejohn drove slowly along the promenade hunting for a place to park. Finally, he managed to ease his car in a gap surrendered by a motorist with a load of children bound for a run round the Island.

It was a scorching day. The sea was like blue-green glass. All the pleasure-boats were out, bobbing about in the bay, and a white speedboat, a large moustache of spray fanning out around it, was skimming round Douglas Head on its way to Port Soderick. You could hardly have thrown a penny between the thick mass of sunbathers on the sands. Portable radios blared out dance music and an almost naked man, his bearded face contorted with his emotions and with a girl in a bikini lying across his knees, was sitting-up strumming a guitar.

Yoo Hoo! Rock ma baby an' me.

He was playing it with such gusto that he looked like somebody in a fit.

Everybody seemed to be moving in a voluptuous daze of warmth. A horse, pulling a passing tram, crossed its legs as it ran, looking drunk in the heat.

The *Bishop's Arms* was half empty. Most of the holiday crowds had gone farther afield or else were sporting in the sun on the beaches. It was a cosy little pub. The landlord collected Toby jugs; in fact he was an acknowledged expert. There were jugs in every available nook and corner and they stood on the shelves behind the bar between the bottles as well.

Although it sported a clerical name, Littlejohn thought it best to leave the Archdeacon outside, in spite of the good man's insistence. So he sent him to buy a new book he'd been talking about all week.

The landlord, Peter Walmer, was at the bar. A stocky, portly, grizzled man in his shirt sleeves, with a heavy, grey moustache, a large Roman nose, and a florid complexion. He gave Littlejohn a queer, questioning look. He'd never seen him before, but seemed instinctively to know he was from the police.

'What'll it be, sir?'

'A word with you in private, landlord.'

Mr. Walmer looked out of patience. In working hours, especially in the high season, he liked to be around the bar.

'You from the police?'

'Yes. I won't keep you long.'

'I suppose it's something about the teddy-boy affair the other night. Nothin' I can tell you. I've been through it all before with the police. It's becoming a nuisance. Everybody's pesterin' me about it. It's good for trade, you might say, but I don't want that sort of trade. It's in bad taste...Well, if you must...I'll call the barmaid. She's takin' a bit of a rest before things warm-up.'

He left the room and quickly returned with a large blonde girl with an overwhelming bust. She looked like a lion-tamer's assistant.

'Come in here.'

A small room, obviously the landlord's private retreat. More Toby jugs. Dozens of them. All colours. Every shape and size. Some of them looked happy; others malevolent. One looked like the landlord himself.

'You've quite a fine collection here, landlord.'

The man's eyes lit-up.

'You interested?'

'My wife is. She has a few of her own.'

'Tell her to call any time. Perhaps it'll be better when we're closed. Then we can compare notes.'

'I'll do that. Meanwhile, I mustn't take up your time. It is about the affair of Saturday night.'

The Toby jugs seemed to have oiled the wheels. The landlord was quite friendly and ready to talk.

'I shouldn't say it, but the murder's solved a problem for me. I guess you know what it is. Everybody's talkin' about it.'

'Your daughter?'

'You're tellin' me! You can't tell what women are up to. I defy anybody to explain 'em. They don't know themselves half the time. By the way, will you take some beer?'

'I don't mind.'

The landlord went out and returned with two pint tankards. It was good stuff, too. A special brew he kept for his intimates.

'Where were we?'

'Women don't know what they're doing half their time...'

The landlord nodded rapidly.

'Take my girl, for instance. Jenny. Though I say it myself, she's a damn' good looker. She's had plenty of chances. Good ones, some of them. Yet, she lets herself reach the age of thirty, unattached, and then goes and takes up with a chap twice her age. I don't mind her bein' unattached.

Since her mother died when she was in her teens, she has been everything to me. I only want her to be happy. She couldn't possibly have been if she'd married Croake...'

The landlord took a good swig of his beer.

'I gave her a good talkin'-to a few times, but it was no good. I asked her if she loved him, although, to my mind, it was a silly question. She said she was *fond* of him. I ask you. I even asked her if it was the money, or the position she was after. She got mad at that. She said Croake was a good man, she wanted a place of her own, and a good man to look after her. She said again, she was *fond* of him. There's no understanding or arguing with women. I admit, I told her she'd marry him over my dead body. I must be honest and tell you I said it because I didn't know what else to say. I was bein' a bit dramatic and don't you go and put me down among your list of suspects because of it. I wouldn't have murdered Croake. As I said, I only wanted Jenny to be happy. If she'd married him, I'd just have had to grin and bear it. But I didn't fancy being father-in-law to a man a year or so older than myself.'

The landlord stopped suddenly. He'd got a bit out of his depth.

'Where do you come-in in this lot? You're not one of the Island police, are you?'

'No. I'm from Scotland Yard. I'm here on holidays and I'm just keeping my hand in helping my friends. I'm not officially on the case, at all. You needn't talk about it if you don't wish.'

'I don't mind. Not that there's much to say. But it comes easy chatting with you and tellin' you my troubles. By the way, don't mention any of this to Jenny, will you? She's upset enough already. What do you want to know?'

'What happened on Saturday night?'

The landlord hurried out and refilled the tankards.

'This is as much as I care to drink. It's a strong brew, Mr. Walmer.'

The landlord grinned.

'Special jubilee brew. It's like wine, isn't it? Saturday night? Croake usually came down from Ramsey to Douglas on Saturdays with his sister. Sometimes, he came down midweek, too. Miss Croake doesn't drive a car, so one of them has to bring her to do her shopping and see her special friends. Until Croake took-up with Jenny, he seemed to escort his sister round the town. Then, he got to calling here. He used to come around six and Jenny brought him in this room. There was nowhere else to put him and I didn't like the idea. It made him like one of the family, and I objected to it. But Jenny won, as usual. It was awkward, you see. He was rabid T.T. He must have been fond of Jenny to do it. But there it was.'

Walmer looked hard at Littlejohn and smiled wryly.

'He must have been a very important person if they've brought in Scotland Yard on the case so soon. And don't you try to tell me it was by accident, or because you happen to be on your holidays. There's more in this than meets the eye, Superintendent. However, to get on with my tale…'

It was very quiet there. They could hear the rumble of voices and the rattle of bottles in the bar. Now and then, the door to the main street would open and close and a newcomer would cheerfully give an order. Everybody seemed boisterous in the lovely sunshine.

There was a door from the room through which Croake had passed to his death in the alley. There was a glass panel in the door and the sun shed a blinding square of light through it.

The special brew began to do its work on Littlejohn. He felt he didn't want to move, or even to think. He just wished to sit there, eyeing the Toby jugs, listening to the pleasant chatter of Peter Walmer, lolling the hours away.

He could imagine the peaceful existence of Walmer and Jenny in their little pub. The pair of them together, calmly eating breakfast, chatting, comparing notes before they opened up for the day's rush. Again, at supper, happy in each other's company when the crowds had gone. And, in the winter, when the season was over, enjoying together the languid days when hardly a soul called for a pint. Then, John Charles Croake had arrived. An outsider, a man out of their class altogether. And Jenny had talked about wanting a home of her own.

'Jenny and me have to go to the inquest tomorrow…'

'Where is your daughter?'

'A friend called and took her out. Said it would do her good to get away a bit. She's upset, as you'll no doubt guess. She should be back before long.'

'How long have you kept this place, Mr. Walmer?'

'Call me Pete; it doesn't sound so starchy. We've been here twelve years. My wife always wanted to come and live in Douglas. I was at sea. Merchant Navy. I got I wanted to see more of my wife and girl, so I looked round here for a pub and found this one. We'd just got comfortably settled when my wife died. Jenny was eighteen at the time. She was going steady with a young pilot in the R.A.F. He crashed and got killed. It was less than a year after Jenny's mother died. Jenny never seemed really interested in men after Will got killed. Until she started this ridiculous business with Croake…'

He stopped, drank and was silent.

The flies buzzed round the room, the Toby jugs all seemed to be looking down at the two men at the table, and through the open window they could hear the winches rolling and unrolling, loading a coaster at the quay.

'What happened on Saturday night, Pete?'

'Croak turned-up, as usual. He was later. It was round about half-past seven. He said he'd been detained with a friend. We keep the side door locked, so Croake used to enter at the main door, through the bar, and come in here. I told him it would be all right that way. What else could I do? I couldn't have him hanging about the bar, a man of his sort. The regulars are always a bit noisy on Saturday and some of them are half soused by the time we close.'

'He came right in here. What then?'

'It was a sort of routine. Jenny would come in and sit with him for half an hour and then return to the bar. She couldn't be spared from seven or eight till Croake decided to go about ten-fifteen. We're busy on Saturdays. When Jenny left him, I'd go in to pass the time of day, but Croake and me never had much to say to one another. I didn't approve, but put up with it for the sake of Jenny. He knew that. So, when I'd had about a quarter of an hour there, I'd go back in the bar. He didn't mind. He'd sit here quietly on his own, reading the paper and drinking his lemonade, quite content. After half an hour at the bar, Jenny would come back for a bit, and then spend her time between talking to Croake and returning to the bar to give a hand. And it went on like that till it came time for Croake to go. Queer, I called it. It beat me. As I said, I'd have shown him the door long ago, if I hadn't known it would upset Jenny.'

Littlejohn filled his pipe and passed his pouch over to Walmer.

'No thanks, I've stopped smokin'. I like snuff best...'

He took a huge pinch from a box from his waistcoat pocket, wiped away the remains with a coloured silk handkerchief and sat back quietly. Littlejohn puffed away contentedly. He was beginning to appreciate Joe Henn's little joke. 'You'll see...' The atmosphere of quiet about the place encouraged the thought that the problems of today could wait until tomorrow.

'What was Croake after?'

'I don't know. Nothing wrong, I can tell you. He never laid a finger on Jenny. Never an arm round her waist, never a wrong look. He might just have been her favourite uncle.'

'But he was courting her in his way, I suppose. I've heard it said he was thinking of marrying her if she'd have him.'

'Jenny said he'd asked her. Just matter of fact, too. He said he'd buy a house, over here or on the mainland, if she wanted. It's no use asking me any more about that. Jenny's the one, but don't ask her yet for a while. I depend on you not to raise the subject till she's got over it. I got so mad when she spoke of it that she shut up about it and it hasn't been mentioned since. I guess she was thinking it over when Croake died.'

'Things went on, as usual, on Saturday night?'

'Exactly to programme, except that he was later than usual. The routine went on. He sat here alone part of the time, Jenny came and spent half an hour with him, now and then. She honestly found pleasure in his company. He was a good talker when he'd got the right listener. He'd travelled and seen things. Jenny'd had a good education. She went to a good girls' school on the mainland. They got on well together.'

'And he left at getting on for half-past ten.'

'Yes.'

'Did he say good-night and just go?'

'He usually did. Said good-night and thanked us for a pleasant evening. Always good mannered and polite. But on Saturday, he didn't quite act as usual. Both Jenny and me were a bit surprised. He stayed a bit longer and at about quarter past ten both Jenny and me went in the bar to get the last drinks and clear up a bit, leaving him on his own. Jenny went in about twenty-five past ten and found Croake had gone. The next thing was, there was a commotion in the side street and we found Croake had been stabbed and was dead.'

'Jenny took it badly?'

'Wouldn't you? Even the murder of a stranger turns you up, doesn't it? To have it done to someone you know and think a lot of is worse. She was terribly cut up.'

'Had he any other friends who came in here to talk to him?'

'Not really. I've my own friends who use this room and now and then, one would pop in on a Saturday night and come through. They'd find Croake here and pass the time of day, but he wasn't the sort to be very sociable if he didn't feel like it. They didn't stay long, as a rule.'

The time seemed to pass slowly, but when Littlejohn looked at his watch, it was three o'clock. He'd been there over an hour. He wondered where the Archdeacon had got to. They'd arranged to meet at the car in an hour. Time to go. It needed a great effort of will to get up and say goodbye. The atmosphere of tolerant indolence seemed to get in your bones.

Suddenly, the peace was disturbed. They could hear the outer door open, pattering footsteps crossing the bar, halting outside the private room, and then the door swung open. There was a stranger standing there. He looked ready to turn and bolt, but Walmer called him back.

'Come in, Ross. This is the Superintendent who's looking after the Croake affair. He's from Scotland Yard... A friend of ours, Superintendent. Mr. Roscoe Bottomley. He's a well-known local artist.'

Littlejohn had been trying to sum up the newcomer. Mr. Bottomley was neat and tidy, but had a touch of originality about him. He wore a soft tweed hat with a little feather in the brim. A heavy local tweed suit, in spite of the heat of the day, an incongruous flannel shirt with a floppy collar, with a foulard bow tie, and very shiny brown shoes. His hair was short and bristly grey, his eyes deep-set behind powerful spectacles in gold frames, and he had a small moustache. He was smoking a cigarette in a holder, he carried a stout ash stick with a silver ring round it, and he wore lemon-coloured gloves. A small man, a bit fragile looking. He carefully removed the cigarette from the holder, rubbed it out in an ash-tray, took off his gloves, and then offered his hand to Littlejohn.

'Sit down, Ross. We were just talking about John Charles Croake. He was an old friend of yours.'

Mr. Bottomley's eyelids trembled and he slowly closed and opened them again. It was a trick of his. Sometimes he spoke with his eyes closed altogether. He grinned uneasily as he spoke.

'John Charles? Yes. He was a friend of mine. Bought a lot of my pictures in his time. Didn't agree with me later. Not educated up to it. Hoped to bring him round in time. Pity he's dead.'

He closed his eyes again, like somebody in prayer. Then he started to roll himself a cigarette, clipped off the spare tobacco protruding from each end with a pair of pocket scissors, put it back in his pouch, and lit the cigarette. He inserted it in the holder baring his teeth as he put it in his mouth.

Mr. Bottomley had, in his time, been a producer of nice little Manx watercolours of popular landscapes which had sold well. Then, overnight almost, he'd turned abstract and appeared with grubby canvases of which nobody could make top nor tail except himself. They embodied objects like nuts, bolts, wire-netting and coat-hangers. He said they were local scenes. They ceased to sell on the Island but, it was said, had a good and profitable market in London and Paris. He'd even had a turn on television. Ross didn't seem badly off. In fact, he'd hit the jackpot by a crackpot brainwave.

'Are you the friend of Caesar Kinrade, sir?'

'I am. He's waiting for me and I must be off.'

'Don't worry about him, my dear Superintendent. I've just passed him, sitting in a car on the promenade, lost to the world in a book. I hope I'm not intruding. I just popped in as I was passing. I got a good tip for the three o'clock tomorrow.'

'You back horses, Mr. Bottomley?'

'A mere bagatelle. I usually share my information with Peter. I must be off.'

It looked like developing into an argument about who should stay and who should go. Walmer settled it by going out and bringing back three tankards of the best.

'I've to drive the Archdeacon home to Grenaby soon. It's not a good thing for a policeman...'

'Nothing of the kind. It'll wear-off between now and when you meet the Rev. Caesar. Good health to all of us.'

Mr. Bottomley drank carefully but steadily and almost emptied his tankard in one. Then he took a deep breath and resumed his smoking.

'Did you wish to ask me any questions about Croake? As Peter says, I know the whole family pretty well. When I used to go paintin' in the north, Ballacroake was always open house to me. Often had me lunch there.'

He closed his eyes again as though seeing it all in his mind's eye.

'What kind of a family are they?'

'Wealthy; but wealth isn't everything. They're all queer, except John Charles. And now he's dead...'

Mr. Bottomley's eyes were closed, as though he were thinking deeply, rummaging in the storehouse of his mind and perhaps his imagination as well.

Littlejohn looked round the room at all the Toby jugs, which seemed to be listening, too; hanging on Mr. Bottomley's words. This little room at the back of the pub seemed in another world. A sort of Disneyland, populated by a lot of little figures which might at any time spring to life and do a fantastic dance. And a crazy artist who'd taken the centre of the stage and was starting to tell a ghost story.

'...There's been too much inbreeding in that family. Too much effort to keep the money intact. Marriages among cousins and near relatives. It weakens the stock...'

Mr. Bottomley opened his eyes and looked surprised, as though he'd suddenly fallen upon one of the facts of life by accident.

'It weakens the stock. They ought to have married outside for a time or two. Like my family did. Manx for generations and then they took on a little fresh blood. A Bottomley and a Dabchick. Improved the breed immensely....'

Littlejohn looked at the man. Bottomley, with his cataract glasses, his bitten fingernails, his chain-smoking, his facial tic, might have been a sort of Greek god instead of a little runt, to hear him talk!

'...There's the eldest, Reuben, who's had to be put away a time or two for alcoholism. A neurotic and a hypochondriac. You should see his dressing-table. Chock full of patent medicines and stuff...Ewan's religious. Not the calm, assured sort, but a fundamentalist...'

Bottomley opened his eyes wide in surprise at his sudden gift of speech. He liked the word...

'Fundamentalist,' he said again proudly. 'A man who believes in hell-fire, sin, eternal punishment and damnation, predestination... The lot. He once took me aside and tackled me. I soon shut him up, I can tell you. I asked him who he thought he was talking to...'

The eyes opened again and Mr. Bottomley looked proud of his dialectical skill. He might have found the answer to the million dollar question!

'... Edward was a doctor. The best of the lot. He died of overwork. Never a strong constitution. Ewan's son went abroad to get away from it all. His father bullied the life out of him. And Joe, Edward's son, looks to be following in his uncle Reuben's footsteps. The bottle...'

Mr. Bottomley remained with his eyes closed. He seemed to be counting, calling the roll of Croakes.

'Oh, and there's Miss Bridget... Bridey, as they call her. She's gone all queer and lives a secluded life, doing good works in a forlorn sort of way. A very decent old maid, but all shot to pieces by a frustrated love affair. She and that bailiff fellow, Juan Curghey, Red Juan, were in love when they were young, but the family soon put a stop to that. Why they didn't run away and get married, I don't know. I guess she was too scared, and Red Juan and his forefathers had been so long with the family, he hadn't it in him to disobey, though he's a man of strong character. I suppose it was next best for him; he stayed on to look after Bridey.'

Mr. Bottomley opened his eyes, started to plut on the lemon gloves and rescued his stick with the silver band. He rolled a fresh cigarette with great dexterity, clipped the ragged ends and put them safely away, lit the remainder, and rose.

'I'll be off. There's just one thing I have to say more. It's my own opinion and I hope you won't mind plain-speaking, Peter. In my view, it's no wonder that John Charles finally decided to make a break and leave it all behind. He found something new in your Jenny, Peter, and nobody could blame him for seeking after it. His only mistake was that he found it out too late and having done so, didn't act quickly enough.'

Bottomley made for the door, put his hat on, removed it again as he made a polite bow.

"Good-bye for the present, gentlemen..."

And he was gone.

'Poor Ross. He's almost as balmy now as the people he's been describing. Comes of a good family and one time he seemed to have a great future in front of him. Then he started to go haywire in his painting. Instead of nice views, he began to paint the sort of things kids do the first time you give 'em a brush. Things like wire bedsteads and corkscrews. Funny thing is, *they sell* in certain quarters over the water. Sell for good prices, I believe. It beats me...'

Littlejohn rose to go. There were more footsteps crossing the bar and they halted at the door of the room again. It opened, and a woman stood there. She wore a grey tailored suit of light material and looked fresh and energetic. A tall, dark, plump girl without a hat, showing her jet black hair. Her dark eyes were clear and smiling.

'Here's Jenny now,' said Walmer. 'This is Superintendent Littlejohn, Jenny. He's from Scotland Yard and he's looking into the affair of the other night, the affair about John Croake you know...'

The smile vanished, and Jenny Walmer looked afraid.

Chapter Six
Teddy-Boy's Lament

As the door of the *Bishop's Arms* closed behind him, Littlejohn seemed to step into another existence again. The hot sun beating down, happy people milling around in their holiday clothes, busy shops, the horse-trams on the promenade, and the still, blue sea with the tide just on the turn.

He hadn't stayed behind to talk with Jenny. She'd just shaken him by the hand and excused herself. She had to change her clothes, she said. And she'd disappeared upstairs.

Her father had been a little apologetic about it.

'Perhaps you wouldn't mind calling again later if you want to talk to her. It's as I told you. She's properly upset. She's been visiting her friends and you know what women are. They've been having a good cry together, I suppose, and she'd got a mood on her. She isn't often like this, but Saturday's affair's been a big shock.'

It was striking four when he reached the car again. The Archdeacon was immersed in his book. He'd read half of it whilst he was waiting. His spectacles were on the end of his nose and his frothy white beard was folded under his chin. He, too, seemed to awake from a dream world when Littlejohn greeted him.

'Have you been busy?'

He told his friend all that he'd been doing and hearing. The old man seemed to understand it fully, to see it, too. The room beyond the bar, where you shut out the crowds and sat quietly talking and drinking, with the Toby jugs looking down. A place where you could relax and let the rest of the world go by. *Traa dy Liooar*, as they said on the Island. Time enough.

Now and then, a friend would drop in for a talk and a smoke. Men like Bottomley, at a loose-end, eccentric, perhaps laughed at by the rest, fetched-up there and found peace and companionship in the torpid, careless atmosphere.

And then John Charles Croake had found his way there, too. Whether it was his fondness for Jenny or pure coincidence which had brought him, Littlejohn couldn't say. It was a mystery as deep as the cause of his death. They'd have to find that out. But he'd arrived, the lazy mood of the place had infected him, and he'd started to make a habit of calling whenever he was in town. Tired of battling with his family, lonely, seeking somewhere where he could relax, he'd found happiness in the warm laziness of the back room at the *Bishop's Arms*. And then...

Littlejohn realised that he'd forgotten all about the affair of the teddy-boys. They didn't seem to fit in. And yet, one of them was likely to stand trial for murder because of Croake. That was a straight police investigation for the local men. Littlejohn's share in it all seemed to centre around the strange mansion in the marshes at Lezayre and in the back room of the *Bishop's Arms*. He was glad of that.

'We'd better call and see how Knell's getting along. Then it'll be time to go home.'

Littlejohn suddenly felt tired of it all. Already he was eager to get back to the vicarage in the hidden valley of Grenaby, infested by ghosts and strange things that walked by night but never did anybody any harm. No murders there. Just his slippers by the log fire, the parson reading, Mrs. Littlejohn doing needlework, the dog snoring by his side, and the old clock ticking the idle hours away.

'You'll see...' Perhaps, one day, Joe Henn's prophecy would come true. He'd settle down like the back-room boys of the *Bishop's Arms*, and stay for good!

People were strolling back to their lodgings for tea. The pleasure boats were returning home and tying-up at the quay. The afternoon boat to Liverpool was just visible, disappearing over the horizon. A man passed, carrying a saxophone, on his way to the Palace. Day was on its way out and people were getting ready for the night.

They stopped at the corporation car-park on their way to the police-station. The attendant looked disappointed when they didn't drive in. He noticed the Archdeacon and greeted him. A little man with a monkey face and a stiff leg.

'Did Mr. Croake and his sister call here last Saturday?'

'Yes. They always did. Reg'lar customers.'

'What time?'

'As far as I can rec'lect, between three and four.'

'Did you see where they went after they'd parked the car?'

'They did as they always did. He went one way and she went the other. She couldn't drive, so she got the 'bus uptown. She carried a shopping-bag, too. Mr. Croake crossed to the Mona Steamers' office. He's a director. I guess he went to run them round a bit. It's said that he did the rounds of his companies every Saturday. At five o'clock, he was here again, took out the car, and went off in the direction of the promenade. Then, he was back about seven and parked again. He walked away towards the promenade.'

'You were still on duty at half-past ten?'

'Yes. His sister came back about quarter-past and seemed a bit surprised he wasn't here. She took a stroll along the North Quay and I saw no more of her.'

'What happened to the car?'

'It was in the police garage till around half an hour ago. Then, Mr. Joseph Croake called and took it away.'

'Thanks. You've been a great help.'

'You're welcome, sir. My respects, Archdeacon.'

Knell was engaged when they arrived at the police-station, but they sent for him and he appeared, smiling as usual, but a little excited.

'Young Joseph Croake's here. He's been collecting the family car and called to ask for news of the criminals. He's come down to Douglas for the inquest. Would you like to see him?'

'Just to meet him. We're going to the funeral tomorrow, so may as well get to know as many of the family as we can, Knell.'

'Anything fresh today, sir?'

'Not really. We went to Ballacroake this morning. It was hardly the time to conduct an enquiry. We lunched in Ramsey and came back here. I spent a while with Walmer, the landlord of the *Bishop's Arms*. We passed a pleasant hour together, but I didn't get much information. What about the prisoner?'

'He's quiet now. He's seen a lawyer. He seems well-lined with money. How much is honestly come-by is anybody's guess. He still protests that he didn't knife Croake. He insists he never had a knife. We've had another search for the knife, but no luck. We also did the rounds of the shops, but none of them sold a knife to Cryer. We took his photo with us, but nobody recognised him. Shall we go and see Joe Croake?'

'He's the son of the late Dr. Croake, who practised in England, I believe.'

'Yes.'

'Is his mother alive?'

'No. She was an invalid and spoiled Joe when he was a kid. At least, that's what I've been told by local people who knew all about it. She died and left the doctor with Joe, who was at school at the time. Joe's never done a job of hard work in his life. His father left him some money, but I've heard it wasn't much. He'd been wealthy in his time, like the rest of the Croakes, but his sick wife made a large hole in his fortune, they say. Shall we go?'

If Littlejohn had expected a scruffy drunkard, he received a shock when he met Joseph Croake. Judging from the aroma which met them at the door, he'd had a drink or two, but he carried it well. He was, from all accounts, just about thirty, but he might have been older. His face was lined from worry or else drinking heavily. Tall, thin, well-groomed, clean shaven, he wore a well-cut tweed suit and a club tie. An indulgent mouth; in fact, a weak face. He was perfectly self-possessed.

'This is Superintendent Littlejohn, of Scotland Yard, Mr. Joseph. He's on holiday, but he's helping us on the case.'

Joseph looked quizzically at Littlejohn. He had a care-worn look as though he found life hard for some reason.

'Case, Knell? Case? I didn't know there *was* any case. I thought you'd got the teddy-boy who killed my uncle. Why need any help?'

'The accused talks only of robbery. He says he didn't use a knife. In fact, he says he hadn't got a knife. And we haven't found one...'

'That's absurd. It's obvious who killed him. The little swine did it and chucked the knife away somewhere. Because you police can't find it, it doesn't mean he didn't do it. It's ridiculous. The family's upset enough by the death of my uncle, without the police starting to wash a lot of dirty linen to no purpose...'

'Is there any dirty linen to wash, Mr. Croake?'

Joseph Croake turned his tired eyes on Littlejohn. He was growing annoyed. Probably the main reason was that he was anxious to get off and buy himself another drink or two.

'I'm not answering that question, Superintendent... Let me see, what's your name? I've forgotten it....'

Littlejohn removed his pipe and smiled blandly.

'Littlejohn.'

'Well, I'm not here to answer foolish questions. I called for information, not to give it. If you go on like this, you'll put your foot in it. This isn't a C.I.D. case. It's a murder which is already solved. The Croakes are influential people and I warn you... You're in for a lot of trouble if...'

'If what, Joseph? This is a case which hasn't yet been fully investigated. If the teddy-boy is to face a charge of murder, it must not be based on what *appears* to be true, but what *is* true. Now mind your manners when you speak to Superintendent Littlejohn and don't behave like an ill-bred puppy.'

Joseph Croake turned and faced the Archdeacon in surprise and met the clear blue eyes with his own for a minute. Then he lost countenance.

Littlejohn followed it with another thrust before Croake could recover.

'Where were you at half-past ten on Saturday evening?'

'What are you getting at?'

'I simply asked you a plain question.'
'You've no right. I'm not a suspect, am I?'
'No. Don't answer if you don't feel like it. I can find out if I wish.'
'I'll save you the trouble. I was in Ramsey. My uncle Reuben and I had been fishing in Ramsey Bay. We stayed out rather a long time. We put-in at Ramsey about ten and went for a drink. It was a hot night. We got home around eleven. They got us out of bed to tell us the news about Uncle John. Satisfied?'
'Yes. When did you last see your Uncle John?'
'About one. He and my aunt set out for Douglas immediately after lunch. Uncle Reuben and I left just after. Anything else?'
'No. You can go.'

Croake didn't know what to say or do. He wanted a drink and yet he wished to squash Littlejohn with a cutting retort. He couldn't think of one. He rose with as much dignity as he could muster and made for the door. Then he turned and tried a parting shot.

'I warn you. Cause any scandal or trouble for our family, and you'll regret it. I shall tell my uncle the way I've been bullied here.'

'Very well, Mr. Croake. He will know where to find me. I shall be with the Archdeacon at the funeral tomorrow...'

Croake was already closing the door. They heard him stamping down the stairs, missing two steps and staggering down two more in his haste. Then the outer door slammed.

'A nasty piece of work.'

He left behind him the sickly smell of brilliantine and whisky.

Littlejohn knocked out his pipe in the ash-tray on Knell's desk.

'How's Cryer?'

'All right. As I said, still denying he killed Croake.'

'It might be a good time for me to have a word with him. I'll go alone, if you don't mind. He might be more forthcoming.'

The Archdeacon drew his chair up to the fire and smiled.

'Don't mind me. I'll give Reggie here an improving talk whilst you're away.'

Knell rang and told the constable who answered it that Littlejohn wished to see Cryer.

'He's all yours, sir.'

Cryer seemed surprised to see a visitor. A very clean and comfortable cell. Cryer had been before the summary court and had been remanded without bail. Shortly he'd be transferred to the gaol at the top of the town to await trial at the General Gaol Delivery. He was lying on the bed in his shirt sleeves with his shoes off. He was proud of his shoes. They stood neatly on the floor and he must have cleaned them carefully. He'd ask for shoe-polish and cleaning-tackle and they'd granted them. Now he was resting.

The cock-of-the-north of the inward boat trip was now deflated. He looked shocking. Rings under his eyes, hair disordered, shifty, guilty look. When he saw Littlejohn, he mistook him for another lawyer.

'No need to come here trying to trip me up. I've my own lawyer and I'm sayin' nothin'.'

'Don't, if it suits you…'

The policeman who'd brought Littlejohn down turned on Cryer.

'Keep a civil tongue in your head, Cryer. This is Superintendent Littlejohn, of Scotland Yard. He's here to help you.'

Cryer lost his voice and then found it again, only this time it was weaker.

'Scotland Yard! Crikey! They're not takin' me to London to try me, are they? I want my lawyer. I'm not sayin' anythin'.'

'Listen to me, Cryer. I'm here to try to help you if what you say is true. You insist you didn't kill John Croake...'

'I didn't. I'd swear it on a stack of bibles, if that'd do any good. But it won't, see? They've got it in for me, and they're out to see me swing.'

'Nothing of the kind. They're anxious that justice shall be done. They've allowed me to see you. I'm here on holiday, but in case I can help, they've given me a chance of it. Now, will you talk sense?'

'It'll do no harm, I guess. But what can I tell you, except I had no knife and I didn't kill the old man? I pinched his wallet, but that's all. I'm ready to take my medicine for that. But they're not satisfied. No. They must hang me for a murder I didn't do.'

He slumped back on his bed, muttering to himself.

'Listen, Cryer. I'm going to ask you one or two questions. Don't answer if you don't want. I've no power to make you. Nor has anybody else. But I'm doing it for your own good.'

'You win! What do you want to know?'

'Tell me exactly what happened on Saturday night.'

'Again! I've told the police here a dozen times. They won't believe me.'

'Try me, then.'

Cryer rose up again. He couldn't sit still. He rolled from side to side, clasped his hands behind his neck, finally swung his legs over the side of his bed and put his hands in his pockets.

'Got a cigarette?'

Littlejohn gave him one and lit it for him.

'Now...'

'I suppose I've got to start where that little twerp Wanklyn left me. As I said before, I found myself some digs off Peel Road. I went to my room, unpacked my traps, laid on the bed, and fell asleep. I'd been up late the night before. When I woke, it was seven o'clock. I went out then to get some chow. That made it eight when I started to walk along the prom. I felt like a drink and stopped at a pub on the prom. I sat there drinkin' till ten. I felt better, then. So, I took a walk to where the boats go from.'

'The quay?'

'Yes. It was nearly dark.'

'You had, by then, put the stone in the sock and were ready for anything?'

Cryer hauled himself back on the bed, lay down, and put his hands behind his head.

'If that's the way you're talkin', I might as well stay mum. I thought you were a friend of mine.'

Littlejohn smiled. The idea of being a pal of Cryer's didn't appeal to him much, but it would do.

'We'll forget that part. What next?'

'I got fed-up loafin' round the boats, so I turned up a side-street to get me back to where there was a bit of life. I began to wish I'd got some company...'

'And then?'

Cryer grew graphic. He started to wave his hands and draw pictures in the air.

'This can't be used in evidence against me. I've told them all about it already. They wrote it down and I signed it. So it'll do me no harm to tell you. Although you're a funny Scotland Yard man. I thought they always told you about taking down the evidence and using it against you.'

'This is off the record. Go on.'

'As I was going down the lane, an old bloke came out of the back door of a pub into the lane...'

'How did he come out?'

'What do you mean? He wasn't chucked out, if that's what you're after. He just walked out a bit unsteady, as if he'd had one over the eight.'

'Are you sure?'

''Course I'm sure.'

'Did you tell the police that?'

'I forgot. They asked me so many questions, I couldn't remember everything. They were tryin' to trap me.'

'He came out looking a bit drunk.'

''Sright.'

'Then what?'

'He'd a pocket-book in his hand and he seemed to be tryin' to push it in his pocket, but couldn't. Too unsteady, see?'

'So you decided...'

'Here. What's your hurry? Let me tell it. I'm not havin' things wot I didn't say put down in evidence against me. I was tempted. I snatched at the pocket-book, hopin' to run off with it. Instead, the old bloke sort of lurched over me and got hold of me. He'd a grip like iron. I couldn't shake him off. So I hit him. I hit him with the sock. What would you have done? Let him hold you and shout the place down? He'd started to yell for help...'

'What was he shouting?'

'I don't know. It wasn't 'help!'. It was like somebody howlin'. Like women do when you hit 'em one and they can't cry tears. Just a sort of wailin'.'

'Was there anybody else in the street?'

'Not a soul. I looked round and saw that.'

I'll bet you did, thought Littlejohn. He could almost see it all happening.

'Did the old man start to fight you as he gripped you?'

'No. He just held on. It made me think later how he was like a man who was drownin'. You heard of 'em. They hang on an' even drown them as dive in to save them. Like that, it struck me when I come to think about it after.'

'You hit him and he released you. Did he fall unconscious?'

'I didn't hit him hard enough. I couldn't get my hands free enough. He'd got me tight. When I managed to get me sock out and gave him a tap, he seemed to crumble down an' just lie there. They usually stagger a bit before they drop.'

'You should know. You ran to the main street and were caught. That all?'

'Isn't it enough? I wish I'd never come to this blasted place. I did me best not to harm the old perisher and this is where it's got me. If I'd coshed him good and proper and then took the pocket-book calm and decent like, I'd have got away with it.'

'Don't break my heart, Cryer. Just tell me the facts.'

'That's all.'

'Did nobody come out of the back door of the pub when the old man began to howl?'

'No. I suppose there was so much row going on inside, they didn't hear him.'

And yet, with the inner door closed, shutting off the noise of the bar, it was all peaceful and quiet there.

'You're sure?'

'Somebody might have come out after I run off. I didn't stop to see. I was on my way.'

'How long was it between you snatching the pocket-book and breaking away and running, do you think?'

'Not so damn' long. Too long for me. It was like hours. I couldn't get myself away from him. Like one of those ... those fish with a lot of feelers ...'

'An octopus?'

'As you say. That's it. All over me, he was.'

'And you didn't use a knife?'

'I thought that was comin'. I was waitin' for it. No, I didn't use a knife. How many more times must I tell that I hadn't *got* a knife? It's not my technique. I learned my technique from a pal who'd been in the commandos. You don't need no knives for that. I'll say.'

'And that's the lot.'

'Isn't it enough? Shall I make somethin' up? About knives? Well, you're out of luck. That's all. And now, I'm goin' to sleep. I'm tired-out with police, police, police. I didn't do the old man in, and that's the lot.'

Littlejohn left him at that. He was asking for his supper. He seemed to have lost any idea of time. All he knew was that he was hungry.

Upstairs the Archdeacon and Knell were chatting cosily.

'Isn't it time we got back to Grenaby? Maggie Keggin will be very annoyed if she has to keep back the dinner. You coming with us, Knell? All work and no play...'

'I've finished. You sure it'll be all right. With Maggie, I mean. She might not....'

'I thought you two were relatives.'

'That's right. I'll come, thanks.'

Looking back as they drove home, Littlejohn could hardly believe that the long day's events had been real. Somehow, those he'd met and talked with, and the places they'd visited seemed parts of a fantastic dream. Only Grenaby and the Archdeacon's fireside seemed real. He was asleep when they reached the vicarage and his dog wakened him by bounding in the car and licking his face.

· CHAPTER SEVEN
THE GHOST AT BALLACROAKE

'In a straight line from Ballacroake to Kirk Andreas without breaking hedges or standing corn...'

John Charles Croake's testamentary instructions for his funeral were precise, but he forgot the water-jumps and they had to build a temporary bridge for him over the formidable drainage trench at Ballajockey.

'It's enough to turn your hair white,' said the undertaker, who had previously been over the course arranging with all the farmers for a right-of-way. Nobody thought of demurring, for John Charles was a well-liked man – one of themselves.

The undertaker, Mr. Bertie Corkill Core, was hard-pressed. He was busy building houses for comeovers eager to reside on the Isle. He was put out by a death in August. People didn't die in August on the Isle of Man. It upset the holidaymakers to see funerals knocking about. Passing on, as Mr. Core called it, in the sunny summer time seemed unnatural and like base ingratitude to him. Death in a storm was much more appropriate, if a bit inconvenient.

All the same, for J. C. Croake he didn't mind. He was going to see to it that he got the finest burial the North had ever had. For B. C. Core, the North *was* the Island. He never travelled to the South; it was furrin' to him. Dressed in his ceremonial undertaking attire ('funerals reverently arranged', ran his advert in the Northern paper) and wearing a billycock which showed the wire in half the brim, he toured the farms, obtaining transit rights and issuing invitations. He promised a meat-tea after the ceremony, in the Ballacroake guest-house.

It was a typical summer afternoon for the burying. The hot sun was tempered by a soft wind across the curraghs from the Lhen. Dead silence struggled to reign in a vast square of the Ayre between the main Castletown-Ramsey highway and the sea. The only disgraceful counterblast came from Ballacronkey-Beg, where the farmer, an intruder from across the water with the name of Serene, had decided to sell up. His sale had been mainly boycotted in the North where they knew there was nothing on the farm worth buying, but the South had attended in their numbers and could be heard bidding and shouting the odds for miles around. Someone even irreverently tried out a harmonium – Lot No. 13 – on the lawn. *Riverboat Rock*. The instrument was quite inadequate in wind and pace for this masterpiece and cast it forth on the still air in a form resembling *Lead Kindly Light*. Like a cockeyed imitation of one of those electronic machines into which English is fed and comes out translated into French.

At ten-to-two, a farm-cart, drawn by two fine Manx farm horses, one of which was wall-eyed and seemed to be weeping, pulled up in front of Ballacroake. They had crêpe ribbons plaited in their manes and the cart had been washed clean and painted black; B. C. Core's reverent handiwork. But for the black, it might have been a prize entry at a show. It was followed by B. C. himself, now in top hat and long frock-coat, and buttoning up his waistcoat, for he had been stripped to the shirt (a blue one ornamented with a dicky and white starched detachable cuffs) giving the equipage its finishing touches. He looked round as though anticipating a round of handclaps, but he got none.

'No sign of anybody yet,' he said to the wall-eyed horse. 'So there's time for a drink,' and he sought out Nessie and said he was thirsty. It was to be an all-male funeral and Nessie was wearing her black frock with a black satin apron over it. She had been weeping and looked scared. She went and brought B. C. Core a glass of buttermilk, which B. C. (there were four brothers in the firm, so initials were always used to identify them) drank quickly to be rid of it. His elder brother, A. D., who had just arrived, observed this with obvious joy, for he was himself a teetotaller and suspected B. C. of secretly drinking the profits away. A. D. was representing the firm, not undertaking, that afternoon.

'It's enough to turn your hair white.'

A. D. thought his brother was referring to the buttermilk and his face fell.

The relatives and friends of the dead man began to gather. Many of them had not met for years and the courtyard was massed with handshaking figures dressed in black. They all looked incongruous in the sunshine and the very formal clothes they rarely wore. Littlejohn and the Archdeacon joined them. More handclasps and friendly exchanges reduced to a whisper to suit the occasion.

A few strangers had turned up. Some of them looked like holidaymakers out for the day; others just lost and embarrassed, but they stuck it out in respect for the dead man. There had been murders and violence at Ballacroake before, and here was yet another to keep up the excitement and the reputation of the family and the queer house they lived in.

The coffin appeared, carried on the shoulders of six farmers, of whom Red Juan was one. Dead silence, and then the bidding at Ballacronkey-Beg could be heard rapidly rising. Someone even had the effrontery to fire off a gun which was for sale; the pigeons at Ballacroake and Ballacronkey-Beg took to the air, swept over the funeral gathering in a huge circle, and grounded again. The rooks in the rookery behind the house started cawing and milling about.

The family emerged. The drawn blinds of upper rooms trembled and showed slits at the sides, as the women, who weren't joining the cortège, peeped round for a last look.

Reuben and Ewan Croake; Joseph Croake and Uncle Zachary Finlo Croake, a very aged man but as stiff as a ramrod, who was walking part of the way with John Charles and then riding the rest. Then about a score of near and far blood relatives two by two. The Croakes of Close Croake, and Bride, and Ballavoddey, and The Dhoor. Those of Bride and The Dhoor had been at daggers drawn – a family feud – for almost a century and a half, but, for the day, had declared a truce.

The coffin was placed on the farm cart, two smaller drays, smothered in flowers, emerged from somewhere behind, and took their places, Mr. B. C. Core gave the sign, and the long trek began. It wound down the farm-street to the main road, Mr. B. C. took his bearings and set his straight course, and the long crocodile of black-clad mourners followed.

They slowly tramped their way along the road for a mile or so and then the charted route took to the fields through a gate. At Close Lake, the improvised hearse halted and the coffin was taken on the shoulders of six bearers again. The cart could not be used any farther. The drays with the wreaths broke away and made off on the high road to the church, followed by Uncle Zachary Finlo Croake in his vintage Daimler. By his side sat a little grey-haired man called Rigbee. Mr. Rigbee was a music-teacher, *Professor Rigbee*, according to the brass plate on his door. He was the most brilliant Bach executant on the Island. His neighbours must have blessed his absence at the funeral, for it gave them a respite from his non-stop harpsichord and well-tempered clavier playing.

The mourners behind John C. Croake drove their way straight through fields and ploughed land. Now and then a diversion at a cornfield, the crop of which stood high and golden ready for harvest. They crossed the temporary plank bridge over the deep, narrow drainage trench at Ballajockey.

Through the flat green fields of Ryehill and the domains of Ballavoddan, Ballacoarey, Ballaseyr, with the tower of Andreas church straight ahead of them, like a sailor's navigation mark in a sea of grass.

At all the farms and cottages on the way, knots of men were waiting, and little tributaries in black joined the main stream behind the coffin. Mr. B. C. reverently rushing here and there, showed them their places and marshalled them into orderly pairs. Twice on the way, the bearers were changed; all except Red Juan, who refused to be relieved and stuck to his post over the whole course.

The churchyard at Andreas is large, but it seemed full almost to capacity with another black-clad crowd anxious to join the approaching cortège. The Archdeacon, who was meeting the waiting clergy, left Littlejohn, hastily assumed his surplice indoors and was there to meet the coffin at the door of the church. Left to himself, Littlejohn was better able to look around at the attendance there. The bearers cut their way through the crowd and all those following, except the family mourners, seemed to dissolve into the throng already gathered. The church filled rapidly and Littlejohn remained out of doors.

The view from the slight elevation there was magnificent. The small, trim village stood in the very centre of the flat lands of The Ayre. To the south, the bastion of Manx hills, suddenly levelling out in a spectacular descent; on three other sides the fertile acres of prosperous farms stretched to meet the sea, their white farmhouses and manors surrounded each by its circle of twisted trees, tortured by the winter gales.

To the right of the church tower, now shorn of its top tier to accommodate the flying of the nearby R.A.F. station, stood the Croake tombs. Three huge vaults, the most recent of which had been opened to receive the sad remains of John Charles. There must have been dozens of Croakes lying there. Many had died in foreign parts, some in unknown places, but their names were on the tablets; judges, governors of colonies, generals, most of them dedicated to the service of the British Empire, as it was then. One of them had gone down with the *Titanic*, and another had gone up with his ship at the battle of Trafalgar.

The crowd itself bore witness to the standing of the family and the member who was now joining its dead. A representative of the Lieutenant-Governor of the Isle, Deemsters, lawyers, doctors, business men, farmers and working-men. And Ross Bottomley, the only one present there in a light suit, a red tie, and lemon gloves. He was standing apart from the main crowd, under the trees which hung across the wall of the vicarage. Jenny Walmer was with him. She wore the costume in which Littlejohn had first met her and stood there like a pillar, neither moving nor speaking. Bottomley seemed delighted with her company and tried to carry on a fruitless conversation, fawning on her like a dog.

The service and committal were brief enough and Littlejohn, from where he was, heard little of them. But he got a good view of Reuben for the first time. Reuben was unlike Ewan, who stood beside him. A much smaller man and more slightly built. Clean-shaven, with a narrow face and a great dome of a bald head. His long, straight nose twitched now and then with a nervous tic and his fingers were never still. A troubled, unhealthy-looking man with filmy restless eyes, unsmiling and almost guilty. He half-heartedly attended to what was going on; eager to get away. Joseph was by his side, watching him, as though if he left him, his uncle might break out into something outrageous, something scandalous which might reveal the secret of his brother's violent death.

Ewan stood by the vault immobile, his face like a rock, his grey hair blowing in the breeze. When it was all over, he had to receive the condolences of many there, but they came to him without moving him at all. He seemed eager to be off, too. Ten minutes after the last words, the crowd had vanished. Long lines of vehicles of every kind swallowed them up, leaving a few knots of black-clad people, some ambling round the graves recalling the past, others idling about the village, reluctant to end the half-day's holiday.

The Archdeacon joined Littlejohn.

'The family asked us back for tea. Shall we go...?'

'Yes. I don't mind.'

In the middle of the village, Ross Bottomley was handing Jenny Walmer into his ancient car. A very old model indeed, but as it had mainly throughout its life been used for travelling to Douglas and back from a place only a few miles away, its total mileage was spectacularly low. Bottomley was still smiling jubilantly. The car started at the first thrust of the starter and they were off without even noticing Littlejohn and his companion.

In times past, the original farm which gave its name later to the mansion of Ballacroake, had been one of several on the Island which possessed a guest-house for beggars and vagrants. This place was still retained, well-kept and intact, behind the house at Ballacroake, where it had served as a granary, a studio, and then as a harness-room and been enlarged for such purposes. A two-tiered stone structure, made up of rooms about forty feet by twenty each, an upper and a lower, the upper reached by a flight of stone steps on the outside of the building. The great open fireplace was still there almost occupying the whole width of one wall of the ground-floor chamber.

In the lower room of this beggars'-roost had been set trestle-tables at which those of the visitors who cared could take a meal. There was a good spread of meats, bread-and-butter, soda-cakes, jams and tea, and the place was full of farmers and workmen. Outside, others were wandering around waiting for the second sitting. The dignitaries and friends were entertained in the house.

The Archdeacon showed Littlejohn round the room, pointing out the fireplace, giving him a running commentary about the use and routine of such places and the wayfarers who used them. Meanwhile, the present guests continued their steady eating.

'The upper room was usually the dormitory. Let's go up.'

They went outside and up the stone staircase which climbed the rear wall. The door at the top was locked. The window was in the roof and they couldn't see inside.

'We'll get the key from Ewan after tea.'

Tea indoors was a less substantial affair than that in the guest-house. Nessie and two helping women were serving it. Sandwiches, cakes and tea. The majority of the official mourners had had their daily work awaiting them and had apologised, or taken a cup of tea, and gone back. About a dozen relatives remained, and two or three who had come from distant places and were staying the night. Miss Bridget had not put in an appearance yet, and Reuben, Ewan and Joseph were doing the honours. None of them seemed comfortable. Reuben was talking in whispers with Uncle Zachary Finlo in a corner of the room, Joseph looked bored and eager to get it over. Ewan mechanically moved from group to group indulging in small-talk, receiving sympathy on behalf of the family, seeming to be keeping a hold of himself with some difficulty.

'Have you the key for the upper chamber of the guest-house, Ewan?' the Archdeacon asked him. 'Littlejohn is interested. It is one of the few remaining intact on the Island and I'd like to show him round.'

'Of course. Ask Juan. He'll know. Where is Juan? Nessie! Find Juan, please.'

Nessie with red eyes and cheeks and flurried by the sudden inrush of unaccustomed visitors, laid down a tray and went off. She soon came back with Juan, still stiff in his best black, mopping his forehead after some argument or other he'd been settling with one of the guests outside.

'Yes, Mr. Ewan?'

'Have you the key of the upper chamber of the guest-house?'

Red Juan's eyes narrowed.

'I don't know where it's got to, Mr. Ewan. We haven't used the loft for quite a while. The key's got misplaced. I don't have it....'

'What are you talking about, Juan? I saw you up there a few days ago. Where is it?'

'I seem to remember Mr. Joseph having it last.'

Red Juan had never had much of a fancy for Littlejohn. Now he looked ready to kill him.

Joseph was talking with one of the Deemsters, with one ear cocked in the direction of his uncle Ewan's party. Red Juan gave him a forlorn look and a shrug.

'Perhaps the Venerable Archdeacon could call another day?'

'That's my business, Juan. We're not letting Superintendent Littlejohn leave without seeing the *Shemmyr*. It's only padlocked; you can force off the staple. Go and get it done. I'm sorry, Caesar, for all the fuss. Take another cup of tea whilst Juan does the job.'

Red Juan turned and walked out without a word. Nessie brought them more tea. The Archdeacon laid a hand on her arm.

'What's exciting you, Nessie? I've never seen you look so flushed and bothered....'

In reply, she handed him his cup, burst into tears, and left the room.

'Excuse me a minute.'

The Archdeacon went after her.

All eyes followed him out. It was quite unusual for this kind old man to cause distress to anyone, to say nothing of tears. There were curious looks, too, when he returned smiling himself.

'Well, Littlejohn, shall we go and inspect *Yn Shemmyr*, as Ewan calls it? Manx for "the chamber".'

'Forgive my not going, Caesar. I've my guests to see to. Reuben is still entertaining Uncle Zachary Finlo and Joseph seems to have left us.'

'We'll look after ourselves, Ewan. I've been up there before. We'll see you before we leave for home.'

They crossed the courtyard and round to the back. The lower room of the guest-house was still busy. The hired women were serving the second sitting with food and tea. Out of sight of the house, the Archdeacon stopped and faced Littlejohn.

'About Nessie, Littlejohn. I went after her to find out what was upsetting her. What she told me disturbs me. She says someone's put The Eye on Ballacroake. These people are superstitious, you know, and nothing will shake it out of them. She means the evil eye. I asked her what she was talking about. She says nothing is going right these days and that the ghost is walking again. There's a ghost at Ballacroake. Or so it's said. That of a young man who was killed here in a duel a century and a half ago. I asked had she seen it. She said, yes, and so had others, including Juan. There's also a headless man been seen. We have such visitors at Grenaby, too. Lots of local people have seen them, but I was never lucky enough. But what I do know is that there's something wrong at Ballacroake. Miss Bridget is locked in her room, it seems; Ewan spends half the day saying his prayers; Red Juan is like a bear with a sore head; and Joseph and Reuben are drinking more whisky than is good for them. I tried to pacify Nessie by saying that the murder had upset them all. She turned white, knelt down and asked me to give her a blessing, at that. Which I did. I also gave her a copy of the Lord's Prayer in Manx on a postcard. She thrust it down her dress over her heart and seemed a lot better for it...'

'I wonder what's going on, sir. Something funny, as you say. Let's go and see if we can find Juan.'

They went in the lower room together. The inmates were hard at it.

Joseph was there, sitting by a farmer, tucking in at the ham and talking freely. When he saw Littlejohn and the Archdeacon he gave them a broad grin.

'Sit down and have a bite of real food. I got tired indoors and found it stuffy. I enjoy myself among the homely folk, though I must say it's not playing the game, Uncle Ewan cutting-off the ale. He might have made an exception today. These chaps are thirsty after the long trek to Andreas.'

'Have you seen Juan?'

'No. Why?'

'He was told by your uncle to open up the upper chamber here and let the Superintendent see it. He couldn't find the key and said he thought it was in your possession...'

'My possession? What would I want with the key of the place? It's of no interest to me. He must have been mistaken or else he's gone round the bend. He's been queer lately.'

On the next table, Ross Bottomley was enjoying the ham. He waved at Littlejohn, and spoke with his mouth full.

'Come and join us. I took Miss Jenny back to Ramsey to make some calls. I'm picking her up later. Came back here when I felt hungry. A good meal once in a while does a man a power of good. Tuck in, Superintendent...'

The word 'Superintendent' might have been a magic one. It caused a great hush in the room and mouths ceased to chew for a minute. They'd all thought the Archdeacon's companion was his nephew from 'over'. Now they understood. 'The big fellah' was there after Mr. John Charles's murtherer. It spoiled their appetites, but not for long. As soon as Littlejohn was out of the room, they all fell-to with added zest.

From the foot of the staircase, they could see the door of the upper room with the chain hanging loose.

'Juan must have found the key, Archdeacon. Let's go up.'

The place had been recently occupied and had been swept and dusted. There was a table in the middle of the room and it was covered by a decent white tablecloth. A sugar basin, a salt sifter, a bottle of sauce. The remains of a meal on a tray on the floor. The mice looked to have been at it. By the wall, an iron bedstead which had recently been used, but not by the type of ne'er-do-well for which the guest-house had long ago been erected. There were good grey blankets and clean rough sheets jumbled there and a white pillow-case.

This the two men saw almost photographically as they entered and looked round, but it didn't occupy much of their time.

Swinging from a rope looped over a hook in one of the beams was the body of a woman. It moved gently to and fro as the draught from the open door caught it. It was too late to do any good by cutting it down.

'It's Bridget Croake,' said the Archdeacon, and he covered his face with his hands.

Chapter Eight
The Man in the Upper Room

The two men stood horrified in the oppressive sunny stillness of the room. A wasp was struggling to get out and buzzing at the overhead window. Below, in spite of the absence of alcohol at the gathering, the party was warming up. Hoarse laughter, the low hum of monotonous conversation, shouts of greeting.

Littlejohn stood on a chair, gently raised, then lowered the body in his arms and quietly laid it on the bed. It was thin and frail and hardly any weight at all. The Archdeacon leaned over and closed the eyes with a gesture like a blessing.

The woman was small, with a pointed chin and a face which tapered from high cheek-bones. The hair was long and grey and roughly gathered together in the nape of the neck. The skin was pale and almost transparent, like fine old parchment.

They locked the door behind them, broke the news to the family, sent for the police and a doctor, and cleared the whole place of visitors.

Littlejohn left the Archdeacon to comfort the three men, Ewan, Reuben and Joseph, and strolled alone about the silent house.

Lost in his own thoughts, he casually examined the rooms of the ground floor. The family and the parson were in a study at the back of the house, a small den used by the men as a smoke-room. The Superintendent entered the sitting-room in which he and the Archdeacon had first met Ewan. The blinds had been raised, soon now to be drawn again, and the early evening sun poured slanting beams across it.

The whole house seemed filled with fine furniture, collected by generations of Croakes, particularly in the period of elegance, a century and a half ago. A large, magnificent lustre chandelier hung from the ceiling, with a smaller one on each side of it. As the soft wind from the curraghs blew in from the open windows, the cut-glass pendants tinkled gently. Fine armchairs, a graceful dining-table with dining-chairs standing round it, cabinets, a valuable escritoire, and three large cases filled with china. In two of them, complete and exquisite antique dinner-services, in the other, porcelain figures of all shapes and sizes and obviously composing a priceless collection, made over many years. This collection greatly interested him. Not that he was, himself, anything of an expert on such things, but Mrs. Littlejohn was. They had never had enough money to permit the full exercise of her tastes but she had, at home, a few fine pieces which she cherished. For the rest, she knew almost every public collection in the country and in many places on the Continent, too, attended, as a matter of deep interest, sales of special porcelain of all kinds, and made up for lack of practical collecting by wide reading on the subject and by discussing and learning as much as she could from established authorities. Littlejohn determined to bring her with him to inspect the Croake collection, if possible, before they left for home.

As his eyes passed over the contents of the room, his mind was busy.

Bridget Croake must have had the key of the upper chamber. What had she been doing with it? That is, if her death were suicide; and there was no reason for thinking otherwise of it. A cursory examination had convinced Littlejohn of this after they had found her. The overturned chair below the body from which she had flung herself to death; the absence of traces of violence, drugs, or struggle. Medical evidence would confirm it or otherwise.

The dead woman had kept to her room since her return from Douglas on the night of her brother's murder. Had she been, in life, perfectly ordinary, or a hysteric, or even a schizophrenic...?

He heard footsteps approaching and found Nessie standing at the door of the room, looking timidly at him.

'The very person I'd like to talk with. Come in, Nessie.'

Nessie approached him cautiously. She had been weeping and now began again. Tears ran down her cheeks and she couldn't speak for sobs.

'Poor Miss Bridget...'

'Have you any idea what might have made her take her own life?'

Nessie fumbled about with her handkerchief, her eyes lowered, her face contorted.

'Well?'

'Mr. John was her favourite brother. They always went about together and looked after one another. It was a great shock to her, especially...'

Then she stopped.

'Especially...?'

'She's gone, and out of her troubles. I promised I wouldn't tell anybody, but now perhaps it won't matter. She went to see an eye doctor in Douglas on Saturday. She only told *me*. She didn't want the family to know. She said she was enough trouble to them already...'

Nessie wept again. Like a child sobbing and boo-hooing. Littlejohn waited until the spasm was finished.

'She went to an eye specialist...?'

'Yes. He told her she would go blind... Her eyes have been bad for a long time. I didn't know how bad they were, because she always used to say that it was her headaches made her giddy. She wouldn't see a doctor till I come upon her quickly one day reading a letter so close to her eyes that it nearly touched her nose. She said if I would promise not to tell anybody, she would go to an eye doctor in Douglas.'

'And she kept it from everyone except you?'

'Yes. When she got back on Saturday, of course, after the shockin' thing that had happened, she just shut herself in her room and wouldn't come out. She wouldn't eat and when I went and shook her and told her it couldn't go on, she just up and told me what the doctor had said. She'd be totally blind in a year's time from now and he couldn't do anything about it.'

'How long has this been coming on?'

'Best part of two years. Slowly, like, but surely. Poor Miss Bridey. It's all over for her now. She's at rest.'

'You think she took her life because of what the doctor said?'

'That, and Mr. John. I think she thought that if he was alive and her eyes were bad, he'd have looked after her. With his dying and so horribly, it must have unhinged her.'

'She was normally a very sensible person?'

'She was a darling, sir. Everybody loved her. We shall miss her about the house...'

She burst into weeping again.

'Could I just take a look at her room?'

'I'll show you.'

They climbed the broad staircase with its beautiful slender handrail to a room at the first floor back. A calm orderly room, with a large window giving a view across the flat fertile plain dotted with clean white farmhouses, with views of the church at Andreas to the left and a vista to the Point of Ayre, with its lighthouse, and the Mull of Galloway visible in the background, on the right. The walls were plain ivory and the woodwork white and there were a few portraits on the walls and two or three family miniatures over the fireplace. A large four-poster bed, a Sheraton dressing-table and a few chairs to match it, and a vast antique wardrobe.

Littlejohn crossed to the window and looked out. Directly below the window, was the guest-house, with the door of the upper chamber, now locked, almost opposite the window of the dead woman's bedroom.

'You didn't see Miss Bridget crossing to the guest-house?'

'No, sir. Ever since she came in on Saturday, I've kept an eye on her.'

'Did she say anything about the murder?'

'No. Not a thing. She seemed to have put it out of her mind. But she wept and wandered about her room like somebody in a trance. My room's on the floor above, right over this. I left my door open when I went to bed, in case... I heard her wandering round in the night, too, like a ghost.'

'The ghost you were speaking about earlier?'

'No, not that! That was in the room downstairs. Like somebody bricked-up in the wall, tryin' to get out.'

'Which room?'

'Mostly in the one we just left. The sitting-room.'

'Miss Bridget got away in your absence?'

'Yes, sir. It must have been while I was serving after the funeral of Mr. John. I was so busy, I must have left her for about an hour... I blame myself...'

There were more tears and sad cries and Littlejohn tried to console her.

'You've nothing with which to reproach yourself. You did your best'

'But best wasn't good enough. I shall always blame myself.'

'When the Archdeacon and I were in the upper chamber, we found that someone had been living there. Do you know who it was?'

'Yes. It was Juan. He has a little flat over the new garage; quite a nice place. But Miss Bridget had said somethin' about hearing footsteps in the night. Just like I did. Juan was particularly fond of Miss Bridget. He insisted on movin' into the upper room of the guest-house and sleepin' there. It's right opposite this window, as you can see, and he kept the door open all night, like I did, in case Miss Bridget needed him. She only had to call through the open window.'

Another mystery explained!

'Where is Juan? We were looking for him earlier, but he was missing.'

'He's taken Mr. Rigbee home in the car. He lives just through Ramsey, in Maughold. I don't know what Juan'll do when he hears about Miss Bridget. He'll go mad.'

The droning voices in the room below suddenly ceased. The family conclave had broken-up and the Archdeacon was hunting for Littlejohn in the hall. At the same time, the police from Douglas and Ramsey drew-up in the courtyard and Knell emerged from among them.

Littlejohn had forgotten Knell and the teddy-boys!

The Croake affair had developed from a sordid little crime in a dark back street into a fully-fledged family mystery. If it finally ended by simply pinning the blame on Alfie Cryer, it would be a roaring anti-climax.

The police took possession of the upper chamber of the guest-house and the doctor cursorily examined the body.

'I'll send in a full report later, but, as far as I can see, it's a straightforward case of suicide. We'll see when we do a proper autopsy.'

A tall, gangling Scotsman with a sad, deadpan expression, as though he expected everybody either to be murdered or commit suicide sooner or later. He supervised the removal of the body in the ambulance and then took himself off.

Knell stood with the Archdeacon and Littlejohn watching it all.

'Funny, isn't it, sir? A murder and a suicide in one family within a matter of days.'

'Yes. If I were you, I'd carry on in this room, too, as though you were on a murder case. Fingerprints, careful examination of everything... The lot.'

Knell's eyes opened wide.

'You don't mean...?'

'No. Just as a precaution. Any further news about the Douglas case? John Charles Croake's murder.'

'No, sir. Cryer still denies having killed him. What do you think?'

'We've hardly skimmed the surface of this case, yet. I can give you no opinion, Knell. There's still a lot to be done.'

The heavy stillness of Ballacroake was suddenly broken by the hoarse shouting of Red Juan, who had returned from his errand and received the news. He could be heard berating Nessie for allowing Miss Bridget out of her sight.

It was just his form of grief. He couldn't weep, he was probably too proud to show any real emotion. And his outlet was to find someone to abuse. He stormed his way to his flat over the stables, slammed the door, and was alone with his sorrows.

Back at the house, Mr. Ewan had retired to his room, as he always did with his problems and emotions. He was saying his prayers. Reuben and Joseph were still in the den, seeking their own solace from the usual source.

Nessie passed carrying another bottle of whisky to the pair of them. She halted for a moment to speak to Littlejohn, whose sympathy seemed to have made her his friend for life.

'They ought not to do it, sir. Miss Bridey would be sorry to think of Mr. Joseph drinking so heavy and her hardly cold and dead. She was fond of him. She'd have done anything for him.'

There seemed to be nothing more to do about the place. The body had gone, the officers of the High Bailiff, who presided at inquests, had asked their routine questions and deployed a policeman to check up on events. Littlejohn and the Archdeacon had made statements about finding the body, the family had answered the usual enquiries. Everybody was convinced that the sudden shock of her brother's death had unhinged Miss Bridget's mind and led her to take her own life. And that was all.

Nobody except Nessie seemed to be active. Juan and Ewan shut in their rooms, Reuben and Joseph drinking and hiccupping in the study. There seemed to be no more questions which could decently be asked at present. After all, you don't set about a flagrant case of suicide as if it were a murder!

'Do you mind if I try to get a word with Juan without the two of you there? He's in a pretty dreadful mood, judging from the way he set upon Nessie, and a party of us calling on him is hardly likely to improve him. I won't be long.'

Another outside staircase of stone led up to the flat they had made for Juan Curghey when they renovated the stables and turned them into a garage. Littlejohn found the door at the top locked and knocked loudly.

'Who is it?'

'Littlejohn.'

'Go away. I'm busy.'

There wasn't a sound inside. Red Juan must have been silently brooding on his troubles.

'You'd better open up. This is important. I shall wait till you let me in.'

Heavy footsteps, and the bolt was drawn and the door flung violently open. Littlejohn hardly recognised Red Juan. He seemed to have shrunk in size. His body dangled loosely and his face was smaller. He was in his shirt-sleeves with his collar and tie unfastened. Even as he stood there, he seemed to find them oppressive and tore them off and flung them away.

'I don't want to see anybody. Especially you. And I can't do with you hanging about, either. You get on my nerves. So go away.'

'I want a word or two with you about Miss Bridget…'

'What has she to do with you? She never tangled with the police and dirtied her good name. And I'll see it always stays good, too.'

'Hadn't we better go indoors, instead of shouting the odds all over the place.'

Red Juan hesitated.

'Come in, then, but you're not staying. I don't want company the way I feel just now.'

'I won't intrude for long.'

The man stood aside and let him in.

There were two rooms, one a bedroom, with a kitchen partitioned off the large living-room. The latter was almost like a monk's cell in its simplicity. White walls, a couple of chairs and a table, a few books on shelves, a gun on a hook over the stove by one wall. A large casement window cut in the gable-end with a view across the curraghs to the hills. Evening was drawing in and shafts of late sunlight entered at an angle from the south-west. There were a few old framed photographs on the walls, and an enlarged snapshot of Red Juan, with a gun in the crook of his arm and dressed in his best coat and breeches, with Miss Bridget, wearing a large straw hat and smiling by his side.

'Well, what is it?'

'Have you any whisky here?'

'Yes. Why?'

'I recommend you to take some. It'll pull you together.'

'I'm best judge of that. What do you want to ask me?'

'You've been living in the upper chamber of the guest-house, I believe.'

'What of it?'

Red Juan glared and looked aggressive, as though being accused of a misdemeanour.

'I gather you were there because you'd heard of some strange happenings in the house. What were they?'

The man's face was set and hard.

'Keep your nose out of my affairs. They're my business. I want to keep 'em so.'

Littlejohn sat on one of the chairs and stretched out his legs. He slowly began to fill his pipe.

'Look here, Curghey, isn't it time you dropped this surly, unfriendly manner? Your master has been murdered and Miss Bridget has taken her own life. A matter for the police.

And we've a right to everyone's co-operation. It's time you joined in and helped us.'

'What more do the police want? They've found the boy who knifed Mr. John and they've taken away the body of poor Miss Bridget. Isn't that enough?'

'No. If I told you that the teddy-boy might not have murdered Mr. John, would you be surprised and more helpful...?'

'What are you sayin'?'

Red Juan towered over Littlejohn as though preparing to shake the truth from him.

'I'm saying I've my doubts about the teddy-boy, and we've to be sure that someone else didn't commit the crime.'

'Why didn't you say so before? If it's someborry else, the sooner he's caught, the better.'

'Tell me, then, do you know anyone who would benefit by the death of Mr. John, or who might have wished him out of the way for some other reason, say revenge?'

'Noborry would want revenge on Mr. John. He was a good man who never did harm to anyone. He was a man of money, though, and some might benefit from his will when he died.'

'The family, you mean?'

'Yes. But it's silly to think of any of them.'

'Where were you on Saturday night?'

'In Ramsey at my sister's. They'll tell you it's the truth. I go there every Saturday and stay to my supper. I left about eleven o'clock.'

'These funny happenings at the house; what about them?'

'Miss Bridget told me she'd heard people prowling around. Nessie said it was a ghost. But there are no ghosts at Ballacroake any more. It must have been someborry of the family. It wasn't my business to go asking questions. Miss Bridget was frightened, though, so I told her to keep her window open, and I'd sleep in the upper chamber of the guest-house, which is right opposite her room. The nights are warm and I left the door of the chamber open. It seemed to comfort her, but I never heard anything.'

'You had the key?'

'Yes.'

'You told Mr. Ewan you didn't know where it was when he asked you. Why?'

'My things were there. I didn't want anybody messin' about among them. I thought you'd no business there.'

'Where was the key?'

'It's kept on a nail in the kitchen. But it was in my pocket when you asked for it.'

'How did the place come to be locked then, when first we went up, and unlocked again when we found Miss Bridget?'

'I'd locked it.'

'Why?'

'Just to keep you out.'

'Knowing that Miss Bridget's body was hanging there!'

Red Juan looked stricken and angry at the same time.

'Of course I didn't know. It was simple. I overheard you and the Archdeacon talking about going up there, prowlin' about my things. I didn't want you there, askin' why I was sleepin' there and not in this place. Why I was there was between me and Miss Bridget, and nobody else. I slipped up the steps, turned the key to lock it, and went down again without lookin' inside. Then, Mr. Ewan told me to open the place for you. Instead, Mr. Reuben asked me to run Mr. Rigbee back home to Maughold, as he was late for a music lesson. So, I rushed up the steps, unlocked the door without goin' inside, and ran down again to get the car for Mr. Rigbee.'

He then sat down at the table and beat his fists upon it. His teeth were clenched so tightly that it gave him a hideous rictus, like one who had taken poison.

'... If I'd only looked inside, instead of hurrying to keep you out, I'd perhaps have been able to save her.'

'You wouldn't. She'd been dead for half an hour or more.'

'Is that the truth?'

'It is.'

He seemed relieved.

'You've nothing more you want to tell me, Curghey? Anything strange happening in the family. Any suspicions you might have?'

'I've nothin' to say about that. As far as that goes, I've been with the family over forty years and I'm one of them. I don't go gossuppin' about 'em. And I've no suspicions.'

'You know why Miss Bridget took her own life?'

'I've some idea.'

He sprang to his feet, shouting.

'Anyborry who has anythin' to say about Miss Bridget will have me to answer to. *You* remember that, too.'

'I will. She was distressed by the death of her brother. But there was something else...'

'She told me. She told me most things.'

It was a sad thought that, these two old lovers, kept apart by Bridget's timidity and Juan's fanatical loyalty to the family, should have been content to remain at Ballacroake, each because the other was there, and should have exchanged secrets and confidences to the end.

Red Juan beat the table with his fists again, and then, for the first time, raised his stricken face and addressed Littlejohn in friendly, almost affectionate terms.

'She was going blind, the doctor said. As if that mattered! It was me who used to wheel her about in her invalid chair the time when she broke her thigh, and carry her around like a baby till she found her feet again. She used to come to me for comfort when things were wrong in the family. Couldn't she have known I'd be her eyes as well, when her own failed her?'

Littlejohn let him quieten down.

'You mentioned when things went wrong in the family. What do you mean, Juan?'

Curghey showed no sign that the use of his Christian name pleased him, but Littlejohn felt a softening of the atmosphere around them, as though the first barrier between them had been broken down.

'Things go wrong in the best families. The Croakes were no different to anybody else. When her brother, the doctor, died, she was heartbroken. He was her favourite. She was always trying to persuade him to come over and start a practice on the Island. Her father and mother dying, too. That nearly broke her heart. And then, this. She told me before anybody else what happened to her brother. How she found him dying in the street and when he saw her, he seemed glad, and just said Ah! and died. And how the doctor had told her what was wrong with her eyes. The noises in the house at night, too. It was said to be haunted. She asked me to look into things. All I could do was to sleep as near as I could to her; I wasn't allowed inside after the family had retired. And...'

He recited it in a dull monotone, but Littlejohn noticed that now that Red Juan was talking of things nearest to his heart, his aggressive loud tone vanished, and he lapsed into the gentle dialect of the Island with its soft reminders of old gaelic.

Curghey hesitated, as though wondering whether or not to go on and then, impulsively:

'And Mr. Joseph. She was very fond of him and he was a trouble to her. At first, he'd come over for a l'il holiday; then for the whole summer. Now he nearly lives here. He drinks too much and he's got Mr. Reuben takin' too much again. They've got to loafin' and drinkin' together and gettin' themselves talked about. And all so that Joseph can get money out of Mr. Reuben. Until Mr. Joseph took to livin' here, the house was quiet and life went on peaceable and easy day by day. Now, with Mr. Reuben and his whisky and Mr. Ewan prayin' and talkin' of sin, it isn't like the same place. Miss Bridget got more and more quiet and unhappy and the days when she used to play the piano to them all after dinner and the sound of it went out from the open windows and made everybody else happy, those days is gone, too...'

Red Juan pulled himself together, took a bottle from a cupboard on the wall and poured out two glasses of whisky.

'I think I'll take your advice, sir. You'll join me?'

He filled up the glasses with soda and they drank together.

Littlejohn thought how easy and agreeable the life of Ballacroake must have been in the old days. A fine house, filled with fine things and in good taste, with nothing to offend the eye, inhabited by kindly, intelligent people. Ewan managing the estates and reading his books; Reuben pottering around harmlessly and good humoured; John Charles making his trips to town to sit on his boards and watch the family monies; and Bridey looking after them all, even Red Juan, and playing to them when the day was finished. And then... Something had occurred which ruined it all.

The wretched little sneak-thief, with his pointed shoes and his greasy hair, now in gaol at Douglas, seemed too paltry, too far away to be involved in such a catastrophe and, as likely as not, had nothing whatever to do with it.

CHAPTER NINE
CROAKE'S SATURDAY
AFTERNOON

The Hot weather persisted. Littlejohn strolled, his hands in his pockets and his pipe in his mouth, along the North Quay. The Archdeacon was in Douglas on some official business and Littlejohn had driven him there in a car he had hired. He was now killing time until his friend returned to meet him.

Killing time. That was it. Since the suicide of Bridget Croake, things had been at a standstill. It wasn't right to call at Ballacroake and start asking a lot of questions before the second victim had been buried. The case seemed to be on ice.

All around was in a state of great animation. Crowds standing on the quays watching the cargo-boats loading and unloading. Groups of holiday-makers round shop windows choosing souvenirs, streams of people making their way to the top of Douglas Head.

Littlejohn was quite happy on his own. The lethargy produced by the heat and the holiday feeling were on him. He lit his pipe and leaned across the iron rail of the quayside. Below in the river the tide was low. A small cargo-boat, which made you wonder however it stood up to rough seas at all, was tied to a bollard, the rope strained by the lowness of the river. A woman was hanging-out washing on lines across the deck and a little boy in jeans and a little sailor cap was playing with a shaggy mongrel dog.

If Cryer had killed Croake, his motive had been robbery and violence. But there were plenty of other motives around. Ballacroake for example. Ewan Croake had shied off when Littlejohn mentioned the possibility of his brother marrying Jenny Walmer. It was the reaction of a man, wealthy, intelligent, a member of the old Manx aristocracy, to the idea of an outsider, a barmaid, entering the family. Ewan was a fanatic. A man of strong passions, even in his religion. He was said to be at home, preparing his next day's sermon, at the time of the crime. Nessie said she hadn't disturbed him all the evening. He'd been in his room, thinking and writing in the quietness. Or else, he might have been in his car, unknown to the rest, on his way to Douglas and back.

Or Joseph, whose hopes were to inherit a fortune from his uncle, and meanwhile was sponging on the family. He wouldn't take kindly to the intrusion of a young wife for Uncle John and a new Will in the making. Or even Reuben, who depended so much on John Charles for the comfortable existence and financial stability he enjoyed. The risk of his brother dividing his attentions and the family fortune with a young wife, or even taking her off to live elsewhere wouldn't be very attractive...

Joseph and Reuben had, according to their story, been out fishing in Ramsey Bay all the time on Saturday. An easy run into Douglas harbour, on a calm, sunny day.

The thoughts passed through Littlejohn's mind as he watched the activity of the quay. There were a number of small yachts and speedboats tied to the groin where the river entered the harbour and a man on one of them was hot and annoyed at his engine which, every time he tried to start it, simply coughed and went dead. Some idlers leaning over the rails kept shouting advice, which made him worse.

John Charles Croake's sudden obsession with the *Bishop's Arms*... Why, when proud of and devoted to his family at Ballacroake, had he suddenly changed, almost gone haywire about a girl who served at the bar of her father's pub? A second-rate place, infested by holidaymakers and locals who made fun of him. And especially noisy and unruly on Saturday nights when he spent his time there.

Croake didn't take alcohol, either. Just lemonade or bitter lemon, as an excuse for calling there, and when Jenny was free, she'd join him and they'd talk together. Sometimes, if she was too busy, he'd have to be content with Peter Walmer or Ross Bottomley, a couple of drifters who hadn't a thing in common with him.

Every Saturday, John Charles and his sister left Ballacroake after lunch and arrived in Douglas around three or half-past. Last Saturday, Bridget had called on the doctor and received the fatal news about her eyes. After that, nobody knew where she'd been. All they knew was that she was back at the car-park to meet John Charles at nearly half-past ten. And where had her brother spent the time between five, when the car-park attendant saw him leave for the second time, and seven, when he turned up at the *Bishop's Arms*?

Littlejohn knocked out his pipe against the bollard and strolled across to the side street in which Croake had met his death. The side door of the *Bishop's Arms* was locked and he went round to the front, entered, and made his way through the bar to the little room in which he'd been before. The room with all the Toby jugs which seemed to stare vacantly at you all the time. A potman was mopping the floor of the bar.

'Looking for Mr. Walmer, sir? He's out.'

'Is Miss Jenny in?'

'She's upstairs cleaning the house. Shall I tell her you're here?'

'Yes. Superintendent Littlejohn, please.'

'I know.'

They all did!

Jenny came down almost at once. She looked fresh and comely and quite cheerful. Hardly the way you'd expect a girl to look after the murder of her husband to-be a few days before. Her father had said she was terribly cut-up about it. She'd soon recovered!

'Good morning, sir.'

'Good morning, Miss Walmer. Can you spare me a few minutes?'

'Yes. Still enquiring about the matter of Saturday night?'

'Yes.'

'What can I do to help?'

She wore a blue smock over her dress and her hair was a bit unruly, presumably after her hard work. She didn't seem as nervous as when first they'd met.

She asked him to take a seat and they sat at the table where her father had liberally supplied the beer when last Littlejohn was there.

'How long had you known Mr. Croake?'

'Quite a long time, by sight, but he's only been calling here a little more than a month.'

Littlejohn must have looked surprised.

'It wasn't my doing, Superintendent, that made him take to calling so regularly. We first met at a garden-party they held for charity at Ballacroake. A friend of mine in Ramsey is interested in the charity and asked me to go.

Mr. John was there and Mr. Joseph introduced me to him...'

'You know Mr. Joseph, then?'

'Yes. He often calls here for a drink when he's in Douglas. In fact, he and my father are very friendly. Mr. Joseph is interested in Toby jugs and so is my father. Father sometimes talks of going back to England and opening an antique shop in the south. It's just talk, though. He's quite happy here.'

'I saw you at the funeral with Mr. Bottomley...'

'I saw you, too. Mr. Bottomley took me in his car. He's quite good that way. You see, we have no car of our own just now. In fact, Mr. Bottomley took me to the charity fete at Ballacroake the other week. He went with me, left to do some painting near the Lhen bridge, and called to pick me up when it was over.'

'And after that, Mr. John Croake began to call here?'

'About a fortnight later. He just turned-up and asked for a bitter lemon. They were hardly his sort in the bar, so we asked him in our private room... this one.'

'Since when, he's been a regular Saturday caller.'

'Yes. Excuse me, but may I ask what all this is about? I don't see how it affects the teddy-boy killing Mr. John.'

She asked it, not in anger, but in a civil kind of curiosity. She even smiled nicely as she put the question.

'The police are anxious to find out Mr. John's movements on the day he was murdered. It's pure routine.'

'I see. It seemed strange, that's all.'

There was a pause. Littlejohn filled his pipe.

'Mind if I smoke, Miss Walmer?'

'Not at all. Light up, sir.'

'Was anyone in the room with Mr. Croake when he left on Saturday night?'

'I don't know. I don't think so. I'd left him there alone to see to the last drinks in the Snug before we closed. Father was in the saloon-bar. Mr. Croake went out without speaking to either of us or saying good-night.'

'He didn't even say good night to your father, who was in the saloon-bar next door to this room?'

'That's right. I asked father and he said Mr. Croake had suddenly left without a word to either of us. We thought it funny.'

'He stayed alone there, then? Why would he do that?'

'I don't know unless he was just waiting till the time he'd arranged to meet his sister.'

'May I ask you rather a personal question, Miss Walmer?'

'Yes, if you like…'

She set herself tensely, as though it might be something dreadful.

'Did Mr. Croake ever speak of marriage to you? Did he ever propose marriage?'

She looked exasperated.

'Not another! Really, Superintendent, this has gone too far…'

'I'm not the first to ask you, then?'

'Perhaps the first to put it so directly. But father and Ross Bottomley and the rest of them seem under the impression that Mr. Croake was courting me. If I'd thought that, I'd soon have stopped him calling here. I'm sure there was nothing like that about it. I think he'd got at a loose end and somehow found the atmosphere genial and free-and-easy. I won't say he might not have liked my company. I liked his. He was a perfect gentleman and he was well educated and could talk interestingly…'

She set her face and looked him seriously in the eyes. Then she spoke emphatically.

'Never once since he's been coming here, has he said anything about marriage to me. Nor has he ever said a wrong word. Nothing rude, nothing suggestive. No making passes at me, like some of them do. I shall always remember him with great respect.'

For the first time her eyes filled with tears. Littlejohn waited until she was herself again.

'What did he talk about when he called here... when you had time to spare to chat with him?'

'He talked about all kinds of things. He seemed very taken-up with Toby jugs and porcelain of all kinds. Old English, Dresden, Continental figures... And yet, he didn't know much about them. He said his sister had a collection at Ballacroake and he was interested in that. But when it came to showing any real knowledge, instead of mere interest in them, he didn't know the difference between a Staffordshire chimney-ornament and a valuable Dresden piece. He asked me a lot of questions about the Tobies and the like. He seemed to want to learn about them. Why, I don't know.'

'He came here for that?'

'Not really. He liked it here and I think he wanted to show he was interested in things. He wanted to be civil.'

'And who did he talk with when you were busy?'

'My father or Mr. Bottomley, who's one of the regular customers here. I think you've met him. Mr. Bottomley's an artist. I think Mr. Bottomley fancied that one day he might sell a picture to Mr. Croake. Mr. Croake did ask me once, if my father and Mr. Bottomley were interested in porcelain, too. I said yes, in a general way, and he asked what I meant. I told him they were both interested in artistic things, like the Toby jugs and pottery of all sorts. He asked me if they ever dealt in them, but I told him not that I knew of. I wondered if he thought of selling some of the things they have at Ballacroake.'

'Did you see their collection when you were at the house?'

'No. I got talking with friends. Some of those there went in the house, but I missed it. Mr. Croake never asked me there. I suppose the family wouldn't have liked it.'

'You know, don't you, Miss Walmer, that there was a bit of talk about you and Mr. John Croake around the town?'

She flushed but smiled and took it the right way.

'Of course, I do. There always is talk about things of that kind, isn't there? Father and Mr. Bottomley used to pull my leg about it, too. Father said he was sure Mr. Croake was taking a fancy to me, and got quite cross about it. He didn't believe me, I know, when I told him there was nothing of that kind about it.'

'Then why did Mr. Croake keep calling?'

She looked bewildered.

'I don't know why you should ask that, Superintendent, after all I've told you. Why do people frequent public houses? For company, or because the beer's good, or because they're lonely or bored and want a change. You can choose any of those and pin it on Mr. Croake.'

'I agree. Thanks for being so patient and helpful. Has Mr. Joseph been in lately?'

'He was here about a week ago. He was in town and called for a drink and a talk with Dad. I don't suppose we'll see him here again for some time, with all the trouble at Ballacroake. It's awful. I hear Miss Bridget has committed suicide. I suppose it's the death of Mr. John has hastened her own. They were very fond of one another. He often spoke of her most kindly and affectionately. I'm sure he would never have married anybody while she was alive. He seemed to regard it as his duty to look after her. I admired him for it.'

There was nothing much more to ask about, so Littlejohn ordered a drink of the good ale he'd tried before and then left to find the Archdeacon.

The Reverend Caesar Kinrade had been doing some detective work on his own.

'I called at the office of the Croakes' lawyers. They're my own, too. Kallen, Kinrade and Co. Michael Kinrade is a nephew of mine. He says John Charles made a new Will in 1954, just after Dr. Edward Croake died, and hasn't altered it since. He also told me that John Charles was in his office only a week ago and never mentioned his Will. He'd surely have said something about it, however casual, if he'd intended getting married or including Jenny Walmer as beneficiary.'

'That's true, parson, and I'm grateful to you for finding it out. If the Walmers didn't benefit under his Will, they'd not much to kill him for, had they?'

'That is a strange sentiment, Littlejohn! You surely don't think they were involved in the crime.'

'I don't know, sir. I'm thoroughly confused about the whole thing.'

'Let's go and find some lunch. Perhaps we'll think clearer after it.'

They lunched at an hotel on the promenade and when it was over strolled along the long, colourful stretch of seafront, enjoying the fine day and the sun. The beach was crowded with sunbathers, the promenade animated and gay. In the distance, the incoming boat from Liverpool was making for harbour across a placid sea.

'Shall we take a stroll round the town, parson?'

'Shopping?'

'No. Trying to find out what John Charles Croake did after he left his car at the car-park last Saturday. The attendant said his first port of call was the offices of the Mona Steamers at the quay. Let's begin there.'

A small office in a converted shop with a warehouse next door. They entered the office.

A barely furnished place. A counter, a desk, a table and a few chairs. Filing-cabinets, cupboards, and a large old safe. The walls were covered in notices fastened on by drawing-pins. Sailing schedules. The company owned two cargo boats, each of which made regular trips to the mainland twice a week, and odd journeys to Eire. Posters, large and flyblown, gave details in fine print of various shipping acts and regulations. There were advertisements there, too, praising Irish and English resorts.

A man rose from the desk and received them at the counter.

'Good day to you, Archdeacon.'

'Good day to you, Mr. Ponting...'

Mr. Ponting was a little, small-boned man with a bald head and a smooth pink face. About fifty or thereabouts. When he shook hands, it felt like gripping a piece of soft India rubber. The boneless wonder! He'd always been ambitious and anxious to get on. Now, he was secretary of a line with two cargo boats and he had a staff composed of a girl of twenty-one, who was manicuring her nails at the desk, and a junior clerk who was, at present, out and about the town buying the components of afternoon tea and buns.

This was a profitable little venture and Mr. John Charles was one of its four directors. Mr. Ponting stayed on duty every Saturday afternoon to accommodate Mr. Croake, and took Thursday afternoon off. He was ready to talk.

'Yes, Mr. Croake called as usual on Saturday afternoon about three-thirty. He didn't stay long. Just looked through the day-book, cargo lists, and cash book. The Bank of Mona closes at noon on Saturdays. Their half-day. But Mr. Croake used to meet the manager there on Saturday afternoons for a quiet hour. He liked to get to the bank around four. He left here to schedule...'

Mr. Ponting fiddled about with papers on the counter nervously.

'A great pity he met such an awful and untimely end. We all come to it; but not like that, I hope. Have you any idea, Reverend, who'll be taking his place on our board of directors, as it will be very important? I hope it's somebody who's as much a gentleman as the deceased....'

The girl finished her manicure, patted her hair, rose and, after a glance at the clock, went out and returned with an electric kettle which she plugged in somewhere under the counter. She was blonde and plump and seemed in a daze. She kept humming the same tune to herself....

Riverboat Rock....
Yoo Hoo!
Rock ma baby and me.

Mr. Ponting looked ready to do violence to her, but probably remembered that staff were hard to come-by in the high season.

The junior entered with a packet of tea and a stack of iced buns, enough for a dozen people. Littlejohn and Archdeacon thanked Mr. Ponting and left him to his feast.

At the Bank of Mona, they had to ring the bell at the side of the door, which was locked, bolted, and barred. There was also a gate in front of the door, padlocked and formidable. After ringing three times, they saw a junior clerk emerge from a side door higher up the street and look them carefully over to make sure they meant no ill to the bank or its cash balance.

'We're closed,' he finally said as they approached him.

'We wish to see Mr. Carmody. Tell him it is the Archdeacon, and please be quick about it.'

The boy vanished, carefully locking, bolting and barring the door behind him. Two minutes later, Mr. Carmody appeared, shook the Archdeacon by the hand, and asked if it were urgent, as they'd locked-up the cash and the books, and distributed the keys hours ago.

Mr. Carmody was an ageing man with white hair and a troubled look. He wasn't troubled about his banking. He had his customers well in hand. On toast, as some of his staff described it. He soon made his fears known after he'd taken his visitors to his room and established them on a hard chair apiece.

'I wonder who'll succeed poor Mr. Croake on our board...'

They all seemed alike. As though John Charles's presence had somehow acted as a soporific to the staff and there was now danger of some new director succeeding him and giving them all hell.

'Two names have been suggested and I'm naturally anxious about the ultimate choice. One is a person you know well, Mr. Archdeacon.'

Mr. Carmody placed his hand over his heart, blushed, and bowed slightly, to indicate that he was that person.

'The other is Mr. Macollister.'

His lip trembled at the very sound of the name and he seemed to shrink in his chair.

'It would be very awkward for me in the latter event.'

The Tormentors

He whispered it to the Archdeacon as though laying bare his sins in the confessional box. Somehow, Mr. Carmody reminded Littlejohn of Donald Duck!

It would, too! Mr. Carmody had taken off quite a lot of time shooting, fishing and bird-watching under the benign and sympathetic regime of Mr. John Charles Croake. With Mr. Macollister, it would be a different cup of tea. He was *anti* everything. Anti-shooting, fishing and bird-watching, in particular. To him, everything but increasing dividends was ridiculous.

'Mr. Croake called here last Saturday about four, Mr. Carmody?'

The Archdeacon interposed to introduce Littlejohn. Mr. Carmody said it was a pleasure to meet him. Anybody who was a friend of the Reverend Archdeacon was also his friend.

'Yes,' he replied. 'That's right.'

'How long did he stay with you?'

'About an hour. I always waited for him. Whatever the time the office had finished, I waited.'

It sounded like a sentimental ballad!

'Did he say where he was going when he left you?'

'We talked about the bank and the week's work. You see, Mr. Croake was vice-chairman of the bank and, as the chairman himself isn't as active as he used to be, Mr. Croake was almost a member of the executive. A great help ... a tower of strength to me.'

He indicated the tower with a tremendous gesture of his arms.

Mr. Carmody sighed and gave the Archdeacon an appealing look. He almost solicited the Archdeacon's full support at the forthcoming election of a new director, but he thought he'd better not with John Charles Croake hardly in his grave.

'You were saying, Mr. Carmody... The time Mr. Croake left.'

'Around five o'clock, Superintendent.'

'He seemed quite himself?'

'Yes. Perhaps a bit tired and worried looking. But then, he had a heavy burden of duty on his shoulders.'

Mr. Carmody squared his own shoulders, trying to show that he was well-endowed with the equipment for bearing heavy loads as well. He squared them so hard that he almost had a blackout with the strain and started to cough hoarsely.

'Did he say where he was going from here?'

'Yes, although he need not have done so. His movements on Saturdays were as regular as clockwork. He went to a bookshop along the promenade to find out if there was anything new. A great reader. And then on his way back with his car, he'd call at the Inis Falga Club, a private gentlemen's club, and have a meal. I've been there myself and seen him. I'm a member. Then he'd look at the papers and magazines and leave, usually about seven. He often made calls on his friends after that. He and his sister usually met and went home about ten. Miss Bridget was a dear lady. Very friendly with my wife. She used to leave her brother whilst he did his business. She preferred the 'bus in town. Didn't like driving in crowded traffic. She always called on one or two of her old friends here and stayed to tea with one of them. Then she went to meet Mr. John."

'Well, many thanks for your help, sir.'

'Is it true that it wasn't the teddy-boy who murdered Mr. Croake? I've heard a whisper that the police are continuing their enquiries.'

'They have to make sure, you know, before making a charge so serious as that.'

'It's been a pleasure to help you...'

Mr. Carmody swallowed hard and braced himself.

'May I ask you, Mr. Archdeacon, if you think me worthy of it, to support my election as a director should my name be put forward at the meeting? You are, I know, one of our shareholders. If...'

'My dear fellow; of course I will. Nobody is better equipped. I'll make a point of being there.'

Mr. Carmody almost danced a jig as he let them out. With the support of the Rev. Caesar Kinrade, he was as good as in! And he was right. His election caused Mr. Hosea Macollister forthwith to take his overdraft from the Bank of Mona to a rival bank. But that has nothing to do with the case....

Chapter Ten
The Treasure of Ballacroake

Tea time seemed to clear the promenade and main streets of Douglas just as does the siesta in Spain or *l'heure de l'apéritif* in France. Those who were waiting for dinner flocked into hotel lounges for cocktails; those whose board and lodging included *high-tea* settled down for an hour and a square meal; and those who were casual about it all left the beaches or the motor-coaches and crowded into the bars and cafés for a break in the monotony. When Littlejohn and the Archdeacon left the Bank of Mona there was hardly anybody about. The sun was shining, the sea like glass, and the heat seemed to hit them in little soft, warm puffs which almost took the breath away.

They drove along the promenade and turned left up Summer Hill, at the top of which stood a number of large Georgian mansions with splendid views over the bay. Many of them had been turned into expensive flats; one of them was the Inis Falga Club. The Archdeacon had suggested it might be a good place to call at for tea. He was a member.

'We may as well finish John Charles Croake's itinerary on the day he died. He ate his last meal at the club.'

It seemed a good idea.

There was also a bit of peace there. No noisy holidaymakers; no wandering yachtsmen dropping in; no golfers making it the nineteenth hole. It was the club for permanent residents on the Island; clergy, lawyers, doctors, business men, scholars, architects, artists, politicians. Those who run the Island when the crowds have gone.

The hall porter greeted the Archdeacon with respectful delight.

'It's good to be putting a sight on you again, Reverend.'

The hall was thickly carpeted and furnished in the good old style. Heavy mahogany, with a portrait gallery of dead, gone and prominent Manx worthies who had once been members there. They took tea in a small quiet room with books lining two of the walls, a large fireplace, and well-padded easy chairs built for large men. A waiter who had been there for forty years or more served them. After he had brought in the tea and toast, the Archdeacon chatted with him.

'I hear that Mr. Croake was here not long before his death, Alfred. A very sad business.'

Alfred said it certainly was.

'Such a good, decent gentleman, was Mr. Croake. A man who'll be sadly missed by everybody.'

'Did he dine alone?'

'Yes. There weren't many in, sir. Saturday's a slack evening. Most members are with their families, then, dining in what, by your leave, Reverend, I'd call the livelier places.'

'Was anyone else here dining at the time?'

'One or two. He greeted them with a friendly word and went on with his meal. Just as he was ready for his coffee, Mr. Cantrell, the antique dealer, called. Mr. Cantrell was waiting for a client who must have been late. Mr. Croake and he talked together for half an hour before Mr. Croake left. Then Mr. Cantrell's friend arrived and they went to their own reserved table for dinner. Mr. Croake seemed to be having a very earnest and, from all appearances, interesting talk with Mr. Cantrell.'

'Were they friends, then?'

'Not what you'd call firm friends, sir. They passed a cheery time of day when they met. But I've never seen them with their heads together so much as last Saturday.'

'Do we follow that up, Littlejohn?'

After the waiter had left them, the Archdeacon asked the question like a good dog who has found a scent.

'Why not?'

'Cantrell's shop is in the promenade arcade during the summer, when he does a very good trade. In the off-season, he just keeps his other little shop on the quay warm by opening a few days weekly. The rest of his time he seems to spend in buying on the mainland or sending off antiques to the English dealers and auctions. A very knowledgeable and decent fellow.'

They drove back along the promenade again. There was a feeling of approaching night in the air now. The sun was hanging over the west as though undecided whether or not to set for the day. People were indoors changing for the evening and the bandsmen were turning in at the dance-halls. Littlejohn himself felt ready for the quiet of the parsonage at Grenaby, the peace of the hidden village, and the late meal with his wife and his friend in the old gracious house. Talk by the fire and then the undisturbed sleep in the big four-poster in which, eighty years ago, the Reverend Caesar Kinrade had been born.

S. H. Cantrell. Antiques. The windows without too much in them. A tasteful piece here and there, but in the shop behind, a mass of temptation to enter and buy.

Cantrell, himself, was a small, slim man of around sixty, with white hair. He was immaculately turned-out and might easily have fitted in Bond Street or Rue de la Paix, instead of Douglas.

This was no junk-shop, nor was its owner a broker. In the summer time, there arrived for holidays on the Isle of Man a section of people with money to spend on other things than simple holiday-making. They were newly-rich visitors, who based their tastes for the large houses they were buying on the mainland on advice given by widely circulating women's monthly magazines. Mr. Cantrell saw to it that they found what they needed in his shop. And when the Douglas season ended, he shipped the connoisseur goods he had been cautiously buying during the Spring and Summer, to England and the Continent. In December, he was to be found in Paris; in February and March, in Nice or Monte Carlo. He met his two visitors at the door.

'Good afternoon, Archdeacon. This is a great pleasure.'

Mr. Cantrell knew the treasures in antique furniture and porcelain quietly reposing in the homes of the patrician Manx. Although isolated from the mainland, their ancestors had been interested in the world around, had made the grand tour of Europe in the days of elegance, and freely bought for their homes anything which took their fancy on the way. Much of it had already been sold and shipped elsewhere. There was still plenty left. The vicarage at Grenaby retained its fair share.

The furniture in the shop was well polished and nicely arranged. There were cabinets of china along the walls. Prints and pictures here and there and the light from the window caught the glass of a fine chandelier hanging from the ceiling and cast a large rainbow on the white wall behind.

Mr. Cantrell was delicately made, like some of the china in the showcases. He had small hands and feet and moved noiselessly across the Persian rugs on the floor. The place was more like a well-kept museum than a shop. It paid good dividends by attracting the right kind of buyers.

'What can I do for you, gentlemen?'

Mr. Cantrell saw in his mind's eye the genuine Hepplewhite dining-chairs, the double-pedestal table, the tallboys, the four-posters, the exquisite Rockingham dinner-service, the miniatures...All the treasures, in fact, which the Kinrades had amassed with the passing of time.

When the Archdeacon introduced Littlejohn, the antique-dealer's face fell and he looked scared. There is no better trade than antiques for attracting confidence trickery, false pretences, and fraud. Now and then, Mr. Cantrell was reminded of it in a practical manner.

'I believe you had a long conversation with the late Mr. John Croake on Saturday evening, a few hours before he met his death.'

'That is true. But surely they've apprehended his murderer. How do I come to be involved in it?'

'Perhaps the Superintendent will tell you.'

Littlejohn had been taking a good look round the shop and had made-up his mind to bring his wife along before they left for home. He smiled politely at Mr. Cantrell.

'You aren't involved, sir. We're just clearing-up one or two matters which have arisen out of Mr. Croake's death. I wonder if you would mind telling us if, when you were talking together, he discussed anything particular with you?'

Mr. Cantrell looked relieved. He asked them to sit and indicated a couple of superb wing-chairs for the purpose. He gave them sherry in Jacobite wine-glasses and fondled a fine Siamese cat which had leapt on his knees.

'We talked antiques all the time. Mr. Croake seemed suddenly to have taken an interest in china and was asking me about it.'

'Did he seem worried, at all?'

'I'd hardly describe it as worried. Earnest, that's the word. If he'd been entering the antique trade himself he couldn't have asked more questions. It was rather unusual. I've never known him so inquisitive, although he'd every reason to be. The collection at Ballacroake is one of the finest I've seen in a private house in my life.'

'Valuable?'

'Priceless! Worth a fortune. It began with Miss Julia Croake, who lived in the middle 1700s. A very old family, the Croakes. She and her husband visited Germany at the time when the so-called Dresden china was at its best. There are Meissen figures and services there...well...it would be difficult to put a price on them, except at a London auction. Now that the Americans are frantic for such figures again for film and television settings, it appals me to think of the value of what is reposing in the cases in the parlour at Ballacroake. They are insured, I agree, but for a paltry sum at present values and I could not persuade the Croakes to protect them more adequately. They just laughed at me and said what has been good enough over the past two hundred years, is good enough now. With the exception of Miss Bridget, poor soul, who knew all about china, nobody seemed to bother. The whole collection might just have been a few old pots! They used to say that there were no burglars on the Island. It's a good job the burglars didn't know the value of the collection...'

'Miss Bridget knew of them?'

'Yes; but she, too, was too good for this world. She would never have been persuaded to believe that anybody would steal sixpence from her.'

The Archdeacon had been taking a profound interest in it all, his white frothy beard sunk on his chest. He raised his head.

'Wherein lies the value of it all?'

'The value? My dear Archdeacon! Let me show you something.'

Mr. Cantrell gently placed the cat on the floor and went in a room behind. He returned carrying a small object in his fist and gently placed it in the Archdeacon's hand.

'What is it?'

It was a coloured figure, about eight inches tall, of a harlequin in motley, seated on a pedestal. It was beautifully modelled and balanced, but one hand had been broken off.

'It's damaged.'

Mr. Cantrell laughed.

'If it weren't, it would not be here, I can assure you. As it is, it is worth hundreds of pounds. It was modelled around 1740 by J. J. Kändler, the great *Modellmeister* at Meissen. He created the art of porcelain modelling in Europe. The greatest of them all! In the Croake collection, there are, at least, a score of Kändler figures in perfect condition. Groups, harlequins, animals, birds...'

The little man flung his hands in the air.

'I can't enumerate them all. Miss Julia Croake bought the lot in Dresden at ridiculously low prices and they've been at Ballacroake ever since, cared for, in each generation, by a devoted woman of the family. Why, there's a set of monkeys there, playing instruments, which is absolutely priceless! And that's not all. There's fine tableware, too, and some Nymphenburg figures, also bought by Julia Croake, modelled by Bustelli, which are fantastic. I've never seen them repeated anywhere in public or private collections...'

Mr. Cantrell was intoxicated by the very thought of them. His voice rose to an ecstatic shriek. It looked as if he were settled for the night.

'And Mr. John Croake was beginning to be interested in them?'

'I hardly know why he had suddenly grown so enthusiastic. But he was asking about the features of the genuine articles. I tried to outline them, but I told him, one had to *see* and particularly *feel* the models to know the genuine from the fake. I wondered if he were thinking of selling some of them. I asked him to remember me if he was.'

'What did he say to that?'

'He laughed. He assured me that he had no such thoughts in his mind. He added that they were his sister's property, and that they had always passed to the distaff side of the family. He then asked me if I would care to call at Ballacroake some time in the near future and see them for myself again. I jumped at the invitation and he said he'd telephone me this week and make a date. Alas! He died a few hours later and now, I hear, Miss Bridget has taken her own life. Probably it was out of grief at the loss of her brother. They were very fond of each other.'

'Did Mr. Croake speak of his sister in the course of conversation?'

'He said he was going to meet her later. I'd enquired about her. He said she wasn't very well. She was spending the afternoon and evening with Miss Cannell. She visited her once a month. They were at school together in England when they were girls and had remained the closest friends ever since.'

That seemed to be all. They left the antique dealer in his darkening shop and made for their car, parked on the promenade. It was past six o'clock, and the evening sun was casting a golden light across the calm water of Douglas Bay. The air was turning chilly with the approach of night and everybody seemed to be moving faster. Offshore, a man in a blue sailor-jersey was gathering up the little pleasure boats, roping them together, and towing them away to the harbour. Another day gone. The band at the *Palace* was already playing and the drums and saxophones were pouring out throbbing noises through the open doors.

The Archdeacon looked at his watch. He was evidently on another trail.

'Shall we call at Miss Cannell's on our way home? She lives up at the top of the town.'

Far be it from Littlejohn to spoil his old friend's pleasures! The Rev. Caesar seemed indefatigable. He would have made a splendid detective!

'Right. If you wish it, parson.'

Miss Cannell lived in a large house in the old residential part of Douglas, built on high ground, with tree-lined roads and, now and then, a view of the sea from an unexpected gap. Great gates, a long drive, and then the huge porch. They rang the bell and a maid in a white cap appeared. She didn't recognise the Archdeacon! She must have been a stranger or else an oddity.

'Is Miss Cannell at home?'

'Is she expecting you?'

'No, I don't think so, but you might tell her Archdeacon Kinrade is calling.'

'Very well, sir.'

She left them in the hall. A vast place with a marble floor, Persian rugs, heavy mahogany furnishings. A large staircase, with a wrought-iron balustrade. Heavy pictures of flowers and dead game and fish on the walls.

There seemed to be two entertaining rooms, each with a double door, and a small library, the door of which stood open revealing shelves with books in rows all bound alike. Miss Cannell was reputed to be well-to-do. Her father had been a banker.

The maid had disappeared upstairs and now returned. She was middle-aged. A very industrious and worthy woman who, belonging to a sect called the Pentecostal Wrestlers, was unimpressed by Archdeacons.

'Will you please wait in the library? Miss Cannell will be down in a minute.'

'If she isn't well, perhaps we could call again.'

'She said she would be very pleased indeed to see you, sir.'

The maid gave them both a look which said she wondered why the pleasure!

There was a fire in the library and the maid asked them to be seated. The walls were panelled in oak and over the fireplace was a portrait, presumably of Banker Cannell, in his masonic regalia. A stern man with cold, blue eyes and a black beard. There were heavy oil paintings of Manx scenes on the walls and a lovely water-colour of the Baldwin Valley, by William Hoggatt, illuminated by an electric strip. On the mantelpiece, a clock under a glass cover, the pendulum of which consisted of four mounted brass balls twisting on a wire. Littlejohn felt that if he looked at them long enough, he'd sink in a hypnotic trance.

Not a sound in the house and not a sound from outside. Miss Cannell seemed to live in a realm apart, a massive Victorian retreat, sealed from the noise of the world beyond.

They did not hear her descend the stairs, but suddenly found that she was with them. A small, grey, kindly little woman, not much unlike the sad Miss Croake who, only yesterday, they had handled so gently and so dead. Miss Cannell almost ran to the Archdeacon and took both his hands in her own.

'I'm so glad...'

She had been weeping before she entered. Now she wept again.

'I'm so sorry, but...'

It seemed a contradiction of her greeting, but, in her confusion, she seemed to smile and weep at the same time.

The Archdeacon did his best to comfort her for the loss of her best friend. Then he introduced Littlejohn. She looked taken aback.

'From the police?'

'A dear friend of mine, staying with his wife at the vicarage on holiday. He is helping me in this sad business.'

That was a good one! Littlejohn caught the eye of Rev. Caesar, which sparkled as he seemed to apologise ironically for this feat of diplomacy.

'We're sorry to disturb you at this time, but the police are naturally concerned in the two recent tragedies in the Croake family. Miss Bridget Croake was with you on Saturday evening, I hear, and we thought perhaps it would disturb you less if an old friend like myself came instead of the official investigators.'

She sat down wearily and offered them chairs as well.

'But how should I be concerned, Archdeacon?'

'As her friend, she might have confided in you something which could give a reason for her untimely end.'

Miss Cannell twisted her handkerchief in her fingers.

'I cannot understand why... Except that she loved her brother very much and must have known how sorely she would miss him.'

'Did she mention him when she was here?'

'She said she wished to get the 'bus from the end of the road at ten-fifteen as they'd arranged to meet at the car-park. I told her she could go in my car; I'd drive her down. But she avoided motoring whenever possible and insisted on going by 'bus. I wish I'd insisted. To think of her arriving there and finding her brother breathing his last, murdered. I can't get it out of my thoughts.'

She looked stunned.

'Forgive me, but may I ask if she mentioned anything about her brother's friendship with a young lady in the town.'

Miss Cannell's emotion seemed to have passed. She looked angry.

'No, she did not, Archdeacon. She was the last person in the world to make or imply any criticism of her brother. She was upset when she arrived, but I don't think that was the cause of it. She trusted John sufficiently to know that he couldn't do a wrong thing.'

'She arrived here after a visit to Dr. Cussak?'

There was a silence. Miss Cannell's lips trembled.

'I know, Miss Cannell. She was going blind, wasn't she?'

Miss Cannell broke down again and it took some time for her to recover her balance.

'But who told you? She made me promise to keep her secret. She didn't wish her brothers to know.'

'She told Nessie, and, after her death, Nessie told me. Did she intend telling Mr. John?'

'I don't think so. Not yet, at least. She said he would be terribly upset.'

She glanced at Littlejohn and smiled as though apologising for not including him in the conversation.

'What do you think about all this horrible business, Superintendent Littlejohn?'

'I think, Miss Cannell, that Mr. John knew of his sister's eye trouble. Whether or not he feared she was going blind, I can't say. But he had, I think, noticed something wrong.'

'But she had tried hard to keep it from him... In fact, to keep it from all her family. I was the only one to know that her eyesight was failing. I persuaded her to see Dr. Cussak.'

'All the same, I think Mr. Croake was aware of it. Did Miss Bridget talk to you about her collection of porcelain lately?'

Miss Cannell looked surprised. Such things seemed irrelevant now.

'No. Why should she do that?'

'I wondered. You see, Mr. John Croake had suddenly grown interested in porcelain. He must have realised that his sister would soon be unable to look properly after her most treasured possessions. So, he tried to learn something about it himself. Perhaps he intended to take care of it for her. I suppose nobody else touched it or even cleaned it when Miss Croake was alive.'

'That is true. She daren't trust it to anyone else. It was so delicate and valuable.'

At the thought of this tenderness and pathetic concern, Miss Cannell wept again.

Chapter Eleven
The Little People

Bridget Croake committed suicide whilst the balance of her mind was disturbed. That was the verdict following the inquest and, after that, she was buried with the crowd of her ancestors at Kirk Andreas. It was a quiet funeral. No beelines across farmlands and drainage-trenches; no procession; no funeral feast afterwards. Only her brothers, Joseph, and Uncle Zachary Finlo, who would have been outraged had he not been invited, were there. The Archdeacon attended to assist at the interment and Littlejohn, who drove him to Ballacroake, stayed at the house with his wife until all was over.

The weather had changed. It was hot and sultry without a breath of the usual air from the sea. By noon, heavy clouds began to drift across the water from the direction of Ireland and an hour later, all seemed set for a thunderstorm.

Nessie served Littlejohn and Letty with tea whilst they waited for the return of the mourners. She had been weeping again and her eyes were red and her face swollen. Red Juan was nowhere to be seen, but Littlejohn guessed that he had gone, by a roundabout way, to watch the last of the woman he had so strangely loved.

'Are you here alone, Nessie?'

She was setting out the tea things with trembling hands.

'Yes, sir. She didn't wish for a funeral like the late Mr. John's. She always said it was to be quiet and only the men of the house were to be there. She also said she liked flowers best when she saw them growing on the plants; so there are no flowers, either.'

She pointed to the window of the darkened room, as though the blind were not drawn.

'She was born in a thunderstorm and now, it looks as if she'll go-out in one, too. I don't like thunder.'

'By the way, Nessie, I hope you haven't had any more disturbances in the night since you mentioned them.'

'I haven't heard any more noises, but that's because I've slept all night. I took sleeping tablets, as I couldn't get Miss Bridget out of my mind. When I don't sleep, I can't do my work properly. So I took something to make me sleep. There's enough trouble here without me confusing things more....'

She paused.

'But there's still something funny about. The dogs have been howling and barking after midnight, and twice Juan has been up. One night he went and whipped them, but that didn't stop them. I heard him searching round the buildings, but there seemed to be nobody about. In the end, he took the dogs to his flat and had them in with him. They were disturbing all the family.'

'Perhaps some tramp or intruder....'

'I think it's the haunting beginning all over again. The trouble's on this house again and I don't know what's to become of us all. I'm frightened, sir.'

'Don't worry, Nessie. Would you like us to send a policeman to look around in the nights until things get straight again?'

'No, sir. These aren't things the police can settle.'

She picked up the tray ready to go.

Mrs. Littlejohn whose eyes had frequently wandered to the three locked cabinets in the room, asked if she might see the contents.

'With pleasure, madam. That china has been in the family for generations and was poor Miss Bridey's great pride and joy. She'd like you to see them. I'll draw the blind a bit and let the light in. And, as I know you'll handle them carefully, I'll bring you the key and unlock the doors. Excuse me, please.'

She hurried out and was soon back with a ring on which were the keys of the cabinets.

'Where are the keys kept, Nessie?'

'In the drawer of Mr. John's desk, sir. Just a safe place to keep them. If we left them in the locks, people might handle the things and damage them. I've heard it said some of them are very valuable and can't be replaced.'

She unlocked the cases and opened the doors.

'There you are, madam. When you've finished, I'll lock them again.'

She left them alone together.

At first, Mrs. Littlejohn seemed afraid to touch the treasures so freely placed at her disposal.

'I just can't understand this, Tom. There must be thousands of pounds worth of china in this case alone. And here we are, nobody about, free to do as we like with it. Have they always been like this about it?'

'I believe so. It's one of their family possessions, almost an heirloom. They say that nobody on the Island would think of trying to steal them, any more than they would think of carrying off the Hepplewhite chairs or the Sheraton tables. I wonder if they've even taken the thought to insure them.

They all lie there, unguarded, protected simply by the trust of the Croake family in its friends and neighbours. They seem to be that kind of people. They think everyone is as honest as they are themselves.'

The cabinet which Mrs. Littlejohn was examining had five shelves. The middle shelf, the one best seen from the room, was entirely occupied by a magnificent set of animal figures, 'The Monkey Band', consisting of a conductor and a fair-sized orchestra of monkeys, each playing a separate instrument. Mrs. Littlejohn gently took them out one by one, examined the exquisite colouring and modelling, sought the marks on the bases, and replaced them carefully with apparent reluctance.

'They're wonderful, aren't they, Tom?'

'Although I'm no expert, I'm inclined to agree with you....'

'And these... They take one's breath away.'

Figures of animals. Goats, dogs, horses, fishes, Tritons blowing horns. Then a tailor astride a goat, brandishing his scissors and with his smoothing-iron protruding from his pocket and his pistols in their holsters. The tailor's wife, with her babies in panniers, also riding on a goat...

Mrs. Littlejohn didn't seem to be there at all. She was lost in another world, that of the artist Kändler, of whom she'd heard and read very much, but whose work she had seen only at a distance in museums. To be able to handle it and see closely its flawless workmanship and artistry was a fantastic treat.

On the third shelf, harlequins, actors from the Italian comedy, women in crinolines, groups of lovers...

The remaining two shelves carried a mixture of workmen, soldiers, dancers, huntsmen, horsemen, peasant groups, courtiers... Mrs. Littlejohn recognised the well-known catalogued figures of Nymphenburg, Höchst, Fürstenburg and Meissen and turning to her husband uttered names he'd never heard before; Bustelli, Kändler, Feilner, Linck... He nodded as though they were old friends of his, just to please her.

Mrs. Littlejohn had been examining the items which, with the exception of the monkeys' band, formed the front ranks of the shelves. Now she began carefully to remove those behind them. The first exhibits she had seemed to take for granted. Now, she began to inspect the rest more critically. She took some of them to the window, balanced them in the palm of her hand, weighing them gravely, stroking them gently to get the feel of them. Finally, she borrowed Littlejohn's pocket magnifying-glass and spent a long time studying the glaze and the paste.

'Whatever's the matter, Letty? You've done everything with some of those things, except try to eat them?'

'There's something wrong somewhere...'

'Wrong, my dear? How can there be? I was told the Croake collection was one for connoisseurs like yourself, and one of the finest of its kind outside the museums...'

Letty looked very upset. She returned to the cabinet and began taking out figure after figure, comparing one with another in looks, weight, in the feel of the surfaces and the reaction of the glaze to light. Then, she placed them all carefully away, locked the cabinet, and sat miserably on the couch.

'I don't understand it, at all.'

She looked so unhappy that Littlejohn felt nettled.

He'd brought her there for an afternoon's enjoyment, thinking of how much she'd revel in the pleasures of seeing and handling so many figures at once and realising a long expressed wish to inspect and enjoy the works of art she'd studied and spoken about with, in many cases, only pictures in books to guide her.

'I wish I'd never set eyes on them.'

Littlejohn sat down beside her.

'Look, Letty. If it's thinking of Miss Bridget and her little figures and the idea of her never playing with them again has made you miserable, let's forget it. We'll go out for a run to the sea and come back for the Archdeacon when it's all over. A bit tactless of me to bring you here on a day like this...'

'It isn't that, Tom. It's the fact that many of the figures, except those in front of the shelves are copies or else fakes.'

He was flabbergasted.

'Are you sure?'

'I'm positively sure. I wouldn't tell anyone but you, until they've been examined by a real expert. But I'm dead certain. At least a dozen or more of the figures in that case are modern copies, cheap replicas of masterpieces, or simply modern models turned out in thousands in Germany as souvenirs.'

'I suppose even the real ones were souvenirs at one time. That's what the generations of Croakes who've collected them have bought them for. Souvenirs of happy holidays. And in course of time, through scarcity, they've become almost priceless.'

'Except that in the old days, the figures happened to be those of great masters whose work was timeless. Now, many are done by mediocrities for sale in their hundreds. Whatever has been going on here? I'm sure Miss Bridget would never have given house-room to some of the stuff hiding itself behind the lovely figures on the front rows of the cabinets.'

Mrs. Littlejohn unlocked one of the cases again and thrust her hand behind the front row of the top shelf and drew out a pretty figure in a crinoline.

'That one is quite modern. You remember there's a shop in Cannes, just off the promenade, which sells all kinds of modern pottery and porcelain. I always stop there and take a good look at what they've got when we pass. They have a whole case full of figures like this. They tell you openly that they're modern work, and they cost the equivalent of three or four pounds each. A genuine Meissen of the great years, you might, with a bit of luck, get at thirty or forty pounds. That's a simple figure of what, so to speak, was the bread-and-butter porcelain. But Miss Croake's best figures were modelled by the all-time masters of the art. Some of them, I'm sure, judging from the prices they make at auctions, would go for hundreds, perhaps thousands each ...'

They were both silent and bewildered, wondering what strange affair they had stumbled upon almost by accident. Finally Littlejohn turned and tugged at the old-fashioned bell-pull by the side of the fireplace. They could hear the bell tinkle in the kitchen. Nessie appeared almost at once.

'You were wanting me, sir?'

'I wanted to return the keys to you, Nessie. Thank you very much. The china is very beautiful. It must be very valuable. Is it insured?'

'Of course, sir. It was valued years ago and Mr. John looked after the insurance. I don't know who's going to attend to them now both Mr. John and Miss Bridget have gone.'

'Did Mr. John interest himself in the china?'

'No, sir. He only looked after the insurance. Miss Bridget was the only one of the family who had anything to do with the cleaning or handling of it. The men regarded it as feminine and left it to her.'

'Did she handle it much... You know, dust or wash it?'

'The cases are supposed to be airtight, sir, and didn't let in the dust. That's what they said, but there was some dust got in. You can't keep it out however hard you try.'

'How long is it since Miss Bridget handled the porcelain or examined it?'

'Three or four months since. Of late, she seemed to lose interest in it a bit. It must have been her eyes. They've been troubling her and she was perhaps too bothered to attend to her potteries.'

'Did other visitors come to see the collections, like Mrs. Littlejohn and I are doing?'

'Yes. But not lately. Miss Bridget didn't seem to want company and the little people, as she used to call her figures, have been neglected.'

'Do you know anything about such things, Nessie.'

'Very little, sir, except what I've learned by looking at them and hearing poor Miss Bridget talk.'

'What company looks after the insurance, Nessie?'

'I don't know the name of the insurance company, but Mr. Filey, from Douglas, has been down a time or two about it. He has all the insurances here.'

'Well, thank you very much, Nessie.'

'Do you mind if I bring in the tea-things, sir? I can see from the back window the cars are returning from the funeral and they'll want a bit of refreshment, I'm sure.'

'Of course. We'll just stroll in the garden. It's still fine?'

'Yes, sir. The clouds are blowing over, I think.'

Littlejohn and Letty strolled about the rose garden at the side of the house. They were very quiet.

'What are we going to do about this business, Letty?'

She actually laughed at him.

'You are supposed to be the expert in these queer matters, not I. Isn't Ewan Croake head of the family?'

'Not exactly. Reuben's the elder brother, but he's not much good at anything. John Charles used to deal with the intricacies of family life. Ewan is in charge of the estate and is a local preacher.'

'Why not speak to him, then?'

'I don't know. It seems to me that neither Bridget nor any other member of the family would think of mixing cheap modern figures with such a magnificent, almost unique, collection of genuine ones. Suppose someone has taken advantage of the men's indifference to the collection and Miss Bridget's increasing blindness and stolen genuine figures, sold them, and, to keep up the packed appearance of the cabinet, substituted cheap almost valueless fakes. The key is easily accessible and the house frequently half deserted. It would be easy.'

'Do you think, Tom, that there might have been a motive in all this for the murder of John and the suicide of Bridget?'

'It might be quite a likely theory.'

'Could Bridget have sold them for some reason?'

'Most improbable; almost impossible. These were a family collection and she cherished them accordingly. From what I've gathered about her, I think she'd rather have died than see one of them go...'

'That's a strange thing to say. She *did* die. Could she have known about it?'

'I'll tell you what... We'll not mention this to a soul at present. If we tell Knell and the Douglas police, it will probably have public repercussions. The Croakes may have sold some, or else the cabinets were filled-up with cheaper figures behind the good ones, just to make the shelves less bare. We'll talk it over with the Archdeacon first. Then, we'll decide what steps to take. Right?'

'I think that's best, too.'

The cars were arriving and mounting the slope to the house. The family entered together. Uncle Zachary Finlo, who had an immense appetite for sweetstuff, was complaining about being hungry.

'...And tell her to put out the big cups for the tea. It takes about ten cups from those little doll's tea-services to quench your thirst...'

The Archdeacon joined Littlejohn and Letty and told them Ewan would be glad if they'd remain for refreshment.

The family had gathered in a little group round the large chair occupied by Uncle Zachary Finlo, who was already sampling Nessie's soda-cakes approvingly.

The Archdeacon introduced Mrs. Littlejohn to them all and Uncle Zachary Finlo insisted that Mrs. Littlejohn should preside over the teacups, one of which was larger than the rest – almost half-a-pint measure – to please him. Even that was an exquisite green Rockingham breakfast-cup with a handle in the shape of a lizard. This was not lost on the aged one.

'A very nice cup, this. Who's going to look after all the pots now that Bridey's gone? I suppose the girls at Close Croake, being the next in line, will get them...'

The use of the word *pots* to begin with, made Ewan wince. The idea of the collection leaving Ballacroake got him on the raw.

'Certainly not! They stay here, where they belong. We'll decide later what has to become of them. The girls at the Close are too heavy-handed, for one thing. Please see that the matter isn't mentioned to them, Zachary...'

The old man was affronted.

'I wouldn't think of such a thing. It's unkind of you, Ewan...'

A family row seemed imminent and the Archdeacon tried to change the subject.

'Mrs. Littlejohn is keenly interested in porcelain figures. Have you seen the collection, Letty?'

'Yes. We took the liberty of looking over the cases whilst you were all away. The collection is beautiful. It takes one's breath away. Outside the big museums, I've never seen anything so wonderful.'

The ice was broken. The contents of the cabinets made a good topic of conversation in the circumstances. Uncle Zachary Finlo suggested the cabinets be opened for Mrs. Littlejohn's inspection. Littlejohn didn't, on any account, wish this to happen at present. To have the assembly examining the figures and perhaps discovering the fakes might cause a very premature commotion.

'We'd both like to see them, but perhaps it would be better if we called another day. I'm sure it might cause some of you a certain amount of grief in the circumstances... The associations, you know...'

Reuben, who had been standing with Joseph, his unshakeable companion, suddenly awoke and started to be gallant. He asked for some more tea for Mrs. Littlejohn, said he was delighted they had an expert with them, and invited her to come round for tea again in a day or two to see the collection in detail.

'There's an inventory of the collection in John Charles's desk. You might like to take it with you and study it before you come again...'

Both Ewan and Joseph seemed taken aback. It wasn't often that Reuben talked so freely in a gathering.

'I'll get the list...'

Reuben hurried out with purpose large on his face. It wasn't often he hurried, either. He was absent a long time, greatly to Ewan's consternation. He had an idea that this was an excuse for a visit to the bottles in the study.

'Go and see what Uncle Reuben's doing, Joseph...'

The two of them were back very quickly. Reuben was red in the face and his cheek was twitching with his tic.

'Who's been rummaging in John's desk? The papers are all anyhow and the inventory isn't there...'

They managed to calm him down and the conversation turned to other matters. Now and again, however, Reuben made disgusted noises and showed he was still thinking about John's desk.

'I've got his keys, but I didn't lock it. I never thought anyone would presume to rifle the drawers. Was it you, Joseph...? Or you, Ewan...?'

'Let it drop, now, Reuben. We'll discuss it when our guests have gone.'

The blind had been raised and Littlejohn saw Red Juan crossing the lawn to his flat. He was dressed in black and wore a billycock hat which had seen better days. His eyes were on the ground and his shoulders sagged. He was taking it all very badly.

Nessie entered to enquire if they needed more tea. Uncle Zachary Finlo, who apparently had a soft spot in his heart for the girl, complimented her on her good looks. But there was no time for compliments. Reuben was still worrying about the inventory.

'Nessie, have you seen anybody looking through Mr. John Charles's desk? The papers have been interfered with...'

Nessie's eyes grew wide and full of fear and she dropped the cream-jug on the carpet.

Mrs. Littlejohn relieved the situation.

'Let's go and find something to wipe up the cream,' she said, and led Nessie away to the kitchen.

Chapter Twelve
The Inventory

When they left Ballacroake, the clouds were mounting up again for another thunderstorm. They slowly drew in from the west, covered the hillsides and peaks, and hung there, menacing, making the whole countryside hot and oppressive. Then, by a peculiar freak of weather, the flat lands of The Ayre stood out in full daylight, whilst over the mountains, it was almost as dark as night. Across the water, over the Mull of Galloway, the sun was shining.

Littlejohn drove on through Ramsey. Although it was high season, everyone seemed to have fled from the streets in anticipation of the storm and the place appeared deserted. Like those arid streets in wild-west films, emptied in anticipation of the arrival of a couple of gunslingers intent on shooting it out.

Letty, the Archdeacon and Littlejohn hardly exchanged a word, except laconic, polite comments about the weather. They all had important matters to discuss and seemed to be turning these over in their minds, framing them properly before confiding in their companions.

'We've got to have a conference,' said Littlejohn, finally. 'I'll drive up to Maughold and pull-up by the church. It should be quiet there.'

To the left just beyond Ramsey the road forked, undulated across the railway line to the little village of Port-y-Vullen, with its small colony of charming villas and a magnificent view of the whole blue sweep of Ramsey Bay right to the Point of Ayre. From where Littlejohn halted the car, they could see the storm begin over Ramsey. No thunder; no lightning; not a sound to break the ominous stillness. The heavens just opened and emitted a deluge. When they reached Maughold, a little more than a mile away on the same narrow road, it was quite fine and the grass of the village green was dry.

Littlejohn pulled-up in front of the ancient church, passed a box of chocolates from the pocket of the car to his wife and whilst she and the Archdeacon started to enjoy them, filled and lit his pipe.

'May I speak first?' said Mrs. Littlejohn, opening her handbag and taking out a folded paper, which she laid on Littlejohn's lap. He opened it and she laughed at his surprise.

It was an inventory of the china contained in the three large cabinets at Ballacroake.

'Where did you get this, you cunning woman?'

'Nessie gave it to me.'

'And where did *she* get it, may I ask?'

'You remember Reuben leaving the room suddenly to find the inventory? He rushed out and took it from John Croake's desk, where the key to the cases was kept. Nessie told us. As Nessie passed the door of the study, she was just in time to see Reuben take out the paper from the drawer and hide it in a book on the shelves at the side of the fireplace. It seems she doesn't trust Mr. Reuben. She thinks he and Joseph are up to something.'

'When did she tell you all this?'

Mrs. Littlejohn smiled.

'You remember how she upset the cream-jug and I went out with her to wipe her down and bring back a cloth to clean up the carpet? I asked her what caused her such a fright. She wanted someone to confide in and she told me. She removed the paper from the book where Reuben had hidden it and then got scared. She didn't know what to do with it, except put it back, and was afraid someone might see her do it. So, I persuaded her to let me have it and said I'd be responsible for it. Here it is.'

There were two pages of it, composing what must have been a complete catalogue of the Croake collection. It was carefully typed and obviously a professional job.

Almost a hundred figures listed and identified, with the names of the artists.

A hundred more without the artist's names.

Two complete dinner-services in Meissen; one in basket-work pattern and another described as having tureens in the shapes of vegetables. Details of the work and the decorators' names were given.

A complete Worcester service in blue and gold with a panelled crest of the Croake family on each piece...

The value of the whole, for insurance, was stated at ten thousand pounds!

'It's not nearly enough,' said Mrs. Littlejohn.

'Probably it's just a nominal figure placed on the whole;' said the Archdeacon, 'to value the lot would be really impossible. Some of the figures, for example, could not be repeated. I'd guess there are only one or two like them still in existence.'

Then Mrs. Littlejohn told him of her discovery of the fakes mixed among the treasures.

'What are we to think of it? And what are we going to do?'

The Archdeacon lowered his head and his white beard spread across his chest.

'What a hornet's nest the teddy-boy seems to have stirred up.'

'Ought we to tell the police?'

'What about me?' said Littlejohn.

'I mean the Douglas police...'

'We must make up our minds before tomorrow. As I said goodbye to Reuben, he asked me to bring you both along to take a proper look at the collection then, when things will have settled-down there.'

'But who could be at the bottom of this queer business? It can't have been Bridget, Littlejohn. She was too sweet and uncomplicated to sell off precious pieces of the china and replace them by cheap imitations. For the rest, what good would it do anyone of the family? They don't need money. They wouldn't be likely to take and sell any of the figures. Except Joseph. He's always without money. Could it be that he has been robbing the cabinets, selling figures, and, to avoid suspicion, filling-up the gaps with cheap modern reproductions?'

'The only one who might have found-out the fraud would be Bridget. I suppose. Joseph may have discovered that her sight was failing, her interest in the collection waning, and therefore, he took advantage of it.'

'I wonder if Bridget did find out what was going on, Littlejohn. And did she confide in her brother, John? Could it be that, in some way, this business is connected with the death of John Charles?'

'It is appalling to think that a member of his own family murdered him.'

The Archdeacon stared ahead through the window at the magnificence of Maughold Head, the old church in the foreground surrounded by its ancient burial-ground. The sun was shining again and catching the distant sea with shafts of golden light. All very far away from the sordid affair they were discussing.

'Someone will have to tell Ewan about all this. He is so occupied with his own solemn affairs, that he has probably noticed nothing untoward going on.'

Littlejohn shook the last of his pipe through the window, and slowly refilled it.

'We have to remember that if Ewan is told, he may, being of a fiery disposition, start rampaging right away and spoil our chance of ever discovering who stole the figures and killed his brother. We'll have to be careful.'

'Meanwhile, the first thing to decide is, do we, or do we not, keep all we know to ourselves?'

'I think we'd better confide in Knell and ask him to keep it quiet for a day or two. We shall certainly need official help in the course of the investigation. Besides, I don't like the idea of keeping Knell in the dark in a matter like this. We'd better tell him.'

They drove on to Douglas. On the way, they ran through several storms and when they arrived, the last of the rain, which had swept the promenade clear of holiday-makers, was vanishing out to sea to the mainland. Here and there, anxious visitors were turning out gingerly to explore the weather, testing it with worried faces, like skaters on uncertain ice.

Littlejohn and the Archdeacon called at the police-station and Letty went to do some shopping. Knell received them with delight.

'How's the teddy-boy, Knell?'

'Still protesting he didn't kill Croake. He's trying to persuade his lawyer to get him out on bail...'

Knell chuckled.

'*He'll* be lucky!'

'No news about the knife?'

'No. Nobody seems to have sold one to Cryer, who persists he's never possessed or used a knife illegally in his life.'

'I think we ought to get a little more information about Walmer and Ross Bottomley. The principal characters in the drama now seem to be Cryer, the Croake family, Jenny Walmer and her father, and Ross Bottomley, who seems to haunt the scene, too. Will you set about it? Find out where Walmer and Bottomley originated, and what they did before they started living here. Have you any records?'

'No, sir. They've never been on the wrong side of the law, as far as I know. Excuse me. I'll just go down to the office and set things moving. Somebody over here must know quite a lot about them.'

He was quickly back.

'We can get a line on Walmer from the brewery, I think. As a licensee, he must have applied for the pub from the brewery, who would check his credentials. As for Bottomley, one of the sergeants says he thinks that before Bottomley came over here to settle, he was an art master at some boys' school in England. He thinks it was Colchester way. He'll find out from the art shop. The owner's been a friend of Bottomley's for years.'

'Also, will you enquire if any antique dealers, say in Liverpool to begin with, have been offered valuable Meissen figures lately?'

'If the information comes to hand before evening, Reggie, would you like to join us for supper at the vicarage?'

Knell, for ever seeking invitations to such gatherings, was radiant.

'Of course, Archdeacon. I'll see the job's done before I set out for Grenaby.'

They joined Mrs. Littlejohn on the promenade, which was now completely dry and crowded with people again, all looking tremendously bucked at the change for the better in the weather.

Littlejohn took the old Castletown road back. He always enjoyed that way best, with its quiet farms, fine trees, surprise views of the sea, and wild coastal scenery.

'I've just remembered...'

This meant that Littlejohn had to pull up, and he did so. His wife was sitting in the back of the car and to listen properly he needed to give himself crick-in-the-neck and at the same time risk running off the road.

'I was just thinking what a fuss the dog will make of us when we get back after a day away and I suddenly remembered something Nessie said to us. It was about Red Juan's dogs. They hadn't barked in the night for years. Suddenly, the other night, they started, and he couldn't stop them. Could it have been that the thief who took the Dresden figures was about Ballacroake? If so, he couldn't have been one of the Croake family. The dogs know the Croakes and, it's unlikely they would have barked the place down if any of them had been afoot. You remember the Sherlock Holmes story about the dog that didn't bark? It may be the same here.'

'That's a point we might investigate when we go over to Ballacroake again tomorrow...'

'There's another thing, too. Nessie keeps talking about the ghost of Ballacroake walking again. Was the ghost somebody prowling about the china cabinets when the rest were in bed?'

'Nessie didn't seem to think so. But we can look into that, too. I don't know how we're going to manage it without causing a lot of questions and suspicions among the Croakes, but we'll try.'

After a day on unpleasant business, Grenaby seemed more delightful than ever. Joe Henn was prowling about his summer-house – his 'ut, as he called it. He thrust out his head.

'You've got a reception committee up at the vicarage, parson.' And then he turned to Littlejohn with the usual prediction.

'Feeling like coming to live over here, yet? One day you'll come and never go back. You'll see....'

There was a motor-coach at the gate of the vicarage, filling-up with a crowd of excursionists. There was a label on the windscreen. *Mystery Tour.*

'This is the vicarage of Grenaby, said to be haunted by a ghostly pig, known as the Purr Mooar. There is also a phantom dog, called the Moddhey Dhoo. The Archdeacon lives 'ere. The Archdeacon of Man is an expert on crime and his friend, Superintendent Littlejohn, of Scotland Yard, often stays here when on murder cases. All aboard, ladies and gents. We're now on our way to the cottage built by his own and his wife's hands, of the late Tom the Dipper, the famous Manx poet....'

The charabanc full of satisfied customers moved on, to reveal, hitherto concealed by its huge bulk, a small red sports car.

'We've visitors,' said the Archdeacon.

Maggie Keggin received them on the threshold. She seemed pleased with herself. Whoever the caller might be, he must have been charming to move her to such a smile.

'You've company, Master Kinrade....'

Sitting drinking tea in the dining-room and perfectly at his ease, was Joseph Croake.

Chapter Thirteen
The Confidences of Joseph Croake

It was not very surprising that Maggie Keggin had found the company of Joseph Croake agreeable, for he was a tall, well set-up man, with a natural grace of manner. When he rose to meet them, he bowed over Mrs. Littlejohn's hand and shook hands with the other two with a charming sophisticated gesture, which made it difficult to believe that here was a young man with a reputation for heavy drinking and a love of soft living. Now, he was different from the man who had treated Littlejohn so rudely at their first meeting.

In repose, Croake's face still wore a worried look. Almost petulant, as though he were sorry for himself and the way life had treated him. Something had happened to him since last they met, however. The indulgent mouth was still there and always would be. But the weak face seemed in some way to have grown stronger, more tense, as though some challenge had arisen and he had made up his mind to face it.

He was well dressed and wore the same club tie. But all his arrogance had gone. He was out to please now, or else make his peace with Littlejohn.

Mrs. Littlejohn left them to themselves and joined Maggie Keggin in the kitchen. As soon as the door closed behind her, Joseph Croake apologised.

'I'm sorry to intrude on your peace, Archdeacon, and I hope you'll forgive me...'

He turned to Littlejohn.

'And you, too, Superintendent. Last time we met officially, at Douglas police station, I was very rude to you. And since, when we've seen each other at Ballacroake, I've not had a decent chance to make my peace with you. I ask your pardon. I was worried when I saw you in Douglas. I still am. That's why I'm here. There are things we must talk over before they grow worse.'

Maggie Keggin brought in more tea and smiled at the newcomer as she poured it out.

'Mr. Joseph's a perfect gentleman,' she told Mrs. Littlejohn in the kitchen later. 'But then all the Croakes are that way...'

Joseph wasted no time in explaining his visit.

'I've not called to discuss my Uncle John's death with you, sir. That, I take it, is settled officially, and the teddy-boy will be tried for it....'

'It is not settled, Mr. Croake. I feel I ought to make that quite plain before we begin. The case is purely circumstantial and there are a number of things to clear-up before the teddy-boy is even charged with it. He is being held at present on a charge of robbery with violence.'

'But my uncle died through the violence. Surely...'

'The teddy-boy admits that he hit your uncle with a stone in a sock. That is all. Mr. John Croake died of a knife wound, as you know. The accused, Cryer, denies that he ever possessed or used a knife.'

'That is a mere tale, an excuse to save his neck. He is obviously guilty. He must be.'

'Suppose we leave that part of the argument, for the time being, Mr. Joseph. What did you want to say to me?'

Croake's expression was decidedly sulky. He liked his own way and resented opposition of any kind.

'I called to ask for your help. But before I explain, I wish you to know that this is an unofficial matter. I could have gone to the police, but that would probably cause a scandal, which my family could not tolerate. I can only speak my mind, if you will regard what I say as confidential. You are a close friend of the Venerable Archdeacon and your reputation is well-known on the Island. I know that if you give me your word, the matter will go no further.'

'That depends. If there is nothing criminal or illegal about your problem, and you merely want advice, I'll try to help. But if this matter is involved with the recent crime or any other, I can make no promises. You'd better make an honest statement about it to the Manx police.'

The sulky look was back again and it seemed that Croake was controlling himself with difficulty. He looked ready to rise and leave the room.

The Archdeacon intervened.

'There have been many strange things happening of late at Ballacroake, Joseph. If your visit here is in connection with them, I beg of you to tell the Superintendent what is on your mind. If you do not, and there are any other tragedies there, you will be responsible. I'm afraid we haven't yet seen the end of it all. It is up to you to take all the steps you can to put an end to it. Superintendent Littlejohn is the man to help you. You'd better overcome your family pride and reticence and confide in him.'

Joseph Croake took a drink of tea as though it were some powerful stimulant to decisive action. And then, as though determined to take an irrevocable step and pass a point of no return, he suddenly thrust his hand in his jacket pocket, withdrew it quickly, and placed something carefully on the table at his elbow.

It was a Kändier figure of a harlequin!

Littlejohn lit his pipe slowly.

'So that is what you wish to talk about?'

Croake was surprised and disconcerted.

'What do you mean? I've never mentioned it to anyone. How can you know what it's all about?'

'My wife happens to be something of an expert on porcelain figures. The one at your elbow is, I imagine, worth several hundred pounds. Many like it have recently disappeared from the cabinets at Ballacroake. My wife, in looking them over this morning, noticed that a number of cheap replicas have taken the places of some very valuable ones. Now, Mr. Joseph, what do you wish to tell me?'

Joseph tapped the little figure with his forefinger.

'I found that in the bottom drawer of my dressing table after you left today. It was hidden under some clothing.'

'Did you expect to find it?'

'No.'

'Why the sudden search of bottom drawers after we had gone?'

'Nessie told me to look for it and put it back in the case. It seems that, over a week ago, she went in that drawer to get out some new underwear she wanted to air for me. She saw the figure, but thought nothing of it. She thought it was perhaps a present for Aunt Bridget I'd hidden for an appropriate time. Later, however, when Uncle Reuben started kicking up a fuss about the inventory, she remembered, too, that you and your wife had seemed very interested in the collection. She asked me about the figure in my drawer. I said I didn't know it was there. Which was true. I've called,

Superintendent, to ask what it's all about and how you have suddenly become so seriously interested in the collection of figures. You seem to have given me the answer. They're being stolen. And it looks as if whoever's doing it, is trying to frame me. How would it look if the figure was found hidden among my belongings? It would seem that I've been stealing and selling them. How much did you say they were worth?'

'As far as we can gather from the inventory, the whole collection is priceless, because many of the pieces are unobtainable now. Mrs. Littlejohn handled several fakes today, and a simple calculation might imply that many thousand poundsworth of figures have been taken. That is, of course, assuming that for each fake, a genuine piece was stolen.'

'They were all genuine. Aunt Bridget wouldn't have found room for phoney stuff. Until she began to lose her sight, which, as Nessie told me, made her lose heart altogether, she regularly examined and kept them all clean. What does it mean?'

'It certainly means that someone was going to accuse you of the theft, Mr. Joseph. Whoever planted it would have demanded a search of all the rooms and furniture in the place.'

'What do I do next?'

'Put the figure back in your drawer. Tomorrow, your Uncle Reuben has invited Mrs. Littlejohn to examine all the china in the cases. She will then be able to disclose that much of it is mere cheap replicas. If the theft is publicly made known when it's found out, someone may try to spring the trap involving you. Let's see what happens.'

'But it surely couldn't be one of my uncles. Why should they do that?'

'You know the reason better than we.'

The Archdeacon suddenly intervened. He had been sitting quietly, curiously eyeing Joseph as he told his tale.

'There is a reason, isn't there, Joseph? Do you think it fair, when you expect the Superintendent to help you, to withhold half the tale? What is all this about? And why are you afraid or ashamed to tell the truth?'

Joseph looked ready to flare up again. Then he flushed and subsided.

'I think Uncle Reuben put it there.'

'Have you any proof of this?'

'I said I *thought*...'

'Why?'

'Because he hates me and wants me out of the way.'

'I thought you and he were great friends. You go about everywhere together.'

'That doesn't prevent his hating the sight of me.'

'Are you suggesting that your uncle stole the other figures and was trying to put the blame on you if the thefts were discovered?'

'I don't know.'

The Archdeacon made an impatient gesture.

'This is getting us nowhere, Joseph. You were going to tell us the background to all this. Instead, the Superintendent is having to tear it from you in monosyllables. If you can't do better than that, you'd better go. In such case, the Superintendent will pursue his enquiries and find out himself. I might tell you he already has several leads.'

'It's very difficult and concerns intimate family matters.'

'Far better to divulge them discreetly here than have a public display of them if the official police take over. Well?'

Joseph Croake looked a picture of misery now. All his nonchalance had gone and he was like someone undergoing torture.

'Very well. Early this year, Uncle John came to see me in England. He asked me to come over, stay at Ballacroake, and take care of Uncle Reuben, who was drinking heavily again. I suppose you know he's been in a home for inebriates in England twice already. Uncle John and Uncle Ewan couldn't take on the job of being a sort of full-time keeper and seeing that he kept sober. So, I was the choice. It was a job I felt I'd like and could do. You see, I've always loved Ballacroake, although some people might not think so. I came. That's the reason why I've been described as Uncle Reuben's shadow. And that's also the reason why I know Uncle Reuben had nothing to do with the thefts of the porcelain figures. I was never away from him long enough for him to rifle the cabinets.'

'Was your effort to keep him sober successful?'

'Yes. I earned a certain amount of odium because I used to drink with him. But that was part of the treatment. I slowly decreased the doses and, in time, I got him down to reasonable proportions. You see, he had to do as I told him. Otherwise, as my uncles warned him when I came over, he'd have to go to England again for a third course of treatment. I'm hoping that before long I'll be able to wean him from it altogether...'

He paused and wiped his lips. He looked ready to ask for a drink himself, but took a large swig of cold tea instead.

'Funnily enough, but quite scientific in such cases, he grew to hate me. You see, it humiliated him to have to beg for drinks in the first stages of the treatment. He never forgave me for that. But, he had to put up with it. The alternative was England and he swore if that ever happened again, he'd go mad. He's like the rest of us. Ballacroake is in his blood and is just heaven to him.'

Littlejohn understood. In his mind's eye he could see the place. The fine house with its vast windows facing south and the incomparable views. The neat courtyard in front, the flowers, the spreading tidy fields, the hills, and sea beyond. And the close-knit, happy family, until all this disaster had fallen upon them. Far better than the turmoil of the world outside.

'He grew to hate me and did everything he legitimately could to shake me off. I think he planned to have me found guilty of pilfering Aunt Bridget's collection, selling the loot, and then coming back for more. He wanted me to be sent home again, which would have satisfied him. You see, he was almost cured and thought he'd manage nicely on his own. He was wrong, but that's what he thought.'

'And you think he'll still carry out his plan and have your belongings searched and then denounce you.'

'Yes. I do. Unless the real thief is found, I can't prove myself innocent. My reputation in the family isn't too good. I'm said to be a lazy spendthrift, a good-for-nothing. It's the way I was brought up and I have to fight it, just as my uncle has to fight his love of the bottle.'

'And what do you wish me to do, Mr. Joseph?'

'To find out who really took the figures and free me from suspicion.'

'But, the figure having been found before your Uncle Reuben springs his trap, you should be in the clear.'

'I don't want it that way. I want to use this opportunity to find out if Uncle Reuben definitely had anything to do with the missing figures.'

'Returning to your uncle's chances of taking the figures, you weren't able to watch him in the night. He might have done it then.'

'He was given sleeping-tablets. We weren't forgetful of the fact that he might get up and start tippling when we were all asleep. He usually slept until early in the morning and, soon after that, Nessie and Juan were around the place.'

'Nessie talked of the ghost of Ballacroake walking again. Could that have been Uncle Reuben? He might have been crafty about the sleeping-tablets and merely pretended to take them.'

'Noises in the night, you mean? There are always noises in old houses. I heard nothing.'

'Are you a sound sleeper?'

'Yes, I must admit it. And I didn't propose to have my sleep spoiled by my uncle night-prowling. I always saw he got his full dose of sleeping-pills and took them. They were necessary for his state as well as to immobilise him while the rest were asleep.'

'Did you hear Juan's dogs barking the other night?'

'Yes. Juan shouting at them roused me more than the dogs themselves. I guess some prowler had got around. They do, you know, in the holiday season. They get roaring drunk and can't find their way home and then go roaming the countryside.'

'That's a bit overdone, isn't it? They'd hardly get as far as Ballacroake. Who else might it have been?'

'I haven't the foggiest notion.'

He rose as though ready to go.

'You haven't any views on your uncle's death?'

'I've already expressed them. I think the teddy-boy did it. Who else could it have been? It's what you'd call an open-and-shut case, isn't it?'

'No. We must remember that whilst the teddy-boy approached your Uncle John from the front, there was an unlocked side-door to the *Bishop's Arms* at his back.'

'But wasn't he stabbed in the chest from the front?'

'Yes. But who's to say he hadn't been stabbed when he lurched into the street and almost fell into the arms of the man who was trying to steal his pocket-book?'

'I'm sure I don't know. But what I do know is, that the thefts of the porcelain aren't connected in any way with my uncle's murder.'

'How do you know?'

'That would involve the family in it. Which is absurd.'

They were indeed a closely knit family, the Croakes. They'd see an innocent crook hang rather than admit that any of them could have killed another member of the clan, either by accident or design.

Maggie Keggin showed her smiling face again.

'Will Mr. Croake be staying to supper, sir?'

'It will be a great pleasure if he will.'

Croake excused himself. He had things to do and he thought he'd get back to Uncle Reuben, who had gone off for a drive with Uncle Zachary Finlo, a monthly event which he detested but had to endure. Uncle Zachary Finlo had a farm at Ballajora, which he let to a cousin and he made frequent visits there to see that it was being well run.

'So, I'll do as you say, Superintendent. Put the figure back where I found it and you'll be there to pursue the matter tomorrow?'

'That's right.'

'I'm very grateful. I'll not forget. Thank you for your patience.'

They saw him off at the gate. His little red car passed, at speed, another small vehicle also driven at speed across the bridge by a man in a slouch hat.

'Here comes Knell for his supper. Won't Maggie Keggin be pleased!'

Chapter Fourteen
Feminine Gossip

Knell, with his usual industry, had been hard at it, gathering the information needed by Littlejohn and already he had a lot to tell the Superintendent before supper. The Archdeacon, however, would not allow him to impart it.

'Maggie Keggin, knowing you were calling for a meal, Knell, has magnanimously provided one of your favourite menus. Game pie, followed by apple charlotte. It will be good manners to partake of it before starting a night's work...'

And the good man ordered the meal to be served.

When it was finished, Knell admitted that he felt more like tackling a murder case and, lubricated by an excellent port, discovered by a former Lord Bishop of Man and supplied by a grocer in Kirk Michael, he grew positively eloquent.

'It looks as if we're on to something!'

Dead silence as Knell waited for someone to ask what it was. Nobody did. The dog snored loudly and yapped at her dreams. Once, she even leapt up from sleep and chased a ghost round the room, subsided, and snored again.

'It's true that Ross Bottomley was once an art master at a school in Colchester. But that's not all. Wait till you hear the job he had before that.'

Knell looked round at them all to see if they were hanging on his words. Maggie Keggin entered and began to clear the table. Then she halted and stood looking at Knell expectantly. Their eyes met.

'You might say if you liked your supper, Reginald Knell. It's like you to say nothing about it when I've specially prepared it for you.'

'I'm sorry, Maggie. It was lovely and I thank you for it. I didn't intend to be rude. You see, I'm very busy, and I was just concentrating...'

'Concentrating on what?'

'A murder.'

'It's funny, when the Inspector's here, you're always getting people murdered. When he's not here, you're busy reading the numbers of motor-cars that can't find places to park in, or else runnin'-in little boys who're doin' nothin' wrong...'

She swept an enormous pile of dirty dishes on her tray and tottered away with it. Knell rose to open the door for her.

'I don't need your help. I can manage myself very well, thank you.'

Knell breathed heavily.

'I've put my foot in it again. Where was I?'

The Archdeacon opened his eyes.

'You were waiting for us to ask you what Bottomley did before he taught art at Colchester....'

'He worked in the porcelain department of the Victoria and Albert museum in London.'

Knell paused as though waiting for a round of applause. The dog leapt up, whining, and rushed for the door. They let her out and she followed the trail of cold game pie to the kitchen.

'Good work!' said Littlejohn.

The Archdeacon didn't seem impressed.

'Are you asking us to believe that Bottomley modelled the fake figures himself?'

'I'm not expecting anything of the kind, sir. I'm just suggesting that he knew the value of the real articles and might have wished to get hold of them himself....'

'And sell them and make his fortune?'

Knell smiled archly.

'I was coming to that. We 'phoned Liverpool police, as the Superintendent suggested, and in less than two hours, they seem to have visited all the local antique dealers and drawn a blank.'

'Good work!'

Knell rose, helped himself to more port, drank it off in two, and seemed much better.

'But an antique dealer called Flewker, in Church Street, told them something very important. He told them that a man, answering Bottomley's description, had met an American at his shop by appointment. It seems the man is the representative of... of...'

He consulted his large black notebook, snapped the elastic band in place decisively, and intoned the name.

'Of... Of Devine, Mashiter & Co. Inc., Dealers in Fine Antiques, of New York. Bottomley has been selling him Dresden figures!'

Everyone sat up.

'I thought that would interest all of you.'

'Have another glass of port, Knell. You've earned it.'

'Thank you, sir. I don't mind if I do.'

Knell was even more eloquent after that. Mrs. Littlejohn's knitting-needles clicked, like a metronome keeping time for a Greek chorus.

'It seems this American buyer calls about once a month at Flewker's, which he sort of makes his headquarters when he's over. He buys antiques for the American market and this isn't the first time that Bottomley has sold him things. As a matter of fact, Flewker told the police he'd always thought Bottomley was in the antique trade himself.'

'Has Bottomley been over there recently, Knell?'

'About a fortnight ago, to meet the Yank. He sold him some figures. Flewker saw them afterwards. They were Meissens.'

'Genuine stuff, like the figures at Ballacroake?'

'I don't know that, but Flewker said they were very valuable. The American was delighted and it seems he and Bottomley arranged to meet again next time the man comes over.'

'When is that likely to be?'

'It should be next week, if the American comes over every month.'

'In which case, if Bottomley has been stealing the figures from Ballacroake, he'll have them hidden somewhere until he meets his friend again in Liverpool.'

'That's quite possible. We ought to get a search warrant and give his place the once-over.'

'Where does he live?'

'Just outside Douglas. At a place called Keristal. A bungalow above the cliffs on the Marine Drive. It's a wild place, but it seems to suit him.'

'What about Walmer, Knell? Any news of his past?'

'The brewery say that he's a record of service at sea. Merchant Navy in the last war and then when the war was over, he opened a second-hand junk-shop in Liverpool. Whilst he was doing that, he got interested in antiques and used to go off into North Wales, which, I understand, is a rich field for collectors. He'd gather them up and sell them to legitimate antique dealers. The police in Liverpool asked Flewker if he knew him. He said he did. It seems Walmer had a mania for Toby jugs and now he's got one of the finest private collections in the British Isles. He came over here after he'd had a fire in his Liverpool shop. Flewker hinted that Walmer might have set fire to the place himself...'

'So we've two experts in antique figures at the *Bishop's Arms*. Add to that Mr. John Charles Croake, whose family have a fortune invested in porcelain figures, and we have a very pretty mystery. What were they up-to between them before John Charles got himself killed?'

Knell looked confused, either by the port or the problem of the three men and their porcelain.

'Could it be that Bottomley was thieving down at Ballacroake? Wasn't Nessie saying something about a ghost walking. It might have been Bottomley.'

'It might.'

It certainly might! He looked like a fantastic object that walked by night, with his thick glasses, his silly moustache, his cigarette holder, his yellow gloves and his stick.

'He may try it on again, then. Do you think we ought to put a man on to watch the place?'

'Not just yet, Knell. We'll hold our horses until the Archdeacon and I have been to Ballacroake tomorrow. We're taking Mrs. Littlejohn to inspect the little people...'

Knell's jaw dropped. The only little people he knew were the fairies, and, as a Manxman, he placed great store by their friendship.

'Miss Bridget Croake used to call her porcelain figures her little people...'

'Oh, I see. Even if Bottomley burgles Ballacroake tonight, we'll get the loot back when we search his place, won't we?'

'I hope so. Meanwhile, what about getting to know something more about Bottomley? We know he's been to Ballacroake and is aware of the existence of the valuable collection. But how does this tie in John Charles and his visits to the *Bishop's Arms*? Bottomley's a big pal of Walmer's and almost one of the family there.'

Maggie Keggin had arrived with the coffee. The old clock in the hall had just struck eleven, and this was her intimation that it was time for Knell to go. A stirrup-cup. She laid out the cups and poured out the coffee.

'I wonder if Bottomley's been indulging in a little blackmail with the Croake family. I wouldn't put it past him.'

Maggie Keggin paused and gave Littlejohn a strange smile as he said it.

'Why that enigmatic smile, Maggie?' said the Archdeacon.

'I was just thinkin' of the day when Mr. John Charles Croake threw him out of Ballacroake. Picked him up and threw him right out into the front garden.'

'Whatever for?'

'He caught him tryin' to kiss Nessie in the hall. It must have been ten years ago, that. It was when the Reverend Archdeacon was vicar of Andreas. Bottomley suddenly got sweet on Nessie, who was a good-lookin'girl then. He wouldn't leave her alone. Mr. John Charles, who was a powerful man in those days, just threw him out like a sack of rubbish. It's all forgotten now, but at the time, Bottomley swore he'd get even.'

'Who told you all this?'

'Nessie and me were big friends at that time. We still are, but we don't see much of one another nowadays. She was housekeeper at Ballacroake and I was mindin' you, sir, at Andreas Vicarage.'

'And you used to meet for a gossip, a *li'l cooish*, now and then.'

'We did.'

'Any other gossip you could tell us about the Croake family, which might help the Superintendent and Reginald in their investigations?'

'You were saying about blackmail. Is that when you threaten to tell about someone if they don't pay you to keep quiet?'

'An excellent definition, Maggie.'

'Most families have somethin' they don't want others to know about, haven't they?'

'That's true. What have you in mind, Maggie?'

'The Croakes are no different than the rest, I suppose."

'They could be blackmailed?'

'I suppose so, by someborry who knew things about them.'

The Archdeacon sat up in his armchair and frowned on Maggie Keggin.

'Put that coffee-pot down, Maggie, and stop trying to be mysterious. If you've any secrets to tell the Superintendent, you can tell them here and now. Nobody of us is going to betray them. No need to look so hard at your second-cousin Reginald. You can depend on him, especially as he's one of your family. Well...?'

'Well, it's well known that Red Juan Curghey wanted to marry Miss Bridget when they were young. She wanted him, too. She was lovely in those days. The family stopped it and she lost all her good looks after that. They tried to marry her off to someborry else, but she wouldn't. And Red Juan stayed on and was faithful to her all his life. It was a scandal and a shame. A daycent man, too...'

'Yes; I think that's more or less common property among the gossips of the North, isn't it?'

'Well, you asked me, Reverend Archdeacon...'

'Can you tell us something we haven't heard before, Maggie?'

She began to pluck at the strings of her apron nervously. The next revelation was obviously one of those things which daycent women didn't divulge in public gatherings, especially with men present. It was the sort of information whispered in corners, at sewing-meetings, or in the kitchens preparing for a tea party at the chapel, and unofficial judgment passed on it forthwith.

Mrs. Littlejohn put down her knitting.

'I'll give you a hand with the dishes, Maggie. It's late and time you were getting to bed, too.'

They went off after bidding Knell good-night. Shortly afterwards, the Inspector left in his little car. Littlejohn stood at the door for a while after he'd seen him off.

He could hear the river rushing under the little stone bridge and the swish of the trees as they caught the breeze in their spreading tops. Somewhere in the wastes of Moaney Mooar a dog was howling and a couple of owls were screeching at each other in Joe Henn's garden. His dog joined him at the door, licked his fingers, and then vanished into the garden for her final prowl among the trees. She yapped as she disturbed a rabbit which she didn't know how to harm. She joined her master and they went indoors.

Mrs. Littlejohn and the Archdeacon were waiting for him. They were talking about Manx witches and she didn't seem to have mentioned any revelations made by Maggie Keggin in the process of washing-up.

It was only as Littlejohn, first in bed, was finding a comfortable resting place for himself in the depths of the feather-bed, that she tapped him on the shoulder.

'I almost forgot, Tom. Maggie Keggin told me something over the dirty dishes in the kitchen before she went to bed. The sort of thing that a respectable Victorian lady blushes to mention in front of men...'

Littlejohn sat up.

'Well? I'll put the light out if you'd feel better telling me in the dark.'

'It's just that John Charles Croake sowed a few wild oats in his youth. There was a scandalous affair with a married woman, which was hushed up. It caused a ferment at Ballacroake...'

Chapter Fifteen
The Tormentors

The Archdeacon had heard nothing of the scandal in the life of John Charles Croake, so the secret must have been very well hushed-up by the family. Over breakfast, Littlejohn told the parson what Maggie Keggin had disclosed to his wife the night before.

'There's only one thing to do. If it turns out to be a mere piece of feminine imagination, we'll be foolish to pursue it. But, if it's true, it may lead to a solution for us. We'd better pay a call on old Jasper Clucas Kallen...'

'Who'd he be, sir?'

'John Charles's lawyer. He and I were at school and Cambridge together. He's turned eighty and only does a few hours' work a day now, looking after the affairs of special people of his own age. He's jealous of me because I won't die before him.'

Littlejohn longed for a bit of peace. As far as he could see, the case was as far away from a solution as ever. Now, another exhausting lead had presented itself, perhaps to peter out like the rest. Jasper Clucas Kallen. It sounded like a name invented for the villain in a melodrama.

Outside, it was raining. Straight, gentle rain, which made the air scented with the perfume of wet leaves and eager garden flowers. A soft morning, which tempted you for a long walk under dripping trees and through the wet grass.

Instead, they were off to see Jasper Clucas Kallen!

They drove to Douglas. It was still raining and seemed to have set-in for the day. Instead of looking depressed, the holiday-makers they passed on the way were out in their plastic raincoats or without any rainwear at all. After the heavy heat of recent days culminating in yesterday's thundery damp, the air was refreshing and the rain sweet.

In Athol Street, among the advocates' offices, the Archdeacon indicated a converted Georgian house with a bright brass plate on the door jamb whence by time and energetic polishing, the names had almost been worn away. *Kallen, Kinrade, Kallen & Kewley.*

The offices were of another world, another century. You almost expected to see men in peg-top trousers and beaver hats and women in crinolines knocking around. Instead, a pretty girl with a hair-do like a bee-hive met them.

'Mr. Kallen, senior, please.'

'With pleasure, Archdeacon.'

In spite of the beatnik bee-hive, the girl was all smiles and good manners. The Archdeacon had christened her nineteen years before. But, of course, she'd had no hair at all then and had howled all through the ceremony.

The Reverend Caesar Kinrade recognised her quickly, patted her on the beehive, and asked her how she was. She said she was very well, thank you, and hoped he was the same, and straight away led him and Littlejohn to a room on the ground floor.

The girl announced them and whispered as she left them, 'Speak loudly. His hearing's not as good as it used to be.'

Mr. Jasper Clucas Kallen was sitting very upright in a large swivel armchair, padded and with a high back. He was very old. He seemed to have hardly any eyelashes and was almost bald as well. Yet, the eyes were very much alive and sparkled maliciously as the pair of them entered. Littlejohn found it difficult to believe that Mr. Kallen and the Archdeacon had been boys together.

'Good morning, Clucas.'

'Good morning, Caesar. And you've no need to shout. My hearing's quite good. You're not looking very well, Caesar. You ought to take more care of yourself. You're not as young as you were, you know.'

Littlejohn realised that it was a pious hope. Like a runner in a race, with only one man between him and the tape, who wishes his rival would trip and measure his length on the course. The Archdeacon was the picture of health. Mr. Kallen's skin was tight and shining, and the bones of his skull were faintly visible through it.

'What are you after, Caesar? Want to make another Will? And who's this you've got with you?'

The Archdeacon introduced them.

'Aha. Something about John Charles Croake's murder, I'll bet. Well, don't forget I'm a lawyer, Caesar, and I'm bound to secrecy about my clients' affairs. So precious little you'll get out of me.'

He paused to take breath.

'Sit down. You're too old to be on your feet too much. What do you want?'

He blinked his eyes rapidly several times and licked his dry lips. Treated diplomatically, it might not be a difficult matter to get him to talk.

'You've guessed it, Clucas. It's about Croake.'

Mr. Kallen hooked his hand round his ear the better to hear what was being said.

'Speak up, Caesar. Your voice is getting feeble with age and it's hard to tell what you're talking about with all your mumbling. Croake, did you say? John Charles? What about him?'

'Was John Charles involved in a scandal some years ago? A scandal with a woman?'

Mr. Kallen looked like a wasp about to attack a ripe plum. He was getting ready to enjoy himself.

'You ought to know better, Caesar, than ask questions of that type. You know that matters between a lawyer and his clients are sacred. I can't answer your enquiry.'

The Archdeacon's eyes flashed.

'In that case, I'll turn you over to Superintendent Littlejohn, Clucas. He is investigating a case of murder. The murder of John Charles Croake. I agree about your customers' business being sacred. Even if you *are* a superannuated lawyer. But you also owe a duty to justice as an officer of the law. If at all possible, you ought to divulge anything you know which might result in the murderer being brought to book.'

The lawyer's eyes glinted maliciously again. Littlejohn saw that if he let this battle between the two old men get started, it was going to persist for hours. He cut in quickly.

'The police are, at present, trying to discover if John Charles Croake was being subjected to blackmail at the time of his death, sir.'

Mr. Jasper Clucas Kallen fixed Littlejohn with his dry gaze and then smiled artfully. He thrust his head forward and chuckled. Now, he looked like a jocular old tortoise.

'I like you, Superintendent Little-what's-your-name. My old friend Caesar is growing senile to the extent of indiscretion. You, on the other hand, know what you want. You said blackmail?'

'Yes, sir. If, in confidence and within the bounds of your discretion you could indicate incidents of a nature leading to blackmail, I'd be very grateful....'

The lawyer wriggled in his padded chair and made chewing movements with his jaws.

'I have no right whatsoever to divulge to policemen, inquisitive clergymen, or anyone else, the secrets of my clients. I therefore cannot give you any direct help. I will, however, venture to give you a push in the right direction. Go and ask the same question of Margaret Foster-Leneve. She may be able to help you. That's all... And now it's time I had my malted milk. So I'll ask you to excuse me. Glad to see you both. I hope, Caesar, you'll soon be feeling better.'

And he rang the bell and asked the girl with the beehive to show them safely to the street.

'It's a long time since you and I came first and second in the mile, isn't it, Caesar? I was first; you second...'

'Your memory's failing, old friend. I was first.'

'I'm not going to argue with you, Caesar. It's childish to argue at our age and it might bring a stroke on you. Goodbye, then... Where's my malted milk...?'

Out in the street it felt like stepping back to the present after a spell in the late 1850s. The Archdeacon looked upset.

'Clucas Kallen's in his dotage. It disturbs me to find him so obstinate and losing his faculties. Margaret Foster-Leneve lives up-town. We'd better go in the car. Which doesn't mean I can't walk it with ease, in spite of Kallen's jibes. I'm in a hurry to hear what she has to tell us. I wouldn't put it past that old reprobate to telephone her and advise her against helping us.'

'Who is she?'

'An island aristocrat and, until ten days ago, the wife of a very eminent archaeologist. Margaret is now a widow. It's a bit awkward asking her, so early in her widowhood, to delve into the past. All the same, this matter is urgent. It's taking us far too long to solve the crime...'

Another square, old-fashioned house in a garden of old trees and matured lawns. The door was set back in a large, square, pillared porch and when Littlejohn rang the bell, it was answered by yet another elderly woman in cap and apron, who looked ready to defend the place against all comers. She smiled when she saw the Archdeacon and bobbed a bit of a curtsy to him. He had prepared her for confirmation over forty years ago.

'Good mornin', Venerable Archdeacon, sir. It's good to be puttin' a sight on ye. Were you callin' on Mrs. Foster-Leneve?'

'If you please, Rosie. And how are you?'

'Middlin', sir. Come along in. She's very low and will be pleased to see ye, I'm sure.'

The hall was heavily and magnificently panelled and hung almost from top to bottom with framed drawings and photographs of the results of the archaeological researches of the late Mr. Foster-Leneve. Ancient stone crosses ornamented with ring chain and interlaced decorations, the sculptures of Gaut, the greatest of Norse stone carvers. Carved slabs commemorating Norse heroes and gods. Photographs of excavated Viking ships. Pictures of Manx castles, models of roundhouses, sketches of ancient burial grounds and tombs... Scattered about the floor were cursing and swearing stones, slabs inscribed with ogams and later inscriptions, old burial stones and the keystones of ancient churches. Then, in contrast, along the remaining wall, a lot of ancient Egyptian odds and ends.

The Archdeacon was lost in contemplation and seemed about to forget the reason of his visit, in spite of his earlier impatience.

A tall, handsome woman of sixty or thereabouts suddenly appeared at the door of one of the rooms, made a joyful noise of greeting, rushed to the Archdeacon, and took his hand in both her own, and burst into tears.

It may have been his beard, or his kindly eyes, or his general appearance of soothing serenity, but whatever it was, the appearance of the Rev. Caesar Kinrade always seemed to make the afflicted weep. He comforted her. 'There, there, Margaret,' and she at once cheered up and invited them to take coffee with her.

Littlejohn left the Archdeacon to break the ice of the interview.

'We've just been to see Clucas Kallen, Margaret. I must tell you candidly, that we were there in an effort to persuade him to inform us if he knew anything in the life of John Charles Croake or any of the Croake family, for that matter, which might give rise to blackmail... Some scandal, for example, or some indiscretion which might have got known to some unscrupulous....'

He didn't get any further. Mrs. Foster-Leneve was pouring out the coffee. She turned deathly pale, carefully placed the silver coffee-pot on the table, and conveniently fainted across the couch.

After eighty years of life, sixty of them spent in comforting and ministering to the distressed, the Rev. Caesar Kinrade showed no distress himself. He dipped his handkerchief in the water of a large rosebowl, placed a cushion under the unconscious lady's head, and gently slapped her face with the wet linen. She made gasping noises, sat upright and apologised.

'I'm so sorry. It came as a great shock to hear you mention the death of John Charles Croake and the unpleasant word of blackmail. Would you care to look at the flowers in the conservatory, Superintendent Littlejohn, whilst I have a moment's private conversation with my old friend?'

Littlejohn, who had already noticed a riot of huge begonias and assorted fuchsias in the greenhouse beyond a glass door at the end of the room, said he would very much like to spend a little time among them. He was not exaggerating. In his boyhood, his grandfather at Ulverston had pursued a mania for spending his time in his greenhouses, which he raised to tropical temperatures for the benefit of cucumbers, tomatoes, passion-flowers and other exotic plants. The very scent of hothouses always brought back happy memories to the Superintendent and the delights of stolen fruits; peaches, small oranges, the fruits of egg-plants. Once, in his grandparent's absence, he had stolen and eaten a whole cucumber, and been removed to the cottage hospital with suspected appendicitis.

The Archdeacon quickly joined him.

'Mrs. Foster-Leneve asks if you'd like to leave us alone for a long chat, Littlejohn. Not, she says, that she doesn't trust you, but the matters she wishes to talk about would embarrass her so much if she confessed them to anyone but me, that she'd not be able to talk freely. I think it would be best for you to agree.'

'Of course. I'll take a little run round Douglas and rest from thinking about the Croake case....'

They arranged to meet again at the Inis Falga Club in time for lunch.

Outside, the rain had ceased and the sun was drying up the town. Everybody seemed to have turned out at once along the promenade. The place was packed from end to end with holidaymakers celebrating the return of good weather again. Children were paddling along the edge of the incoming tide and there were bathers in the water.

Littlejohn drove slowly through the crowds to Onchan Head. The Fun Fair was in full blast, fortune-tellers were busy, and a hypnotist was giving a show in a marquee. The fairground was massed with people. The weather had changed for the better too late for morning excursions, and they were filling-in the time before lunch. The rides were all busy, many of them jammed to capacity with screaming sensation-seekers and the sideshows were flourishing.

Littlejohn had never been there before. He parked the car and mixed with the crowds. He even felt like taking a ride on the dodgems; the spirit of the place seemed to infect him. He fired a lot of shots at a rifle-range. His rifle was faulty, but after several wides, he was able to adjust his shooting and landed a couple of bulls. He drew his winnings in bars of chocolate. At the coconut-shy he failed to dislodge several nuts which seemed to be screwed down, but finally knocked one over and carried it away under his arm. He was at the Inis Falga Club in time to meet the parson.

The place was half-full, but they found a quiet table in a corner. The Archdeacon had obviously had a successful interview with Mrs. Foster-Leneve and had much to tell him.

'I am amazed at how well the secret has been kept. It is like a story in a novelette. Mrs. Foster-Leneve agreed that I might tell you what she confessed to me. I explained to her that we had suspicions that the teddy-boy might not have been responsible for the death of John Charles Croake. I told her again that you thought he was being subjected to blackmail, although I must say, I was surprised when you used the word. What was he being blackmailed about and how did you arrive at the conclusion?'

'You have probably learned what it was about, sir. I got the idea that he might have been involved that way because he was paying off, not in cash, but in valuable Dresden figures. We now know that Bottomley was selling figures to American buyers. Croake was certainly not selling them to Bottomley. The Croakes aren't short of money. I got the hunch that Bottomley had some sort of hold over him and wouldn't take cash. He could do better with the figures. The rendezvous was at the *Bishop's Arms* and Croake took the figures there. That accounts for the well-known teetotaller being found frequenting a pub. There had to be a public explanation for this. So someone put around the rumour that Croake was sweet on the landlord's daughter. She never admitted it; neither did the Croake family. Someone, and I think it was Bottomley, had so firm a hold over Croake that he made him surrender his sister's collection of figures at a place where Croake would get a maximum of humiliation. Vulgarly, he made him sweat. And why? I think because, when Bottomley took a fancy to Nessie at Ballacroake and began to hang about the place, Croake threw him out bodily. To a little madman like Bottomley, that was an unforgivable affront.'

They ordered lunch and after the first course the Archdeacon began his tale.

'Margaret Foster-Leneve was the only child of a very wealthy Manxman, Frank Baron Curwen. He left her all he had, estimated at about half a million, earned in the Australian goldfields. He came back home to end his days. Foster-Leneve was a well-known explorer and archaeologist. He'd been up the Amazon, travelled in the Congo, and made a name for himself in the Valley of the Nile. Over thirty years ago, he first came to the Island with a university party surveying gallery-graves. They were here, on and off, for two years. During that time, he met and married

Margaret Curwen. Foster-Leneve was then a handsome man and, I gather, almost penniless. In between his excursions, he lived extravagantly and, although his wife didn't know it when she married him, was a rake who couldn't resist a good-looking woman. She had evidence of this before they'd been married long. He'd obviously married her for her money. She, being high-church and opposed to divorce, took no steps to free herself from him...'

As this climax was reached, the club bore intervened, crossed to their table, shook hands with the Archdeacon, insisted on being introduced to Littlejohn, started to discuss the Croake case and many others in which he seemed to have participated, and finally asked to be allowed to join them for lunch. This was too much for the Venerable Archdeacon.

'Some other time, Benjamin. Some other time. We're at present engaged on private business, which can't be delayed. I'm sorry...'

The bore looked sorry, too, but he took the rebuff in a good spirit. He said he quite understood and tiptoed away, as though trying to escape without being caught. He joined another solitary diner, a bank manager, and spoiled *his* lunch.

'The marriage was a strange one. Foster-Leneve was absent half his time exploring abroad. He returned now and then when he was short of money. Finally, he went off to Patagonia for almost twelve months. The pair of them had then been married four years and Mrs. Foster-Leneve had lived most of the time like the single woman she was before her husband turned-up. Now, this is where John Charles Croake enters the picture....'

The waiter entered the picture too, and his solicitude and the length of time he took in meticulously attending to the Archdeacon almost wore away the good man's patience.

'We ought not to have come here at all! We ought to have taken sandwiches and eaten them in a quiet part of the country where we wouldn't have been disturbed... I was saying, John Charles now enters the drama. People often wondered why he never married. If what Mrs. Foster-Leneve says is true and isn't a product of her romantic imagination, he was in love with her all his life and never married because of it. Manxmen are often slow in declaring their affections, and it seems John Charles delayed too long and Foster-Leneve beat him to the post. So much the worse for everybody. Not long after our explorer friend left for Patagonia, John Charles and Margaret met on a charity committee, which was held every week. Their seats, it seems, were adjacent, and soon they began lunching together, now and then, at a quiet hotel off the beaten track. What puzzles me is, how did they manage it without being caught out! The Manx capacity for detecting such irregularities is usually phenomenal. However, Mrs. Foster-Leneve confesses that soon their moral scruples were drowned in a gust of passion. They were quickly involved in a secret love affair. It did not last long. She soon found she was pregnant and the commotion of dealing with such a grave and illicit emergency seems to have separated them for ever....'

'By jove! It *does* sound like a penny novelette, as you say, parson.'

'Jam pudding, sherry trifle, ices, or cheese, gentlemen?'

The waiter was back, offering his wares.

'Whatever you say, Herbert.'

'As you don't seem keen about any of them, I'll do my best to get some strawberries and cream, Reverend...'

'Penny novelette or not, the pair of them seem to have arranged matters very efficiently. Margaret left almost at once for a village in the South of France, where the child was born. It was a boy. John Charles must have taken his family into his confidence, which is easily understood. They are a very close lot, tightly bound to each other. Edward Croake was practising as a doctor in Birmingham at the time. He was married, but they had no children; nor were any likely, for his wife was, even then, suffering from the complaint which later grew more grave and resulted in her eventual death. Edward and his wife adopted the child. Joseph Croake was that child. I don't know whether or not he knows it. Probably not. Telling him that his mother was one of the wealthiest and most respected women on the Isle of Man, to say nothing about his paternity, must have been quite a fine point, a problem.'

There were no strawberries and cream, so the waiter brought strawberry ices with his apologies. He later told them in the kitchen that the Archdeacon was ageing fast and breaking up. He'd asked for butter and biscuits to eat with his ice cream!

'... Now to tell you where the blackmail comes in...'

'Did Margaret and John Charles start a correspondence about the whole business, sir?'

'How did you know that?'

'They always do in blackmail cases... *and* in crime stories.'

'You're right. She must have written to him from a village near Grasse to tell him of her safe arrival. How frequently they corresponded I can't say, but he wrote to her suggesting she divorced her husband and married him. She kept that letter. Again, he wrote after news of the child's birth. He asked her again about a divorce. She gave her reason, which I mentioned before. He later wrote about the idea of adoption by Edward and his wife. This delighted her and she agreed. In all, she kept six of his letters. They were locked in a drawer of her desk. Five weeks ago, they disappeared.'

'Was the house burgled?'

'No. I asked her when and by whom she thought the letters were taken. She told me quite plainly that she thought either Bottomley or Walmer of the *Bishop's Arms* had stolen them. It seems she, too, had a collection of china figures, as well as one or two Toby jugs. Walmer must have heard of this and called to ask if he might see them. She showed them to him. He offered to buy them. She said she had grown tired of washing and caring for a lot of her china and had already decided to offer some of it for sale. Walmer bought several of the jugs. There were some Chelsea figures there, too. Walmer mentioned that he had a friend interested in buying fine china figures. Could he bring him along. That's how Bottomley entered the affair.'

'They rifled the escritoire!'

'As you so melodramatically put it, Littlejohn, they did. They called as she was writing at the desk, with the keys in the drawer containing the letters I've mentioned. She left the room to get a figure from upstairs. Bottomley bought several figures. After they'd gone, she locked the desk, but before doing so, opened the drawer. The letters were missing. As she asked me, what could she do? If she told the police, the whole affair might have come out. She'd nobody to confide in, and she didn't think of me, as she said, with an apology for not remembering me. She didn't wish to worry Croake. She decided to wait and see what happened. Nothing did. As far as she was concerned, that is. Instead, the blackmailers turned to John Charles Croake. You can guess why. As you told me, Bottomley hated Croake and wanted to make him squirm. Here was his chance. It was full of delightful possibilities for him. He held letters about the infidelity of Mrs. Foster-Leneve, about John Charles's illegitimate son, about the paternity of Joseph Croake, and a chance to cause even greater distress by insisting on payment in china figures from the famous Croake collection. These, sold in the right places, would have made him rich indeed. No wonder he chose Croake instead of Margaret!'

'Were Croake and Mrs. Foster-Leneve still friendly?'

'More than that. Their once passionate liason, after their mistake, developed into a kind of idyllic loving friendship. They never wrote to one another, she told me. They sometimes met at public functions. They spoke to each other over the telephone now and then. They must have obtained some kind of mental comfort from their harmless relationship. He for his perpetual celibacy; she for her unhappy marriage with a roue who cared for nothing but her money.'

'Did she never tell her husband about the love affair in the past and its results.'

'No. She felt he would only use the information to his advantage and felt justified to a certain extent in keeping secrecy, in view of his own immoral life. She was very distressed about the whole matter when it came to confiding in me. But, as I had told her, by being quite frank about it all, she could perhaps help you to run to earth the murderer of her best friend – I call him that out of charity – and she agreed to my telling you, also relying on your discretion.'

'I suppose the blackmailers threatened to tell Foster-Leneve the whole story and John Charles paid up to avoid distress to Margaret.'

'I suppose they did.'

'And he suffered all of it for her sake. No use asking why he didn't go to the police. They never do.'

'They never do, because, regarded objectively, as the police are in the habit of doing in such matters, it would have been just another case, just another opportunity to help someone out of a dilemma. But regarded subjectively, as the victim must do, the threat becomes a nightmare which blackens the whole of existence and makes them unable to think rightly.'

'The great question now is, what happened to cause the death of John Charles Croake?'

'My guess is that he turned on his tormentors. He got a chance to do so and they struck him down.'

'What chance, sir?'

'A week before Croake's death, Peter Foster-Leneve was in Bone, Algeria, consulting with a Moslem expert on a matter of some desert ruins in which they were interested. As they left the museum they were shot down by gunmen. Foster-Leneve was dead when Croake next met his extortioners. The letters had lost their value. He turned upon his tormentors, and they executed him.'

Chapter Sixteen
The Elder Brother

After lunch, they met Mrs. Littlejohn, who'd been giving a talk to a Women's Institute, and set off again to Ballacroake.

It was far too nice to be working on a murder case. Littlejohn told his companions as much and they both agreed. All they felt like doing was sitting in the car and quietly admiring the magnificent views of the distant hills and the blue sea with waves lapping against the rocky coast.

As they approached Ballacroake by the long drive from the road, Littlejohn noticing again the old, settled, timeless look of the great house, felt that it would have been far better approached in one of those patient old country horse-traps which seem to make time spin out. At last, they reached the gate to the courtyard and then drove in. The sun was shining full on the white front of the mansion, there was nobody about, and the noise made by the car seemed magnified in the silence and caused the birds in the rookery behind the house to launch themselves, cawing, from the trees, and then, after a disorderly flight, to perch back again over their untidy nests.

Across the valley from the house, the sunny mass of the Manx hills rose steeply. The high peaks were coloured in the purple of the heather and the brown of the sun-baked bracken. To the left, the flat lands to the Point of Ayre and the mass of the Mull of Galloway across the water, looked like scenes painted on a back-cloth.

Nessie answered the bell and stepped aside to let them enter. The house was quiet, as though itself listening for something. Nessie showed them in the sitting-room which, in its spaciousness and contents, looked more like a French *salon* than the parlour of a country house.

'It's quiet, Nessie. Is there anyone at home?'

'Mr. Ewan, Archdeacon. Mr. Reuben and Mr. Joseph have gone to Ramsey. Juan's somewhere about the place. He's been very quiet since the funerals.'

Nessie looked pale and quiet, too, and was more taciturn in her manner. As though tragedy were hanging over Ballacroake still. She had little to say and, after asking them to be seated, went to find Ewan Croake.

He came right away, running almost soundlessly down the long staircase. His thick white hair was dishevelled and his face was paler and the eyes heavily ringed with dark circles.

'We've brought Mrs. Littlejohn again, this time to see the collection of Dresden figures. Could we leave her with Nessie and have a talk with you?'

Ewan looked at the Archdeacon blankly, as though he might have addressed him in a foreign language which he didn't understand. Then suddenly he seemed himself again.

'I'm sorry, Caesar. How are you all? Talk, did you say? Come upstairs to my room. We'll be quiet there.'

He called to Nessie, told her to make Mrs. Littlejohn welcome, and, after that, get ready some tea.

Ewan Croake's study upstairs faced the south and the Manx hills in front of the house. It was a large room with an Adam fireplace on each side of which books were ranged on shelves from floor to ceiling. There was a large mahogany desk under the window, a four-poster bed in an alcove, water-colours of Manx scenes on the rest of the walls, two tallboys and a huge Georgian wardrobe. Croake motioned to two easy chairs and himself sat in an armchair with his back to the desk.

'What is it, Caesar?'

He said it in a weary voice, as though at the end of his tether with other people's worries and his own. He put on a pair of large gold-rimmed spectacles, the better to see what was going on, and this removed the peering look he had when without them.

'I'd like you to hear a first-hand account from Littlejohn of what he has discovered about your brother's death. I've no doubt that some of it isn't new to you. I'm sure it's on your conscience, Ewan. You have been withholding information from the police, which might have resulted in a young man being convicted of a murder he didn't commit...'

'What are you talking about, Caesar?'

But he knew. He looked afraid in spite of his efforts to remain calm.

'Tell him, Littlejohn.'

'How many people know, Mr. Croake, that your nephew Joseph was the son, not of your brother Edward, but of the late Mr. John?'

No use denying it. Ewan Croake saw that. He paused for a minute, wondering whether to refute it and then took off his glasses.

'As far as I know, nobody but John Charles, my late sister, myself, the child's mother, my brother Edward and his wife, and Clucas Kallen, who drew up a settlement and arranged the adoption.'

'Did Joseph know?'

'He did not and still doesn't and I'd be grateful if, now that you've found out in some way, you'd respect the secret. Had Joseph been a stable, dependable man, we'd have told him long ago. As it is, he's wilful enough to use the information for his own purposes. He has been a great trouble to the family, without giving him reason for being a bigger nuisance. What of it all?'

'The secret got out, however. It seems your late brother, John, exchanged letters which must have contained all the information about the birth, parentage, and adoption of Joseph, with his mother. Those letters were stolen from a drawer in Mrs. Foster-Leneve's desk and used to blackmail Mr. John....'

Ewan's face slowly turned livid with rage and he stood up and towered over Littlejohn.

'Why wasn't I told the full tale before? I'd an idea that something was wrong and that John and Bridget were up to something before they died. If you knew what it was, you should have told me. I'd a right to know.'

'Please sit down, Mr. Croake, and let's talk calmly about this. I've only just found out what was happening.'

'How have you found out?'

'I'll tell you later. The urgent matter is, exactly how much you know of what your brother John Charles did to cause his own death.'

'I don't know anything. You must believe me. I don't know.'

'Let me tell you how far we've gone, then. We know that years ago, during the absence of Mrs. Foster-Leneve's husband on a prolonged trip abroad, there was a love affair between her and your brother. A child was born and adopted by Dr. Edward Croake and his wife. The whole matter was hushed-up and kept a profound secret, I presume to avoid a scandal which would have dealt hard with your family.'

'That is true. It had to be handled cautiously, discreetly, otherwise we'd never have held our heads high on the Island again. Also, it would perhaps have involved my brother and Margaret in divorce proceedings. She is not the kind to tolerate divorce in any circumstances, but a scoundrel like Foster-Leneve would have made capital out of it and squeezed every drop of advantage from it. John Charles, at the time, did wish to go on with the divorce. He always loved Margaret and wouldn't have any other woman. She refused. We all found it difficult to prevent John Charles from acting unwisely. However...'

'The letters appear to have been stolen by one of two men, or perhaps both of them. One was Walmer; the other Bottomley.'

'So that was it! Is that why he began to frequent Walmer's low public-house in Douglas?'

'It's hardly low, but not the place you'd expect to find your brother drinking in.'

'He was a total abstainer....'

'For goodness sake, Ewan, don't be so pompous! This is a matter of murder, not of offending the tastes of Methodist trustees. John Charles did drink lemonade when he was at the *Bishop's Arms*. He never, from all accounts, got drunk. It might have done him good if he *had*, now and then. He might have mustered strength to tell those two rascals to do their worst. As it is, he's dead and he wasn't murdered by a teddy-boy.'

Ewan took it all with his head down.

'He might, at least, have told me of his troubles.'

'If he had done so, you would probably have upset the applecart by your impulsive temper. He told his sister. In fact, he had to do so. His blackmailers insisted on being paid, not in the coin of the realm, but in figures from the Croake collection of Dresden. Bridey's collection. Bottomley, I gather, hated your brother like poison for throwing him out when he tried to make love to Nessie. He took a sweet revenge. He made John Charles pay his blackmail across the table of the *Bishop's Arms* in Bridey's Meissen figures. Not only did it humiliate John Charles, it made Bottomley and his partner rich without causing the publicity incurred when large sums of money are involved. The figures taken to Bottomley were replaced by cheap fakes in the cases downstairs. None of you, except Bridey, ever opened the cases or handled the contents. One figure was as good as another to you and the rest. But not to Bridey. She was growing blind, fretted about the vanishing figures, but gladly parted with them for John's sake. When, on top of it all, John lost his life, she couldn't stand it any more, and she took her own life. All that is the reckoning due from Bottomley and Walmer, and Littlejohn is going to see that they pay it.'

Ewan Croake raised his grief-stricken face and his sorrow turned to rage again.

'I will do that! I'll kill them for this!'

'Be your age, Ewan! Be civilised! If you kill either of them, you'll land in gaol. You'll make a proper job of disgracing the family you've tried so long to protect and keep in its lofty place in Manx society. Did you know about the disappearance of the Meissen figures?'

'I did not. I never gave them a minute's thought. They were Bridey's. I always regarded them as her toys, her playthings. She called them her little people. I thought she was merely being childish.'

'I'm sorry I've taken all the talking in my own hands, Littlejohn. You'd better tell Ewan what you propose to do about all this. Anything rather than have him chasing the pair of scoundrels around Douglas with a shot gun.'

Littlejohn was smoking his pipe. He was amused secretly at the way the Venerable Archdeacon had, in his enthusiasm, taken the case out of his hands and questioned Ewan Croake in a truly professional fashion.

'There are one or two matters still to be cleared-up. Once or twice when I've been speaking with her, Nessie has mentioned a "ghost" which walks in Ballacroake. And one night your man, Juan, seems to have had difficulty in keeping his dogs quiet, as though there were prowlers around the house. This happened after the death of your brother. Have you heard any sounds in the night which might have, say, been attempts to break in here?'

'I cannot say that I have. I am usually a sound sleeper and I must say that even the tragedies of recent weeks have not prevented my sleeping. I haven't found any traces of intruders, either.'

'As a matter of fact, your sister seems to have been disturbed by noises in the night before she died. Juan, for that reason, took a bed to the guest-chamber across the yard and slept there for several nights in case of further alarms.'

'I have since heard that.'

'Now that we have discovered why your brother frequented the *Bishop's Arms* at certain times, we can get on with the job of questioning Walmer and Bottomley. I hope in this way we'll be able to clear-up the mystery of your brother's death. The assassination of Foster-Leneve recently made it possible for your brother to turn the tables on his blackmailers. Obviously, with the husband out of the way, the letters became worthless to Bottomley and Walmer. Was your brother a violent man? Might he have attacked them, do you think?'

'In his younger days, he was a passionate man. He was prone to lose his temper against, let's say, certain acts of injustice and wrong. He was certainly a very powerful man even at his age of past sixty. In his youth, he was at Cambridge, where he boxed and fenced for his college. He was very fit at the time of his death. But if you are suggesting that he might have entered into a brawl with these two men, I'm sure you're wrong.'

'We will see. I'll call at the *Bishop's Arms* on our way back to Grenaby. Perhaps you'll allow me to telephone. I want to take Inspector Knell along with me. This has now become a matter for the official police. I've only been helping them in the case.'

'Of course. The telephone is in the hall. Shall we go down and see if there's any tea for us? There's nothing more you want to ask me?'

A strange man, Ewan. Right in the middle of a dramatic climax, and he bothered about his tea!

'No, sir... Except one thing. The matter of the inventory. When we were last here, Mr. Reuben offered to let us see the inventory. When he went to look for it in your late brother's desk, it had been removed, he said. I have reason to believe that Mr. Reuben had taken it and hidden it himself...'

'But that is ridiculous! What good would it do him to hide the thing? Wait. He and Joseph are just returning from Ramsey, I can see the car coming up the street...'

He hurried to the door and called downstairs.

'Nessie! When Mr. Reuben comes in, please ask him to join us here for a minute.'

It was not long before Reuben Croake arrived. He hadn't been drinking and seemed very pleased with himself.

'We've just been fishing in Ramsey Bay. I caught fifty young plaice. Not a bad day's catch, eh? Good afternoon Archdeacon... Littlejohn... What brings you here?'

His brother faced him sternly.

'Reuben, do you remember last time the Superintendent was here you offered to let him see the inventory of Bridey's china? Then you returned saying that someone had removed it from John's desk.'

Reuben pretended he'd forgotten and had to think hard – so hard that it made him squint.

'Yes. I remember. That's right.'

'I've reason to think you hid it yourself. Why did you do that?'

Littlejohn intervened.

'Also, Mr. Reuben, was it you who placed one of the Meissen figures in Joseph's drawer in his room? Perhaps in case of a search, it might have been discovered and the whole theft of the figures laid at Joseph's door.'

Reuben didn't know where to look but he hadn't the impudence to deny his part in the drama.

He giggled.

'Just a little joke, that's all. I hid them both for a joke.'

Ewan rose in a tearing rage again.

'You mean to tell me, that with two of our family just buried after dying in tragic circumstances, you could find it in your heart to practise silly, childish jokes, first on the Superintendent and then on Joseph. I don't believe you. You must have gone mad. I want the truth, Reuben.'

Reuben cowered as though Ewan were going to hit him.

'All right, then, if you call me a liar in front of these two gentlemen, I'll tell the truth and you're not going to like it. I knew that John Charles was stealing the figures and selling them. Two or three times in the night, I've been wakened by footsteps passing my door. I got up twice and saw Charles go in the sitting-room, open the case, and take out some figures. He'd even got little figures like them and put them there in place of the good ones. I know something about those figures. Bridey and I used to talk about them. As for the fake figures John was putting in their place to make it look as if they were all still there, I took one of them down to Tiller, the antiques man in Ramsey, and he said they were modern stuff of very little value. I don't know why John should want to steal and sell them, but he did....'

'That accounts for the ghost walking, Ewan.'

Reuben giggled again.

'That's right. That's what I thought when first I heard of it. When I offered to produce the inventory, I suddenly remembered that if it were checked, the thefts would be discovered. So I hid it. It's gone. I know who did it. It was Joseph...'

'No. It was Nessie. She saw you hide it.'

'Well, it doesn't matter now. You all know. I was only trying to protect poor John's good name. That's why I hid the figure in Joseph's room. I thought if the thefts were discovered, I could suggest a search and Joseph would be blamed instead of John. The family wouldn't have prosecuted him for it. Only sent him away. I'd rather Joseph take the blame than John. I never cared for Joseph. He's a good-for-nothing, who's always spying on me. Can I go now? I want my tea and after that I'm going to have some of the plaice I caught cooked for my supper.'

'Yes, go, Reuben, before I lose my temper. You've caused a lot of trouble with your clever ideas. Go and get your tea if that is all you can think about.'

Reuben hurried away giggling to himself.

'You must forgive my brother. Sometimes he does silly things. He must be growing senile, I think.'

Ewan seemed to have forgotten that only a few minutes ago, he had himself been eager for his own tea at a time of dramatic gravity!

Chapter Seventeen
Hard Luck on Littlejohn

'Let's go in the room behind and have a talk.'
Peter Walmer was standing with a double whisky in his hand contemplating the bar of the *Bishop's Arms*. There was nobody else about.

Evening was coming on and the sun was hanging heavily over the hills behind Douglas. Even in the street there was little noise. It was the hour before the last meal of the day and everybody was indoors preparing for it. The odd one or two who were abroad seemed awestruck by the beauty of the fading light and sounded to be walking on tiptoe. Across the harbour in a garden on Douglas Head, a blackbird was singing and you could hear it clearly over the water. From one of the bedrooms nearby boarding-house came the sounds of a clarinet playing softly.

Riverboat Rock, sailin' to the sunset,
Riverboat Rock, rock ma baby in my arms...

It sounded quite a different tune, a kind of gentle lullaby.
Walmer hesitated and then led Littlejohn and Knell into his private quarters. It was almost dark there. The tall buildings behind cast long shadows across the windows. Outside,

soft footsteps passed the door through which John Charles Croake had staggered and died.

From their shelves, the rows of Toby jugs all looked alike in the shadows, rows of dark figures crouching like listening men.

'What'll it be?'

'Nothing, thanks, Mr. Walmer. We've just called for some information...'

'No need to be unsociable about it, have you?'

'Wait until you've heard what we have to say.'

Walmer sat down at the table and put his elbows on it and rested his chin on his clenched fists.

'Shoot! What is it then?'

'Where's Ross Bottomley?'

'How should I know? I haven't seen him since noon.'

'He's usually here at opening-time, isn't he?'

'When he feels like it. He's not answerable to me for his movements, you know.'

There was a tense stillness about Walmer. Like someone waiting for the worst.

'Which of you took a bundle of letters from a desk at the house of Mrs. Foster-Leneve the other week, Mr. Walmer?'

Walmer looked at Littlejohn craftily from under his shaggy eyebrows.

'What are you talking about?'

'You were there. I can produce witnesses to prove it. They will also state that before you both arrived and were left waiting for Mrs. Foster-Leneve in her drawing-room, there was a packet of letters in the drawer of her desk. When you both left together, they'd gone. What have you to say?'

'Nothing.'

'We're not leaving until you tell us what happened.'

Knell was standing near the door. He moved and placed his back against it.

'Here. What are you two at? I told you I know nothing about it.'

'Put your coat on, Mr. Walmer. I don't suppose you want to accompany us to the police station in your shirt sleeves.'

'What am I being accused of? I want my lawyer.'

'You can have your lawyer when we reach the police station. Get your jacket on.'

Walmer moved and aggressively put his hands flat on the table as though making up his mind about something.

'No need to make a fuss about it. I can tell you what happened. Bottomley was admiring the desk. It's a fine antique piece. He opened the drawer as you do with such things. It's sort of pleasant to slide the drawers in and out when they're made by craftsmen. They come and go as if they was on silk. Know what I mean?'

'I think so. What about the letters?'

'They were there when he opened it. You know him; or, at least Inspector Knell does. A busybody. Always prying into other people's private affairs. We could hear Mrs. Foster-Leneve walkin' about upstairs. Bottomley opened one of the letters. Then he pocketed the lot, shut the drawer and sat down. I was just going to ask him what he was up-to when Mrs. Foster-Leneve came back. I couldn't very well start ribbing him then about what he'd done. When we got outside, I asked him what he was playing at...'

'And he told you the letters were very incriminating and written by John Charles Croake, and that he'd pay well to get them back.'

Walmer was on his feet trying to brazen it out.

'Have you been talkin' to Bottomley? If he's told you that, he's a liar.'

'He told you what they contained and the pair of you concocted a nice little blackmail racket. Don't deny it. You and Bottomley were in this room together and met Croake when he made his Saturday call to pay his hush-money, or rather pay you in kind, to keep quiet. What happened to the porcelain figures he regularly brought in here with him?'

'I don't know what your talking about. It's double-Dutch to me.'

Walmer licked his lips. Then he turned on Knell.

'What are you standing there for with your back to the door? You can't stop me from moving where I want on my own property. You've got nothing on me. Let me pass. I want to draw myself some beer.'

'You can wait for your beer until we've settled this matter. I've a good idea that Bottomley was responsible for the idea of Croake calling here with his pay-off. He hated Croake and wanted to humiliate him. And to cover up Croake's visits, you put around the story that he was calling to see your daughter. That was untrue.'

'It wasn't. He was crazy about her.'

'That's what you told people. You and Bottomley had him in your clutches and could make him do as you liked for the sake of avoiding disgrace for himself, a woman, and his own family. You and Bottomley are a pretty pair of scoundrels. He blames you and you blame him...'

'What have you been doing to Bottomley and what's he told you...? Because if he's been...'

Walmer stopped.

'You're trying to trick me.'

'To keep you quiet, Bottomley had to give you your cut. He took the Meissen figures, sold them, and shared the loot with you. It was considerable. Altogether it totalled several thousand pounds. What did you do with it, Walmer?'

'Nothing. Bottomley ran the thing all the way through. All I had to do with it was letting them have this room while they did their private business. I know nothing about Meissen figures and blackmail...'

'We'll see how Bottomley bears that story out when we face you with him. You'd better come with us. If what you say is true, Bottomley will probably deny it.'

'You know he will. He'll only try to save his own skin.'

'If I were you, I'd try to save my skin, too. You'll be charged with blackmail and you'll go down for a good stretch for what you've done. And unless you tell a convincing tale, you'll probably be charged with worse than blackmail. This case involves the murder of John Charles Croake, and it wasn't done by a passing teddy-boy, either. He was stabbed here, in this room, and staggered out in the street to die. Who stabbed him? Was it you, Walmer?'

It was dark now, but even in the shadows, Walmer seemed to go to pieces. His body seemed to shrink.

'I'd nothing to do with the murder. Why should I kill Croake? I'd nothing against him...'

'But he'd plenty against you and Bottomley. He suddenly found himself in a position to call your bluff about the letters. The person to whom you threatened to show them was suddenly killed. Croake called here that last night to tell you that and to make the pair of you pay for the weeks of torment you'd given him. He said he was going to the police. There was a row. He was a powerful man, lost his temper, and got violent. You stabbed him to keep him quiet and defend yourself against him. Are you ready to come with us? Otherwise, we'll have to take you as you are, in your shirt sleeves.'

'Wait. Have you got Bottomley at the station and has he been blaming me for all this mess...?'

'You'll see. Facing you with him will provide the necessary element of surprise.'

'I'm not taking the murder rap. I'd nothing to do with it...'

'Who had?'

'Bottomley. He's a little coward. He goes mad at the thought of any kind of physical violence. Once, when a couple of teddy-boys accosted him in the street, he raised the roof with his screams and they hadn't even touched him. When Croake caught him by the throat, he went berserk.'

'What weapon did he use? A table knife?'

'There were no knives about. No. He used the dagger in his stick. It's a short sword in it. He bought it after the teddy-boys attacked him. Nobody knew it was a sword-stick, except me. I saw he'd got it after the teddy-boys affair, but I just thought it was a sort of bludgeon with a weighted top. One day he left it here. He was back like a shot when he found he'd forgotten it, but before he got back I took a look at it. I found out the secret about it. He never knew I discovered it, but I kept an eye on it whenever he had it with him, which was regular.'

'You must admit, Walmer, that the pair of you were almost lucky enough to get away with murder...'

'I had nothing to do with killing Croake, I tell you. It was all over and done with before I knew anything about it. He was alone with Bottomley in here when it happened. I was at the bar and when I came in, Croake had gone, and Bottomley was standing there, all roughed up, as you might say, with the sword-stick blade in his hand, looking like somebody who'd gone up the wall. As a matter of fact, he was a bit mad before all this happened.'

'It was lucky for you both that a predatory teddy-boy happened to pass, and saw what he thought was a drunken old man clutching a wallet, emerging from the pub. He snatched at the wallet, but the old man, now with the mists of death around him, gripped the boy convulsively. The teddy-boy was caught with the wallet and the old man died in the street almost right away. What would you have thought, Walmer, in such circumstances? That the old man had been knifed by the young thug? You see how lucky you almost were…'

'It's nothing to do with me, I tell you. I didn't knife Croake.'

'Probably Bottomley will say the same. He'll try to blame it on you. Shall we go, then?'

'Where to?'

'The police station. The pair of you can argue it out there.'

'Who's going to look after this place while I'm away?'

'Your daughter. Isn't Jennie at home?'

'No, she's not. She left by the afternoon boat to visit her aunt in Liverpool. We've had a row.'

'What about?'

'She's got a bit above herself. Since she took up with John Charles Croake, she's got too fancy to do work about the *Bishop's Arms*. This afternoon, after a bit of an argument, I told her she could go. So, she went.'

'As simple as that.'

'Yes.'

'Do you mind, Knell, asking the local police to send a message to Liverpool and tell the police there to meet the boat and detain Miss Walmer. We'll check her father's story, then.'

'I've told you the truth. You're only giving yourself a lot of trouble for nothing.'

Knell went to 'phone from the instrument in the corner of the room.

'I'll get my jacket, then, if you insist on taking me with you. You're making a mistake, though. You'll look foolish when you find I'd nothing whatever to do with Croake's death. I tell you, I was in the bar when it happened.'

'We'll see about that. Get your coat. Where is it?'

'Upstairs in my bedroom...'

He made for the door.

'I'll come with you.'

'You needn't bother. There's no other way out except by the front door and the side door. The beer comes in through the cellar. So, I couldn't bolt if you asked me to.'

'All the same, lead the way.'

Walmer entered the saloon-bar and then led the way through a door from one corner into a private hall whence the stairs rose to a landing. It was a relic of the days when the *Bishop's Arms* took-in boarders and this was their private entrance to the rooms above. Littlejohn followed on his heels as Walmer made his way up, slowly, like a man suffering from a bad heart.

What followed certainly took Littlejohn off his guard. It was lucky for him that Walmer was short-legged and fat; otherwise it might have been much worse.

Walmer, as they reached the top of the stairs, turned as if to round the banister at the first landing, but instead, made a quick half-circle back and kicked Littlejohn on the point of the jaw with his heel. The Superintendent clutched at the newel-post, missed it, and slid down the stairs from top to bottom. A door slammed as he picked himself up and, hardly able to hold himself together, almost crawled upstairs again. Knell, hearing the commotion, rushed to join him.

There were four doors all alike on the landing and they were all closed. The first was locked and presumably that was the one behind which Walmer was sheltering. Littlejohn was in no shape to lend much help in breaking-in and, as he stood at the stairhead gasping to recover and fingering his bruised jaw, Knell flung himself three times against it before the lock gave way and the screws parted from the wood.

It was a sort of junk-room now. A dismantled bed, a dusty dressing-table, a rolled-up mat, boxes, and odds and ends all over the place. Presumably, if they had to take a lodger in now and then, this was one of the rooms they tidied-up and used. The window was wide open. On the bed Jenny Walmer was lying. Her hands and legs were bound with insulating tape and there was a wad of adhesive plaster over her mouth. To anchor her to the bed, a length of clothes-line, or something such, had been passed round her body and the bed three times.

Knell rushed to the window. It overlooked the side-street where Croake had died a few days ago. Directly below was a small back-yard, with a door to the lane. There was nothing particular happening down below. People were coming and going down the alley quite unaware of the pantomime which had been taking place above them. Below the window was a wooden shed. Walmer, if, as was presumably the case, had used that way out, would have found it easy. A scramble through the window, a short drop to the top of the shed, and then down in the yard and through the door, which was now ajar.

At the end of the alley on the quay, Knell could see that something was afoot. A small crowd had gathered and a couple of them were apparently dandling between them a man who seemed to be being violently sick.

Littlejohn appeared at the door, and then between them they disentangled Jenny from the tape, the plaster and the clothes-line. When they'd finished the job, she fainted.

'Did he beat-it through the window, Knell?'

'Yes, sir. I think I'd better go down and see what's happened at the end of the street on the quayside. There's a crowd gathered there. You all right, sir?'

'Yes. My jaw aches a bit, but I can see straight again now. Just pop along then, old man, see how the land lies, and I'll join you in a minute. I'll find somebody to attend to Jenny and then I'll just take a dose of medicine from one of the bottles in the bar and give my jaw a dab in the bathroom, and I'll be with you.'

'Feel you can make it?'

'Yes. I'm all right now, Knell.'

Knell bolted down the stairs three at a time and ran to the spot where the crowd had collected. Someone recognised him.

'And time, too. It's a funny thing, whenever you want a policeman, you can never find one. Here's a chap been beat-up and 'ad his car pinched. And do you know who did it? Walmer of the *Bishop's Arms*. He must have gone off his rocker. What should he want to pinch a car for? And he was in his shirt-sleeves!'

'Oh, shut up, you! You're only delaying him...'

One of the men holding-up the object which had presumably owned the missing car, looked up and silenced the complainant.

'Look at this chap. Nearly killed him. It seems he was just gettin' out of his car and taking the ignition key out, when the bloke gives him a rabbit punch and nearly puts paid to him. Then he leaves him in the gutter and does a bunk with his car...'

The victim was still heaving rhythmically, like a seasick man who wants to vomit but can't. His complexion was almost grass-colour.

'You'd better take him in the *Bishop's Arms* and lay him flat on a seat and get an ambulance. There are two others there, too, who might need the ambulance. Which way did Walmer go?'

About a score of them were ready to give the exact bearings. One louder than the rest managed to make himself heard above the babble.

'He took off over the bridge and along the road past the Nunnery. He'll be lucky if he gets away with it.'

A police car arrived ringing its bell. Someone had had the presence of mind to telephone the police station.

As though stimulated by the sound of the bell, the man who'd had his car pinched suddenly recovered a bit. He vomited, reared himself upright, and started to talk.

'Who the 'ell hit me?'

He squared-up like a boxer, as though ready to take Walmer on, made a frantic swipe at the air, and then collapsed in the arms of a little man behind him, who, unable to bear his weight, measured his length himself, with the other sprawling on top of him.

Chapter Eighteen
The Cliffs at Keristal

The marine drive runs from Douglas to Port Soderick, a shelf road chiselled along the rock, with views of the sea and mighty cliffs below it. Like the Corniche d'Or and the Corniche Sublime of the Cote d'Azur rolled into one and on a sunny day, with the sea like blue glass and the waves dashing on the rocks a hundred feet below, as splendid as either of them.

That was what Hubert Hinks, on holidays from Manchester, told his wife in simpler terms one afternoon.

'Why go all the way to the South of France like we did last year, when we can 'ave all this an hour away from 'ome?'

He'd hardly got the words out of his mouth before the fun began. It ended in court for Hubert, but he didn't mind. He was only a witness and he got another week on the Island under a subpoena, and paid for.

The Hinkses had covered the first phase of the Marine Drive, where the road forks and one branch leads on and down to Port Soderick, and the other goes off to the main road at Oak Hill. On the right stood a small bungalow, a blot on the otherwise splendid landscape. You wondered how in the world anybody had been allowed to put it up, not to mention stay there with it. On the left, a stretch of fine sea-turf, a drop over the edge, and below, the rocks and the little bay of Keristal. Hauled on the shingle of the cove was a small motor-boat which captured Mr. Hinks's attention and distant admiration, for he did a bit of sailing himself on Hollingworth Lake.

'From here she looks a little beauty,' he said to his wife, who didn't share his enthusiasm for a sport which, one day, she was sure would make a widow of her.

It was late afternoon and there weren't many people about. They were either at tea or else had gone back to town to get ready for the pleasures of the coming evening.

First, a land rover, driven by a man without a hat and with a shock of unruly red hair blowing in the breeze, tore along the Manx Corniche, turned up the ramshackle road to the wretched red bungalow without slowing down, and pulled up at the door. The newcomer beat on the panels with his two fists and finding it locked, he kicked his way in.

Mr. Hinks was a tall, gangling, thin man, who looked as if a puff of wind might carry him off to heaven, but he didn't lack guts. He left his missus after an argument in which she implored him not to interfere in what didn't concern him. He set off at a shambling trot in the direction of the suffering house calling, Hey! Hey! as he did so, in the hope that the intruder would realise that he'd been spotted and would run away. Instead, the red-haired man turned and faced him. He was huge. Like a giant in the excited imagination of Mr. Hinks. A perfect Goliath of a chap, Mr. Hinks later told his friends at home.

'You keep out of this,' the redhead shouted, and Mr. Hinks did. He stood and watched the rest of the drama without doing much about it.

First, the man who'd broken in the place could be heard exploring it. His heavy nailed boots resounded here and there all over the floors. Then he shouted.

'Where are you, Bottomley? No use hiding. You can't get away from me.'

Then there was silence as if the redhead were listening for the heavy, fearful breathing of his quarry. Mr. Hinks could only hear the sound of the water lashing the foot of Keristal and the panting of his wife, who was ascending the rough road in low gear either to drag her husband away by force, or else protect him in some way from the wrath he had brought upon himself.

'Come on, Hubert. Let's go. He's mad and might do us harm.'

But Hubert remained rooted like a pillar of salt.

The uproar started again. The man in the house sounded to be pulling it down piece by piece. Now and then an article of shabby furniture flew through the open door and crashed on the long grass which once had been a lawn. It was all of no use. The man he was hunting wasn't there.

On the Marine Drive, some distance away, other figures appeared, noticed that something queer was going on, and started to mount the rough road, as well. Soon there was a small crowd of spectators standing at a distance asking Mr. Hinks what it was all about.

'I don't know. He just drove up in a car, kicked down the door, and started pulling the house down and smashin' up the furniture.'

One of the party suggested that he might be a holiday-maker who'd rented the place and when he'd found out what it was like, had taken a turn for the worse and was having his revenge.

'Somebody ought to do something about it. What about sendin' for the police?'

Before anyone could act, a further diversion arose. Another car appeared, driven by a man in his shirt-sleeves.

He was fat, excited, and sweating heavily and, at first, drove up the drive to the shabby little house. Then, when he saw the crowd, he halted, climbed out of the vehicle, and tried to look as though he'd made a mistake and taken the wrong turning. As he clambered out of the car, the red-headed man appeared at the door. At first he seemed amazed to see the spectators and then he spotted the new arrival.

'Walmer!' he bellowed.

Walmer had been hurriedly taking a can of petrol from the boot of the car and at the sound of the shout, leapt like someone stung. Then, still clinging to the can, he started to trot in the direction of the cliff edge, where a narrow goat-path ran down to the cove.

The massive red man followed him, running with remarkable agility for his size. Walmer had almost reached the start of the path when his pursuer caught up with him. The men in the crowd hesitated, held a brief committee-meeting about what to do next, and then, like a sheriff's posse, set off after the other two.

Before they reached them it was all over.

The big man seized the little one with his two huge hands, twisted him round and shouted in his face.

'Where's that murderer Bottomley? Where is he?'

The little fat man who was only interested in freeing himself and fleeing down the path, didn't seem to give the right answers. The redhead thereupon took him in his arms like a child and walked to the edge of the cliff, obviously threatening to throw him over if he didn't speak up. The other's resistance and silence finally enraged him. He lifted him in the air and tried to heave him over the edge. As he did so, the clawing fingers of the sweating, terrified little fat man caught the mop of red hair and clutched it frantically. For a second they seemed glued together. Four legs, two bodies twisted about each other, two pairs of hands and arms heaving and thrashing, and then the whole mass vanished over the edge.

The posse behind came up just too late. There was shouting and crying and some of them recoiled at the edge, dizzy from the height. Two who were steeplejacks on holiday hung over and looked below. There were two smashed forms, still intertwined, lying far beneath on a ledge. Then, the calm blue sea, the edge of foam gently lapping on the rocks, and the disturbed seagulls wheeling out over the water and perching again on inaccessible ledges.

Five minutes after the climax, a police car arrived with Knell. Littlejohn followed, still looking a bit shaken, in another car not long after.

By the time further help arrived and the bodies could be brought to the top of the cliff, the two dead men were cold and stiff.

'Perhaps it ended the best way,' said Littlejohn, as if to himself. Knell looked surprised.

Ross Bottomley had disappeared. There were several theories about it at the police station. Something had obviously happened to startle him and Walmer into tragic activity. It might have been that they had quarrelled and Walmer had murdered Bottomley and hidden the body. Or Bottomley might have fled, gone to ground somewhere, and was waiting for a chance to get off the Island. In the latter event, it might be the devil's own job to find him, as the Island was thronged with hideouts of all kinds. Sooner or later, however, he'd have to break ground. He couldn't get away, with ports, the aerodrome, and the coastline all watched.

Gus Watters, the potman at the *Bishop's Arms*, took over the management of the place in the absence of anyone better. The pub filled-up as usual for the evening; a party of birthday celebrants even arrived and ordered champagne. Gus went to the cellars for the bottles. He got a surprise. He stumbled over the body of Ross Bottomley at the bottom of the stairs. He wasn't dead, but fast asleep. There was an empty bottle of cheap port at his side. He was dead drunk.

Whilst Ross answered questions at the police station, Gus told his story at the bar, over and over again, embellishing it as he went along.

'It was like this...'

By the time he'd told it half-a-dozen times, he'd found Bottomley mad-drunk and aggressive, and had only subdued him by sheer physical strength.

Jenny Walmer had recovered sufficiently to attend at the police station, too, and make a statement. She was in better shape than Bottomley, who had a thick head and punctuated his account with many lamentations. Twice, he burst into tears. Then, as usual, he closed his eyes whilst he spoke, as though praying.

'If I'd known when I told Walmer that the collection at Ballacroake was priceless, that all this was going to follow, I'd have kept my mouth shut. That's all I did. Told him about the collection.'

Littlejohn was helping Knell with the questioning, but he'd rather have been at Grenaby. He'd recovered from the kick on the jaw, but the left side of his face felt as though all the teeth there had been extracted.

'Now, Bottomley, let's have it all from the beginning. Then you can sign a statement and sleep-off your bad head. The cells are quite comfortable.'

'What! I'm not going to be put in prison, am I? I haven't done anything.'

'I'm glad to hear it. But there is a matter of murder to be considered. No bail will be granted.'

Bottomley opened his eyes and started to weep.

'You'd better tell a plain, truthful tale and it will be over sooner, then.'

He'd been sick after his excessive potations, had had two cups of black coffee, his head held under a cold tap, and then two raw eggs broken in Worcester sauce, but Bottomley looked in poor shape still. He must have tried to smoke a cigarette in the dark, too, during his vigil in the cellar and had singed part of his little moustache on one side. His face was ashen and his nose red; he looked like a clown in a circus.

'All I have to say is, that a bit more than a month ago, I told Walmer about the collection of Meissen figures at Ballacroake and how valuable they were. I know what I'm talking about on porcelain. I was once an assistant in that department at the Victoria and Albert Museum. Walmer started to ask a lot of questions about Ballacroake itself and I soon tumbled to it that he had in mind trying to burgle the place. I'd told him the figures were unprotected in a glass case in the drawing-room...'

'But the pair of you soon found an easier way. Was that it?'

'I was forced into it. Walmer went to see Mrs. Leneve about some Toby jugs she wanted to sell and found she'd also some china I might care to buy. So he took me to see it. While she was out of the room, Walmer started to examine a desk there; a lovely antique piece. There was a bunch of keys in the top drawer and Walmer opened the drawer and looked in. He pulled out a packet of letters tied up with blue ribbon. He took one off the top and read a bit of it. Then he put the lot in his pocket.'

'Then, to put it briefly, the pair of you started to blackmail John Charles Croake.'

'It was Walmer. He dragged me in it. I owed him money. He said it was a good way to pay off the debt.'

'You, Bottomley, hated Croake, so you arranged for him to pay it off in the form of Meissen figures which you disposed of to a dealer in Liverpool.'

'Who told you that tale?'

'We've traced the dealer. What do you think we've been doing since the pair of you murdered Croake? Sleeping?'

'I didn't kill him. It was ....'

'Let's keep the story orderly. You suggested that Croake should pay in kind ...'

'It was Walmer. He said it would save our handling a lot of cash with Croake and we could sell the figures for far more than Croake thought they were worth. It would seem then that we weren't squeezing him too hard.'

'He agreed.'

'He said he'd let us know. There were six letters in the pile. Walmer said he'd settle for two figures for each letter.'

'His price was high!'

'He was a greedy, heartless man and saw he'd got Croake where he wanted him. Even after Croake's death, he went one night to the house at Ballacroake and tried to burgle it and get some more figures ...'

'But the dogs kicked up such a hullaballoo that he cleared off?'

'You seem to know a lot.'

'More than you think. Go on ...'

It was quite dark now and from time to time one or another of the police would bring in a drunk, sometimes singing happily, sometimes shouting the place down, declaring his sobriety or offering to fight the lot of them.

'Croake came the next night and said he'd agree. He asked us to take cash, but Walmer wouldn't....'

'Nor would you, Bottomley, and don't profess your complete innocence in this affair. It suited you to humiliate Croake. You were getting even for an old offence....'

Bottomley's face fell and he looked ready to weep. Then he closed his eyes and spoke up aggressively.

'I was once courting the housekeeper at Ballacroake. When he found out, John Charles Croake took me by the collar and threw me out in front of her. Do you expect me to forgive that. Me, an artist and come from a good family. I'm as good, nay better than the Croakes any day...'

'We heard a different story. You made a pass at Nessie who resented it and when you persisted...'

'It's a lie!'

'Lie or not, you tried to humiliate Croake by inducing Walmer to insist on the porcelain figures in payment. You, too, I suppose, insisted on Croake, a teetotaller, calling every Saturday, in front of a crowd of regulars, and meeting the pair of you at the *Bishop's Arms* to exchange the letters for the figures. And you kept him hanging-about there, until you chose to call for the pay-off.'

'We couldn't have gone to Ballacroake to collect them!'

'You could have done better than make Croake frequent a pub like Walmer's. And Walmer covered the visits by saying Croake was sweet on his daughter and Croake had to keep quiet to please the pair of you. You really filled his cup full of humiliation, didn't you?'

'It was Walmer's idea.'

'Go on.'

'Walmer had threatened to take the letters to Mrs. Leneve's husband when he got back from abroad if Croake hadn't paid up in time. Well, on the night the teddy-boy killed him, Croake came in a different mood. Leneve was dead. He told us that and said, if the figures weren't handed back and the letters, as well, he'd decided to go to the police and tell them about the blackmail. Walmer sort of dared him to do it and said the husband's death didn't make any difference. We could still blacken the woman's name... And Walmer called her a woman of easy virtue, only he used a worse term I don't care to quote. It was like a red rag to a bull calling her that. Croake was usually a mild man. Now he lost his temper. He was a big, powerful man, as you know, and he caught hold of Walmer and held him off the floor with one hand and slapped his face with the other. I tried to stop him, and somehow we all got mixed up in a fight....'

Littlejohn held up his hand.

'Stop, just one minute, Mr. Bottomley. Before you begin to blame the teddy-boy for the murder, let me make it quite plain – he didn't stab or kill John Charles Croake. It was done in the back room of the *Bishop's Arms* by either you or Walmer. Which of you did it? Walmer told me earlier today that it was you.'

For the first time Bottomley showed a bit of spirit. He'd no dignity left, with his dishevelled clothes and his half-burned-off moustache, but he tried to pull himself up to his full height, which wasn't very much.

'I was going to tell you the truth. It was Walmer.'

'How did he do it? With a table knife or a pen-knife?'

'Of course he didn't. I always carry a sword-stick, with a short blade. I've had it ever since some hooligans tried to rob me last summer in Drumgold Street. The police wouldn't grant me a licence for a revolver. I live in a lonely place, too. It's not right. So I got me a sword-stick. I don't know how to use a sword, but it sort of gives me confidence and might scare off anybody who tried to molest me.'

'What about Walmer?'

'He must have guessed what it was. As the three of us were struggling, he suddenly shook himself free, picked up the stick, drew the blade out, and struck at Croake. Croake took it right in the chest. It might not have been so bad, only Croake sort of threw himself at Walmer to take the sword away and met the blade.'

'And then...?'

'Croak drew himself upright, as though he'd not been wounded at all. We just stood there speechless. I really wonder whether or not Croake himself realised, at first, what had happened to him, because he put his hat on and he actually took out his wallet pulled out a ten shilling note, and said "for my drinks". And, as though the talking upset something, he started to bleed at the mouth. He went through the side door and vanished, with the wallet still in his hand.'

'And ran right into the arms of a teddy-boy, who snatched the wallet, and almost got himself convicted for murder?'

'I guess so. We heard the row going on outside and we went in the bar and mixed with the crowd as a sort of alibi. You see I'm telling you the truth. When we heard the teddy-boy had been taken for the crime, we said we'd lie low and see how things went...'

'Thanking your lucky stars and ready to let him hang for you.'

'Nothing of the kind. The teddy-boy might have stabbed him, as well, because, remember, he was fit to walk when he left the *Bishop's Arms*.'

'What a hope!'

'Is that all?'

'No. What happened today? How did you come to get yourself locked and drunk in the cellar?'

'I called-in this afternoon to tell Walmer that the police were still on the case, there was doubt about the teddy-boy committing the crime, and what had we better do about it. He said he knew and we'd just act normal; nobody would ever think of suspecting us.'

'Where was Jenny?'

'I was coming to that. She was at the bar. Walmer and me were in the private room at the back, where...'

'Where you murdered Croake?'

'I object. I tell you I'd nothing to do with it. You can't pin it on me. Walmer did it and he's dead...'

'And can't answer for himself. Go on with your story.'

'We were in the back room, when suddenly the door of the bar bangs open and someone stamps in. "Where's those two murdering swine, your father and Bottomley...?" It was Juan Curghey, the one they call Red Juan, from Ballacroake. Jenny said after, he'd a twelve-bore across his arm and looked ready for murder. She told him we weren't in. We quietly nipped-out by the side door and round the block. Red Juan, Jenny told us, went round the house before he believed her and then he went out and off in his land-rover somewhere. He went to Keristal, it seems, after me.'

'And what did you do to Jenny?'

'I did nothing. She turned on her father suddenly as though something had dawned on her. "Did you have anything to do with the murder of Mr. Croake?" she says. "Of course we didn't. Red Juan's always been a bit mad. It's turned his head," Walmer says. "I don't believe you," she says. "The very look of the pair of you's enough". Before she could say another word, her father up and slaps her across the mouth. I'm fond of Jenny and I saw red. I pushed him away...'

He looked at Littlejohn and Knell aggressively as though he were going to push them away, too. Then he nodded his head in self-approval. Littlejohn could imagine Bottomley putting up a fight. *Pushing* people, instead of giving them a sock on the jaw.

'...Walmer hit me, too, then. I didn't remember anything else, till I woke-up in the cellar.'

'So you attacked the port down there and got maudlin'-tight, didn't you?'

'I did not. When I came-to and realised where I was, I went up the stairs and tried the cellar door. It was locked. I knew the mood Walmer was in and I'd seen him stab Croake. My sword-stick was in the back room. What would *you* have done? Raised the roof and brought him down again. I didn't feel very well after the clip on the jaw he'd given me...'

Littlejohn sympathised momentarily. He'd had one, too... from Walmer's foot I

'... So, I opened a bottle. I thought, at first, it was brandy. Then, when it turned out to be Burgundy...'

Just like the little fool not to know the difference!

'... I took a substantial drink to pick me up. Before I knew where I was, I'd drunk the lot, although, mind you, I was down there several hours. My head was spinning from the blow and I fell asleep.'

'You did indeed. You and your Burgundy! It was cheap port, like methylated spirit. You must have a stomach like leather.'

'My digestion's not been bad for years, although, now and then...'

'Oh, for Pete's sake... Let's finish all this and then you can go to your cosy little cell.'

'I want a lawyer. My lawyer's Samuel Clucas Kallen. Now, don't make any mistakes when you send for him. It's the youngest. There's Jasper, the very old man; then his son, the old man, who's called Mark; then the middle-aged one, Samuel. It's Samuel I want.'

'You can have him in the morning. You can have all three then, if you like, but we're not upsetting their family party at this hour of the night. Another question; what about the fake pieces of Dresden that appeared among the good ones at Ballacroake?'

'When we told Croake we wanted... Or rather when *Walmer* did...'

'Go on; we know all about it.'

'Croake said he couldn't take the figures without the family missing them. Walmer remembered I had some...'

'His memory assisted by yourself, no doubt.'

'If you don't stop being sarcastic, I won't assist you with the case at all. It's not good enough the way you talk to me.'

That was a good one! The pious burglar... or was it murderer?

'Go on.'

'Walmer remembered I had some at Keristal. You see, I was once agent for some modern figures for a German firm...'

No wonder they didn't sell, if those in the case at Ballacroake were samples! Bottomley probably tried hawking them to the shooting-galleries and hoop-la stalls on the Onchan fun-fair.

'So you handed some over to Croake.'

'That's right.'

'Doing him a good turn, so to speak.'

'I ignore that crack. It's beneath my dignity. What happened to Jenny after Walmer laid me out?'

'He tied her up and gagged her. Then he took her and locked her up in a room upstairs. It seems she told him she'd report it to the police. She was lucky he didn't kill her with your fancy sword-stick, but he thought better of it. Unfortunately for him, as he was doing his thinking and laying further plans for himself over a fortifying glass of whisky, the police, in the shape of Inspector Knell and myself, turned-up. Then, the band began to play again. Red Juan had gone to Keristal in search of you, Bottomley, and Walmer ran straight into him. You know the rest.'

'How did Red Juan know about what happened to Croake?'

'*We* knew, and I was speaking to Mr. Ewan Croake about it at Ballacroake. Red Juan was cleaning out the room next to Mr. Ewan's and both windows were open. Hearing our discussion, Juan listened-in. What he heard made him take out the land-rover and hare off hell-for-leather to murder the pair of you. Nessie told us where he'd been and that she'd seen him leaving. We put two and two together....'

Bottomley's mental image of Red Juan must have been a nightmare one. He turned green, clutched at the table, and staggered to his feet.

'I'm going to be sick.'

They rushed him out to a suitable spot.

Later Bottomley signed a statement and asked about the motor-boat in Keristal Creek, said it was his own, and he'd called her *Nessie*. Strange man! He and Walmer had arranged, if matters grew too hot for them, to take themselves quietly off in her to Dublin. Walmer had evidently decided later that it was wiser to go alone. No wonder! Alone at sea with a crackpot like Bottomley would have been a nightmare.

In spite of the united efforts of the Kallens, Ross Bottomley was found guilty of manslaughter and sent to gaol in England for ten years. He is now head decorator and designer in a well-known prison, where his artistry frequently causes riots among the inmates.

Alf Cryer got two years for robbery with violence. He smiled as he received sentence. After all, he'd just missed hanging or life imprisonment, thanks, of all people, to the police! He bowed mockingly and turned to go, but the Deemster called him back as he hadn't quite finished. In addition to the two years... ten strokes of the birch. Alf Cryer fainted and had to be carried from the dock.

DEATH IN DARK GLASSES

GEORGE BELLAIRS

Chapter One
The Missing Client

The defalcations of John Wainwright Palmer at Silvesters' Bank, Rodley branch, were of small dimensions compared with the hornets' nest of crime they set buzzing in the town. Only two hundred pounds, taken from the till and hidden in the accounts with moderate skill, yet in the mind of the dishonest bank cashier, they had assumed such enormous proportions that, learning the Chief Inspector of the bank was closeted with his manager and then being told the pair wished to see him in the private office, Wainwright Palmer bolted. In his panic and haste to the station, he failed to see a bus, fell beneath it and was picked up dead.

The Chief Inspector of the Bank had called to discuss Palmer's career with the manager of Rodley branch and they were about to offer the cashier promotion in the shape of the managership of a highly sought-after seaside branch. Beautiful, tragic irony of life!

It seemed obvious that Palmer must have had something on his conscience and that, to the bank, meant only one thing. An alarm was sounded which brought to Rodley a large team of investigators from headquarters. Had he lived, Palmer might, out of fear, hope or remorse, have laid bare his whole scheme of modest fraud. Now, the branch had to be turned upside down to trace the causes of the cashier's flight. The process was far from easy. The balances of all the clients who could be contacted were verified. It was proved that Palmer had forged cheques on rarely-used accounts to square his books. Finally, all the customers but ten had been covered. Seven of these were abroad and inaccessible; two were dead; and one would not reply to letters. It was thought better in these cases to call in a handwriting expert to examine the cheques drawn on their accounts. They had specimens of Palmer's writing and in a very short time had sorted out the whole affair. Entries were passed to make good the fraudulent withdrawals, the bank wrote off as bad the unlucky debt created by their faithless servant, and the manager of Rodley breathed again. But not for long.

Mr. Hoffman, the handwriting expert, was still uneasy.

"I can't make this out, Mr. de Lacy," he said, passing his soft white hand over his large bald head. He had a tic in one eye and winked at the manager, who, after weeks of strain, winked mirthlessly back. Mr. Hoffman placed three cheques on the official writing-pad.

"These are forged, too, if the specimen in your signature file is authentic," he said. "But Palmer didn't do it."

Mr. de Lacy slumped in his chair.

"My God!" he managed to say and he placed his hands flat on his desk and gazed blankly into space like a cataleptic.

The cheques totalled seven thousand pounds! They had been drawn to "Self" on the account of one Finloe Oates and they had exhausted the whole of his balance. Nay, with accrued charges, Finloe Oates owed the bank nine shillings and threepence.

After bracing himself by drinking most of the brandy in his first-aid box, Mr. de Lacy rang the bell.

"Bring me Mr. Finloe Oates's file...."

No sooner said than done. The file revealed that five letters, all unanswered, had been sent to this customer in the course of investigations arising from Wainwright Palmer's misdeeds. The manager, his eyes wild and his thin hair dishevelled from his tearing at it, ordered them to get the Chief Inspector on the telephone.

"Hullo, de Lacy.... How are you?" came a cheerful voice from Head Office.

"I'm not so well," answered the manager and fell unconscious under the desk.

The Chief Inspector arrived later that day and this time he was far from cheerful.

"Where does the man live... this Oates fellow...?"

He spoke as though poor Finloe Oates had himself caused all the trouble.

"Netherby... about five miles away in the country..."

They had given Mr. de Lacy more stimulant; so much, in fact, that he was a bit truculent.

"Why wasn't somebody sent out to see him when he didn't answer letters?"

"So busy and confused by all the fuss... I mean, all the worry of the investigations, I quite overlooked it. And if I overlook anything, nobody else finds it. I'm not getting the support I ought to get from Killgrass..." he said between paroxysms of nervous coughing.

"Very serious.... Very serious indeed. Seven thousand pounds! Whatever were you thinking of...?"

The Chief Inspector might have thought Mr. de Lacy had himself put pen to paper and forged Oates's name!

"Send a man out right away...."

They rang for the assistant manager, Mr. Killgrass, who entered braced for the fray. He was a clean, bald, tubby man with the folds of his heavy face set in lines of irony and disappointment. He objected to being assistant to a manager like Mr. de Lacy. He felt he could manage better himself. They told Mr. Killgrass the nature of his mission, waved aside his expostulations, and meticulously instructed him what to say and do, like potentates sending an emissary into a distant alien land.

"We depend on you...."

Mr. Killgrass took a taxi in a show of efficient haste. "The bank can stand it," he thought to himself, and, after all, he was in a hurry.

Netherby is a small village which once boasted little else than a pub for refreshment, stocks for evil-doers, a fine church, and a few workmen's cottages. Now, however, it had grown into a dormitory for Rodley's professional and monied classes. Large, imitation period-houses had sprung up solidly in the middle of the village, surrounded by an outer, more attenuated ring of pseudo-manors and sham-castles in magnificent bad taste, like their owners. Most of the wealthy elders of the community moved about it in large, opulent cars and their offspring tore about it in racing models. Mr. Killgrass, after a pint and a few inquiries at the inn, found that Mr. Finloe Oates lived in a bungalow named, for some obscure reason, "Shenandoah," and situated about a mile outside the village in a country lane, along with three or four similar houses built by a speculative builder.

Shenandoah was closed. Nobody answered Mr. Killgrass's knock. He looked around the place. It was a rustic-brick structure; two living-rooms, two bedrooms and the usual offices. Behind, a small orchard and a vegetable patch; in front, what must once have been a very pretty lawn and garden, but now it was a wilderness. The grass was like a meadow, with coltsfoot and plantain romping merrily all over it; the round rose-bed in the centre was running riot and sprouting burdock; the flowers on the borders had gone wild and were choking under the weight of stitchwort and coarse grass.

Mr. Killgrass was a man of imagination. He had read books by Walter de la Mare, Sheridan le Fanu and Ambrose Bierce. He believed in the benevolence or malevolence of bricks and mortar and knew that houses bore personalities endowed upon them by powerful occupants. There, on a hot afternoon, with no birds singing; with not a soul about but the taxi-driver snoozing in his cab, a fag dangling in his mouth; with somewhere the sound of water running from a pipe and falling from a height; he felt that the house was watching him and that the forsaken, desolate garden was trying to tell him something he could not interpret. He shook off the feeling, remembering that he was expected to return with an answer of some practical kind. He took the liberty—not without looking furtively around to make sure he wasn't overlooked—of peeping in through the windows. The living-rooms were tidy. Over the fireplace of one, a dark portrait in oils looking straight at him, made Mr. Killgrass recoil like one discovered doing wrong. The blinds of the bedrooms were drawn. The kitchen bore signs of habitation, but it must have been a long time ago. The table was laid. On a soiled cloth were the remains of a meal; dirty dishes, a half-empty jar of marmalade, a piece of mouldy cheese, and a loaf of bread turned almost to fungus. There was a mouse busy eating the cheese. Instinctively, the banker tapped on the pane with his finger-nail and the mouse bolted to a dark corner and was gone. The place obviously hadn't been occupied for weeks—nay months, and someone had left it in a hurry.

Mr. Killgrass then peered through the letter-slit in the front door. There was a small pile of letters on the floor and among them he recognised two of the bank's envelopes with the familiar crest on the flaps.

"Wantin' somethin'?"

Mr. Killgrass raised himself and spun round. As if in answer to a prayer, it was the postman himself, a little, stringy fellow, with mean, inquisitive eyes and a face like a wizened nut. His jaws rotated as he chewed and then he spat out a quid on the grass to facilitate articulation.

"I'm trying to find Mr. Oates...."

"Funny place to look for 'im. Ain't been 'ere for near on two months. Went away an' said nothin'. Not even left 'is address. Put a note on the door for the milk-boy. 'Gone abroad,' it said. As if that were any help. What's 'e want goin' abroad for...a feller of 'is age? Made 'is money in distant parts, but never bin away from 'ere since he married and settled down more'n a dozen years since. Seems 'is wife dyin' turned 'is 'ead, if you ask me."

He seemed affronted by the fact that the vanished tenant of Shenandoah had not taken him into his confidence before disappearing. He eyed Killgrass up and down.

"What you wantin'?"

Mr. Killgrass replied by another question.

"Do you still deliver the letters here, then?"

The postman's thin lips disappeared altogether as he compressed them in stubborn malice.

"Course I do. Can't do no other, 'cept burn 'em. Serve 'im right if I did. Why didn't 'e tell me? He could tell milk-chap. I'm more important than milk fellers, ain't I? So, as 'e didn't tell me, I keep on puttin' his letters through the slit in the door. Not that 'e gets many now. All 'is dividends stopped comin' a while since."

Mr. Killgrass started.

"What do you know about his dividends?"

The postman spat maliciously on the grass.

"Don't get no ideas as I opens 'em. I can tell divi letters. Smooth and sleek, like, with, like as not, name and address printed on 'em, 'stead o' written. Mostly circulars now, with penny stamps, or a letter or two from the bank. P'raps he got 'isself overdrawn. Anyhow, by the look o' things, bank'll 'ave to whistle for their money. Somethin' tells me we won't see Finloe Oates agen...."

Mr. Killgrass looked at the postman with respect. His comments on the letters had been worthy of Sherlock Holmes himself! Perhaps he knew....

"When 'is wife up an' died early in the year, Oates tuck funny. For a week or two after the buryin', he was normal. Nay, 'e was more chirpy than usual. As if his missus's death 'ad give 'im more freedom. Then, of a sudden, overnight like, he shuts 'imself up indoors and won't come out. I knew 'e was there. Saw 'im through the winder, moving round. Heard 'im, too. Letters went from behind door and milk was tuck in. I recollect parcels, too. Registered 'uns. 'Leave 'em on the mat,' 'e sez. 'Not me,' I sez. 'You got receipt to sign.' So 'e tells me to put it under the door; then 'e signs it and shoves it back without showin' 'imself."

"You didn't see him, then?"

"Not close to. But 'is writin' on receipt... that was 'is. I'd know it anywhere. Gone queer with broodin' and bein' alone after Mrs. Oates got tuck...."

He waved a grubby hand like a talon at the garden.

"Look at all that. Wrack and ruin. An' Oates that proud of it once. Nobody more proud. In it from morn till night till just after 'is wife died and 'e tuck funny. Even photographed it an' won prizes in ladies' papers for best gardens...."

The postman spat again.

"Since she died... well... as I said, he was normal for a bit. Mowin' the lawns like mad and weedin' them beds like a good 'un, as if it comforted 'im. Then, he stopped, and never done a 'and's turn at it since. I can't understand it. You thinkin' o' buyin' this place, because I don't know whose goin' to sell it to yer if they don't find Oates...?"

Mr. Killgrass informed the postman he wasn't going to buy. He didn't quite know what to do. The thought that the taxi was still at the gate ticking away the bank's sixpences, spurred him to action, however. He bade the postman good-day and hurried off. Whereupon, the postman, assured that nobody was looking, went behind the house, cut a fat neglected marrow from a wilderness of nettles, grass and weeds, stuffed it in his bag, and made off as well.

"Hadn't we better have a word with the police about this?" said Mr. de Lacy to the Chief Inspector when Killgrass had made his report.

"I think so...."

An hour later the telephone in the lobby of Netherby police-house rang. P.G. Albert Mee, digging in his garden, rose to the perpendicular, dusted his hands, and lumbered indoors.

"Telephone, Dad," said his wife from somewhere upstairs.

"I know...."

P.C. Mee always knew. They called him "Johnny Know-all" in the village.

"Yes, Mee speakin'."

"Yes, but who is it?"

"You know very well 'oo it is.... What do you want?"

The man at the other end of the line laughed. It was a perennial joke. "The Super wants a word with you...."

"Yes, sir."

"I believe the bungalow, Shenandoah, in your village is deserted...."

"I know, sir...."

"Don't interrupt, Mee. It seems an official from one of the banks here called there to-day, couldn't get an answer, and said the place looks as if it's been empty for weeks.... The postman said the owner, a man called Oates, is abroad. Is that so?"

"Yes, sir. I knew that. Went away about two months since. I've been keepin' an eye on it."

"Do you *know* he's abroad?"

"Yes, sir."

"Did he tell you so before he went?"

"Not exactly, sir. He left word with the milk-boy. Wrote it on a card and left it.... Didn't want any more milk, sir."

There were tearing noises at the other end of the wire.

"Any idea where Mr. Oates went?"

"South o' France, I think."

"You think! Do you *know*?"

"Not exactly, sir. But 'e always talked of how easy gardenin' was there. 'E'd lived there, or somethin'...."

"Don't make wild guesses, Mee. Better go up and see what's going on there. Take a good look round and get inside if you can without breaking-in the door. Speak to me again if you don't manage it...."

"I'll get in, sir. I know 'ow...."

"Remember, no breaking-in without my permission. The chap may be dead or something, inside. I'm surprised you haven't seen to it before. Go right away...."

P.C. Mee was annoyed. Insinuating that he didn't look after his village properly, were they? He'd show 'em.

"I'm just going up to Oates's place, missus," he called upstairs. "Won't be long. 'Ave me tea ready about five...."

"Somethin's not right there," shouted his wife over the landing rails. "Miss Featherfew who lives next door..."

"I haven't time to listen to what old Featherfew thinks," said Johnny Know-all rudely and then relented, bade his wife a civil good-bye, and pedalled off on his bicycle.

On the strength of the message produced for his information by young Belcher, the milk-boy, P.C. Mee hadn't worried much about the absence of Finloe Oates. He'd heard about Oates becoming a recluse shortly after his wife's death. Well... he'd a right to his grief in peace, hadn't he? He'd get over it. He'd told one or two busybodies who'd wanted him to investigate matters at Shenandoah that. Leave 'im in peace with his memories and his sorrow. He'll get over it. And he'd been right. Oates had gone off for a holiday to the South of France. Or, that was where P.C. Mee imagined him, sporting on the beach with the pretty bathing girls like they showed on the advert. at the station. Maybe, Oates had seen the advert. for Nice on the station. Yes, that was it. Provided the bungalow was secured, hadn't been burgled, or set on fire, P.C. Mee thought he'd no cause to interfere. Besides, Johnny Know-all didn't miss much in his village. No, sir. He'd tell the Super a thing or two in his report. Returning from night patrol on his bike at five o'clock one morning, he'd seen Mr. Oates on his way to the station to catch the first train. You have to get an early train when you're going abroad from Netherby.... He'd shone his light on him.... Mr. Oates in his big coat and soft hat with his limp, too.... When the milk-boy told P.C. Mee, he'd been able to say "Yes, I know...."

Still pondering his case, P.C. Mee parked his bike at the gate of the bungalow. Funny, Mr. Oates hadn't told him properly, though. Always before, when Mr. and Mrs. Oates had been going away for a day or two, Oates had telephoned to say the house would be empty and if anything happened...well...Mee knew where the key was....

P.C. Mee boldly approached the rockery at the side of the house. Beneath one of the large stones was the hiding-place known only to the Oateses and Mee. He raised the rock, peered in the cavity, and brushed away a couple of woodlice and a centipede. Nothing there. Mee was annoyed. He moved a few more rocks without success. At this rate he'd shift the whole rockery! He rose and dusted the soil from his hands and knees. Funny; yet perhaps not. Poor old Oates had taken it on the chin when his wife died. Everybody in the village was sorry for him. The bobby looked round to see that nobody was looking and then carefully put the rocks back in their holes. Then he made no more ado, but took out a large clasp knife, opened it, went straight to a certain window and forced the catch with great ease. He'd done it once before when the Oateses went away and left the cat in. After that, they'd hidden the key for him, just in case. Mee winked to himself and climbed in.

"Pooh!" said the bobby as the atmosphere of stale air, food, yes...and mice...greeted him. He was in the best bedroom. Just as Mrs. Oates had left it apparently. Like the window of a furniture shop. Everything in order, the bed made, the place tidy, but very dusty. The lounge was the same. The other bedroom was the reverse. Bedclothes filthy, bed unmade, clothes—a man's—all over the place. He drew the curtains and started instinctively to flail at the moths which flew out. Dead flies on the window-sill.... P.C. Mee shuddered.

"Pore Finloe Oates.... All gone to pieces," he said.

Clocks stopped, dust everywhere, letters behind the door. P.C. Mee picked up the envelopes. Gardening circulars, a few other advertisements, a number of sealed letters from Silvesters' Bank, according to the name on the flaps....

Oates hadn't been living in the dining-room either. He'd had his food in the kitchen; and what a pigsty! Grease and dirty pots all over the shop. Tins of food, stale bread, the remains of a meal.... P.C. Mee opened the back door to let in the fresh air. A mouse scuttered from temporary hiding and ran to a hole in a corner.

Mee wasn't an imaginative man at all, but he felt cold shivers run down his spine. He felt someone was watching him! He'd see about that! There was only one other place. He tugged a cord hanging from the kitchen ceiling and a door in the loft opened and a ladder descended. He tried the light, but they'd evidently cut it off. He climbed the ladder and struck a match. Nothing there except a lot of old junk. He didn't even go in. It was a small place, a room made of plaster-board and his matches illuminated it to every corner. He turned to descend and then... There, on one side of the little loft-room, was another door, a sort of entrance to the rafters beyond, where, like as not, the water tank was kept. He'd better take a look. But first he climbed down, took a candle from the kitchen window-sill and lit it. Then he went aloft again. The little door opened easily, and P.C. Mee almost fainted. The stench was appalling. The hair under his helmet rose as the bobby realised, knew for sure, that there was something dead there. He braced himself and entered.

The body was lying doubled in one corner and it was in an advanced stage of decomposition. There was no mistaking it, however. The blue uniform with the red stripe down the seams of the trousers, and the peaked cap with the initials C.R., Corporation of Rodley, on the front. Although the Electricity Board had taken them over now, the officials were wearing out their old clothes. It was Jack Fishlock, the electricity meter-man. He'd been a bit of a one for the girls, had Jack, and when he vanished and couldn't be found, they'd said he'd run off with one of them. His wife had sworn it....

P.C. Mee scrambled down the ladder, locked-up the house, was sick with dignity in the garden behind, and then mounted his bicycle. With limbs which seemed turned to water, he pedalled off to the nearest telephone.

WANT ANOTHER PERFECT MYSTERY? GET YOUR NEXT CLASSIC CRIME STORY FOR FREE...

Sign up to our Crime Classics newsletter where you can discover new Golden Age crime, receive exclusive content and never-before published short stories, all for FREE.

From the beloved greats of the Golden Age to the forgotten gems, best-kept-secrets, and brand new discoveries, we're devoted to classic crime.

If you sign up today, you'll get:

1. A free novel from our Classic Crime collection.
2. Exclusive insights into classic novels and their authors and the chance to get copies in advance of publication, and
3. The chance to win exclusive prizes in regular competitions.

Interested? It takes less than a minute to sign up. You can get your novel and your first newsletter by signing up on our website www.crimeclassics.co.uk

Printed in Great Britain
by Amazon